THE WOLVES WITHIN

Based on a True Story

A Novel

J BARTELL

&

GINGER MARIN

DEDICATION

This book is dedicated to my good friends and teammates.

Chauncey Marvin Holt
Michael Agnew Harries
Jeff Cooper
Jim Boland
Dr. K

And a very special thank you to Ginger Marin
for helping me only feed the Good Wolf.
— J Bartell

As well as to all the men and women who work and sacrifice in
order to gather the much-needed intel to help protect us all.

CONTENTS

PROLOGUE

*T**he man in this room is not who he was. What happened between then and now is the story.*

The room was dark, save for the glints of light of a passing police helicopter. Its searchlight beamed in like an artificial sun, wandering from building to building, on a constant search for some faceless perpetrator hiding in the slum streets. But it also found Nick Bryant.

The light invaded his small studio apartment where classic jazz played on a radio. Everything owned was boxed up or tactically hidden. The least hidden was Nick himself, a shadow of a man covered in dark despair, sitting in a shoddy recliner at a fold-up table. His back was facing his boxed-up former life. The boxes were filled with things that would make any man proud: college degrees, licenses to practice his trade, championship trophies, some broken by having to move quickly to escape eviction. At one time, they were on clear display for all to see.

The light continued to rouse him and the beating sound of the helicopter blades overhead drummed like a march of war in the sky as the copter continued its relentless search. All it saw was the decay of urban expansion, whole apartment complexes where renovation was never a possibility. It was supposed to be the City of Angels, but not so in this part of town.

The light burst fully through the balcony glass door, forcing Nick to acknowledge the old photos strewn across his desk. A picture of himself in his prime, ten or more years ago, stared back at him with a pleasant smile. His hair had grown long, undisciplined and unwashed. He looked like he hadn't smiled in years. He was in his late 40s, staring at the man he used to be with nothing but regret.

Also on the desk was his tried-and-true sleeping aid, a bottle of off-brand tequila. The light glinted through the tequila, revealing a ragged Chinese takeout menu, dirty with food stains, that was braced onto the table by a pair of disposable chopsticks. They caught Nick's eye and forced him to remember — a man dying via chopstick. One scene out of a long string of killings and mayhem. The wood was shoved deep into the chest of a diner who was eager to dig into his plate of saucy food and then snapped off, leaving a barely visible stub of wood between two ribs, before he plopped face-first onto his plate. Nick could still hear the accompanying screams of the man's trophy wife.

He swept the menu off the table and, as it floated down, it passed the holstered gun he had duct-taped under the right-hand side of the table. It landed on the floor, hardly disturbing the Siamese cat that was curled up underneath taking a nap.

The golden sheen of the tequila bottle strobed in the glare of the helicopter searchlight. It was the same color of the moonlight that once followed him on his chase through a warehouse where the sound of his heavy breathing was overpowered only by the sound of bullets smashing through windows. He could still feel the shower of glass against his back and shoulders.

The searchlight glinted hard off his knife which was held erect and blade-side down in a cup holder. The knife triggered the memory of the sound of a dying man still echoing through his brain, a Latino with a young wife and two small children, all screaming for the madness to stop. A knife was against the man's throat, in his own hand, as he faced his family with a pitiful resolve. They couldn't do anything but watch. The guns at the back of their heads made the trade clear. He chose a righteous cause, a father's choice, and cut his neck open so his family would live.

Nick reached for the tequila. He needed it. It made him hate it at the same time. Just before he took a swig, Etta James'

At Last started playing on the radio which prompted Nick to pick up a photograph of himself and a woman standing on a beach smiling.

He emptied the bottle and set it back down too close to the table's edge. The bottle wobbled and fell to the floor, its thud startling the cat away. The copter blades approached closer and the light steadied itself through the worn curtains.

When Nick disarmed the tequila, his hand reached for his gun and placed it on his lap. A .45 one-of-a-kind pistol. It too held memories, too many to bear remembering.

Soon Nick could only see his shadow cast against the wall. He turned to it, hoping to find shelter from the light in his own darkness. He watched the shadow lift the gun but didn't feel his arm moving. A click as the safety came off.

The light became blinding.

Then a shot.

CHAPTER ONE
PSYCH 101

Ten years earlier, Nick drove along a Los Angeles highway on a sleek but powerful custom chopper-style motorcycle. The root beer brown metallic paint was accented by dazzling chrome parts, enough to blind the nearest drivers. His dark blonde hair, a fitting length for the times - early 1980s - blew about from the freedom of a helmet-less ride as his arms, toned from past labor jobs and daily rides, guided the bike around the hills and curves of the road. The air, fresh with a hint of exhaust, was actually pleasant to take in. His destination was the Castaic Sheriff's correctional facility in northern L.A. county.

Nick pulled into the parking lot and sat for a few moments, gathering his thoughts before he entered the large, ominous complex. He commanded an air about him that wasn't uniformly respected. Some acknowledged him with a simple nod as yet another off-kilter figure of authority above them. Others would smile at him while some scowled at the outsider.

He wound his way through the facility, past the larger cells, through the corridors of smaller ones, and finally to the end of a hall. Four guards stood side by side in front of a steel door. Solitary confinement. The guards looked unhappy and a little roughed up. He waited for one of them to open the door, then quickly stepped in.

Inside was a man in a fighting stance, shivering with adrenaline-pumping excitement. He rushed Nick first thing with fists still stained with blood — his and another man's.

Nick ducked the first swing and dodged the follow-up before the convict even knew he was throwing it. The enraged felon changed stance at the last second and threw a wild, unaimed elbow that Nick caught in the face. Nick huffed it off and waited for the next attack. He answered a high swing with a leg sweep, causing the man to take a short but hard fall onto concrete. Once down, Nick descended and held the crazed man down by the shoulders. Then quickly whispered "Beach. Family. Calm." into the man's ear. Each word was distinct and said with forceful precision. The man on the ground became calm as images flashed through his eyes of his wife and child on the beach. He could hear the ocean and the giggles of his daughter. His muscles relaxed; his tension quickly faded, allowing Nick the opportunity to use his special process.

The transformation was nothing short of magical, especially when compared to the state the convict had been in just hours earlier. Luis, the notorious prisoner known for his intimidating tattoos, had been placed in solitary for good reason. He had abruptly launched himself at another inmate in the yard, a man who had seemed innocently engrossed in reading from a Bible. This sight inexplicably ignited a fierce and irrational rage within Luis, propelling him into a frenzied attack. He relentlessly pummeled the man, even after the holy book slipped from his grasp and small plastic packets of drugs scattered across the ground like confetti.

It took a cohort of guards to subdue him, as they encircled him with caution. They were met with the imposing image inked across his muscular back — a vivid tattoo that dominated the expanse of his skin. On one side, a menacing red devil, complete with draconic wings and a sinister forked tongue, stared down an ethereal angel clad in pure white, wielding a sword that seemed to burn with righteous fire.

The guards swung their batons with relentless force, each strike meeting the man's seething fury that seemed limitless. Despite their efforts, they struggled to contain him, finally managing to subdue him just enough to drag him into solitary confinement. There, in the dim isolation of the cell, his anger echoed off the cold, unyielding walls.

Once the guards heard rhythmic bangs coming from inside the solitary cell, they opened the door. They prepared themselves for a sudden defense but saw Nick standing calmly behind Luis, who took two measured steps out and kneeled with his hands on the back of his head. With his position assumed, the guards carefully managed him.

Nick stepped out and rubbed his jaw. Just a bruise, another point of fashion for his clean-cut face. "Next time," he said to the guards, "call me immediately." The guards offered a smirk and then escorted Luis back to his cell. Nick turned to leave, only to face a wall of a man, the warden, twice Nick's age and twice the weight in all the wrong places.

"You don't talk to my men like that." The warden spoke with absolute authority, wielding power in his words of warning.

But Nick wasn't part of the system and let the warden know it. "Then tell them not to fuck with my clients," he said, matching the warden's tone before brusquely walking past and out of the facility. He knew Luis would be safe in his cell away from prison yard politics, at least for the time being. That left Nick free to return to his office. And back onto the freeways he went, a little hotter under the collar and facing more traffic than when he started out.

Two freeway interchanges and forty-five minutes later, Nick pulled into a different parking lot where a space was reserved just for him. He made his way into the brick building whose facade was entwined by lush ivy, broken only by the wrought iron around the door and window frames, and took the stairs to the second floor.

A silver plaque cemented to the wall behind a large office counter read *The Costas Academy - Caring Help & Education.* It was one of those therapy and new-age places that was still finding its feet in Los Angeles' self-help scene, still struggling for credibility among more conventional therapies.

Nick entered as clients waited and workers busied themselves behind the counter. Among them was office manager Lynn, a perky and über efficient woman in her mid-30s, who shuffled aside a current 1980 issue of LIFE Magazine in her efforts to spruce up the counter space. Shouting from the cover was Iran's Ayatollah with the headline: *"Khomeini's Fierce Outcry Against America."* Its proximity to a skeleton and a witch sitting next to an overflowing pumpkin candy bowl was not lost on Lynn. She added another witch as a final statement. She had decorated the entire office in anticipation of Halloween.

Nick moved toward Lynn, who immediately spotted the bruise on his face. "Not as bad as last time," she said, as she handed him some messages.

Nick facetiously responded, "A man must suffer for his art."

"Some more than most," she said drolly. "John wants to see you right away." She whispered, "The words 'pro bono' came up."

Nick shook his head — *not this shit again* — and walked into the one place he'd rather not be that day — the office of penny-pinching business owner John Costas, a tightly wound middle-aged man who always wore a coat, tie and an ill-fitting toupee. Standing next to him was his son Stevie, a recent high-school grad with a smart mouth, who was dressed just like dad, except for the toupee. A photo of them in matched set fishing gear, holding up their catches, sat on the desk.

Nick waited as patiently as he could for Costas' attention to veer his way, which could take some time considering that Costas was busy examining the company's new P.R. brochures. He finally spoke. "Looks great," he said to Stevie, as he held up one as if it were a recently discovered gold nugget.

Nick took one of the brochures out of a large box to check it out.

"I'll send them right out, Dad." Stevie smiled, appreciating the compliment, then looked over and noticed Nick's bruise. "Some clients just aren't worth it," he said with his usual smirk.

Nick ignored him with his usual aplomb.

Costas rammed his next words into Nick. "We talked about you seeing people who can't pay. Now I find out you have another one in your office."

Nick deflected, "He's a veteran." But it didn't work.

"I'm running a business," growled Costas.

Nick pushed back. "You knew from the beginning some of my clients were pro bono."

"Well, he's the last one." Costas hit the intercom button as Stevie's smirk grew. "Lynn, send in my next client."

He turned back to Nick and, in a condescending tone, said, "Don't forget to take enough business cards for your class tonight. And make sure you have a full class when that reporter comes next week."

Nick slid the brochure across the desk in Costas' direction. "Unless you want people showing up at the empty lot on the corner," he tapped the cover, "you may want to correct the address." Stevie's smirk quickly vanished as his father's jaw tightened.

On his way out, Nick noted a new photo on the wall — Costas on his yacht with a crowd of people and his new 18-year-old bride, "Barbie".

Back in the waiting room, Nick caught Lynn's attention as he moved to the office coffee machine and poured a mugful. "Remove the Vets from the appointment book," he said.

"Really?" asked Lynn incredulously.

"I'll book 'em myself."

"You're going to have to see them after hours."

Nick acknowledged her with a weary head nod. The resigned look on Lynn's face showed she sympathized as she knew how hard Nick worked seeing clients whenever duty called, including working before regular hours as with the prisoner Luis.

"Oh," she alerted him, "the lecture room for tonight was changed to Royce Hall 190."

Nick thanked her and made his way down a long hallway bordered by classrooms and private therapy rooms. Inside one of those rooms was Morgan, wearing worn-out army fatigues, the only clothes he could afford. A duffel bag filled with his only belongings was on the floor nearby. In his hands was a letter opener. He studied it carefully by brushing the blade lightly against his thumb to see how sharp it was but came away unsatisfied.

Nick firmly gripped his mug of steaming coffee as he reached the door of his office which displayed a polished brass nameplate: 'Nick Bryant - Chief of Staff'. He stepped inside where neat rows of bookshelves lined one wall holding an eclectic mix of titles ranging from psychology and behavior to biographies of Einstein and Picasso and even a few oddities like *"Why Do Clocks Run Clockwise?"* and some on the care and well-being of cats. A Hopalong Cassidy lunchbox was on prominent display next to his framed licenses and professional degrees. Comfortingly nestled in one corner was a plush recliner while some plants injected life into the scene and kept it homey. Of course, there was his well-organized desk. And it was there that Nick saw Morgan standing, still holding the letter opener, as he heard his breathing fill the air with heavy tension. Morgan noticed that Nick saw the letter opener so he put it back where he found it, in a pencil holder cup. He corrected the placement so that it was closer to Nick, who offered him the coffee. The large mug filled his hands, but as he reached for it, he revealed tightly wrapped bandages over his wrists. Morgan moved away, towards the recliner, but didn't take a seat. Nick casually sat at his desk.

"Where are you today?" Nick asked. "Zero to ten."

"Where I always am," Morgan muttered. "With a head full of shit that never goes away." He started pacing the room.

"As a sniper," Nick began, "aren't there certain procedures to follow for a successful mission?"

"Yeah." Morgan lifted the coffee to his face, not to sip it but to relish the aroma which transported him briefly back to the camaraderie he felt with his team.

"And each step is dependent upon the step before," Nick said. Morgan nodded. "So, as a recruit, what if I didn't follow your procedures?"

Morgan stopped and turned to him. "I'd tell you to get your fucking shit together." His tone was now more alert than before.

"Well, I have procedures too," Nick said. "So give me a fucking number." He matched Morgan's disciplined, demanding candor with one of his own to prove he was in charge, but didn't raise his voice in anger. Morgan stared back, until his eyes wandered away for just a moment, in defeat.

"One."

Nick smiled. "Last week it was zero," he said, striking a more pleasant tone. "It might be insignificant to you, but in my book, that's progress."

Morgan took a moment to process. "Okay." He moved toward the recliner.

"You have to admit," Nick said with a smile, "it's better than a stick in the eye."

Morgan lowered himself into the seat. "Really? A stick in the eye?" A brief grin finally broke on Morgan's morose face. "Okay, I get it."

"Good." Nick rose, walked around to the front of the desk, and sat up against the edge. "Let's get started."

Morgan pushed himself back into the recliner and felt the slight push of the cushion against him. It cradled him and kept him secure. "Is there anything else I can do to speed things up? Anything?"

Nick looked above the door where he'd hung his motto. Morgan followed Nick's gaze and read the signage *Today's Shortcuts Are Tomorrow's Nightmares*. It was a steadfast reminder to everyone how the delicate game of psychology was played. They weren't in a battle that needed to be won, but a war they had to survive.

"You'll get there," Nick assured.

That evening, students hurried to the lecture room at the University of California at Los Angeles, UCLA for short. The school had given Nick plenty of space and a decent time slot to teach his special therapy process and maybe get some additional clients for the Costas Academy. At least, that's what Costas was hoping for when he gave Nick his blessing and agreed to pay just half of any leftover costs.

Nick checked in with the student projectionist who stood behind the projector and checked again on the sequence for slide changes, taking a moment to compare it to his notes. The projectionist loaded the slides which caused dust particles to float up and get caught in light that escaped the machine. This was not yet the digital age.

The screen was smaller than Nick expected but big enough for him to present his lecture and build momentum as he made his points. He returned to his place at the front of the room where there was nothing between him and the fertile minds seeking higher knowledge that he could provide.

He signaled the projectionist. The only source of light now was the projector and the white screen. Nick stood and looked out at his crowd. It was standing room only. This seminar was dedicated entirely to his unique Left-Right Brain Conditioning Process.

He began as he always did, with some banter and general discussion of what he'd be covering before finding his way to the main point of this lecture: controlling pain and bleeding.

"You say the subconscious mind is much more powerful than the conscious. How much more powerful?" one student asked.

Nick held up his fist and said, "This will represent your total mind." He extended his little finger away from the others. "My little finger will represent your conscious mind, your logic, and your reasoning. You know, the area you use to convince yourself that you can accomplish something… until your subconscious, represented by the rest of my fist, tells you you're full of shit."

After the laughter from the audience had subsided, Nick continued. "In your first few years of life, you're like a sponge with feet soaking up everything around you. Some of what you're soaking up is the assumption that every injury, from stubbing your toe to major surgery, has to hurt. And a lot of injuries have to bleed. Not so. Pain doesn't have to be paralyzing."

Nick signaled the projectionist, "Mother, soldier."

A slide that came on the screen showed two newspaper clippings. One was a photo of a mother and a young boy standing next to a car. Part of the headline read "- *Saves Son from Wrecked Car -*". The other picture was of a soldier in a hospital bed, bandaged around his head and chest, surrounded by his team all giving the thumbs up.

"The mother," Nick said, pointing to the first photo, "who sees her kid trapped under a car. She's lifting thousands of pounds as her muscles and ligaments tear under the load. Or the soldier, even though he was badly shot up and bleeding, he didn't let it interfere with what he had to do — save his team." Nick raised his fist. "That's power. The conscious, knowing what has to be done, and the subconscious, making it happen. With my process, you can access your subconscious to make what you want to become reality."

"Aren't you mixing apples and oranges?" a nurse in scrubs said, interrupting him. "They're not using a process, their body's on autopilot."

"True," Nick said, "you could describe it as autopilot. But I would describe it as the woman's conscious mind instantly becoming overloaded with the thought of her son dying in front of her. So the subconscious took over and flooded her body with the chemicals needed to save him. In this case, adrenaline and cortisol. Now, what if you could purposely send messages to your brain without waiting for your autopilot to kick in?"

Nick turned and opened his briefcase and took out a sterile, hypodermic needle. He raised it for all to see. "I need a volunteer." With his other hand also held up, Nick began to repeatedly tap his thumb to the tip of his little finger. "I've used my process to reinforce subconsciously that when I do this action, I'm able to increase my control over bleeding and pain." He then jammed the needle deep into his cheek, all the way to the thumb rest; it seemed like it would have been accompanied by a "thwack" but the movement was fluid and natural. The pressure of the needle, the touch of the flesh, all done with the same confident motion as if he were scratching an itch: no pain, no jumping, and no blood. There was, though, a louder than normal breathing in the audience as they drew in a collective, gasping breath. A few stifled laughs of shock followed, but they mostly moaned in earnest surprise. Two attendees whispered to each other in the back.

Nick stood there with the needle stuck in his cheek and smiled as he scanned the crowd. "Any questions?" He recognized one whisperer as his former client Carrie, a tall 30-year-old transsexual who was with a younger, smaller male friend. "Oh hey, Carrie, got a question?"

Carrie nudged her friend and forced him to raise his hand even though he slinked to the side of his seat. All eyes stared his way, and he looked thoroughly embarrassed but spoke up nonetheless. "Can you numb your emotions?"

"Great question!" Nick said with enthusiasm. The young man seemed less embarrassed now and sat up straight, ready to hear the answer. "Normally you're reducing emotions, like fear, anxiety, guilt. But generally, you only want to numb emotions until you're able to identify and resolve the underlying problem. Because long-term emotional numbing can cause a severe barrier between you and your feelings."

The young man nodded and Carrie smiled.

"Now," Nick said, waving his hand to get everyone's attention, "how about a volunteer to come up and pull the needle out?"

Suddenly, everyone became a bit excited. One young woman broke away from the group without asking for permission and strode up to Nick. He turned to her and smiled, causing the needle to move slightly.

"What do I do?" she asked.

"Just pull it out," he said. He held still and leaned forward a bit, trying to be as straightforward as possible about it. Some students laughed nervously. The woman tensed up and shut her eyes tight as she tugged the needle out. There was a little resistance before it was in her hands, right at the tip of her fingers, where she dared not touch it more or bring it closer.

Nick turned and faced the group. There was no wound. They couldn't even tell where the needle entered. As the audience applauded his demonstration, Nick turned to the volunteer and held his hand out. She daintily placed the needle in it and Nick popped it back into his briefcase. The room settled back down and became filled with an uneasy silence. He noticed everyone staring at him with strange expressions on their faces. Someone pointed at his chest, and he looked down to see a dot of red. He cautiously touched his cheek and his fingers came away dry, so he touched his lips. Red. And that's when he knew.

The audience murmured, but Nick proffered them not to start up. He held up his right hand while his left retrieved a handkerchief from his pocket. Then, he did the same preparatory ritual with his fingers and entered a brief entranced state. His eyes closed, his breathing became rhythmic and a few seconds later, he started moving like no time had passed. He wiped his lips clean with the handkerchief and showed it to the audience. That time, there was no blood.

"One thing's for sure," he said, "you know it was a real needle."

The group was relieved and laughed off the error, although some were still unsure if there was an error at all. The volunteer raised her hand with a guilty expression. "Did I do something wrong?"

"Not at all," he said. "I simply pushed the needle in a little further than usual. So it hit my tongue, which I hadn't included in my preparation for blood control." His calm, off-handed nature about what had happened, and the way he faced it all without a single adverse reaction, impressed the men and women in the hall. "And with that, I think we're out of time for tonight. Thanks for coming. See ya next week."

He received another polite round of applause as some of the students swarmed him, fishing for conversation, a few business cards, or more personal questions like how much pain he could tolerate in different parts of his body. He answered each question with precision and grace, never missing a beat.

Nick then felt like he was being watched. When his gaze finally met the figure in the back corner, his eyes widened in surprise; the man wore a vintage fedora indoors, right out of the 50s. Nick felt as if eyes from under the obscured brim of the hat were staring back at him, peering into his soul. Then the mystery man, as quickly as he had appeared, faded away like a ghost vanishing into the crowd of departing students.

Once the last of the students left and the projectionist packed up, Nick got ready to leave as well. The crowd had kept him longer than normal and now he was in a hurry to get going. There were things to prepare for work and a home he wanted to get back to. Nick stood outside on the mostly deserted campus, his gaze lingering on the eerie emptiness of the nightscape. Without a steady stream of student bodies moving around, the odd infrequent traveler looked like a shadow without proper form moving through the night. And he was among them.

His heart skipped a beat when he saw a suspicious silhouette by his pride and joy — a pearl tan 1964 Jag Roadster with a cocoa brown convertible top — which he'd been lovingly restoring for the past few years. He had swapped it out for his motorcycle back home before coming in. The thief seemed to be an experienced hand, heading straight for the door lock rather than through the fabric of the roof. Nick didn't give him a chance to get away; he quickly dashed forward and shouted, knowing if they got away with it, then his treasured car would be gone forever. So Nick didn't give him a minute.

"Hey!" he shouted. The car thief didn't budge. "Hey!" Nick shouted again and louder as he ran. As the thief looked back, he saw Nick now sprinting toward him, his mouth open and teeth grit in rage. The thief took off and vaulted over the hood of the car, kicking off hard enough to leave a dent, if it were made of weaker stuff. The Jag shrugged the hoodlum's weight while Nick ran after him.

Nick was faster, but the thief was more daring. Knowing the distance was closing, the dark figure turned and flicked out a knife from his pocket. Nick stuttered his feet to a stop and held his hands out. He took a low stance and prepared to defend himself.

CHAPTER TWO
CIA CALLING

"You really want to do this?" a stranger's voice said. Nick and the thief were both caught off guard. A man appeared from behind a lamppost that was definitely too thin to fully hide him. He was about Nick's height and slender, completely opposite in build from the thief. He wore a fedora — *the fedora*, unmistakable even in the low light. The thief found himself outnumbered and ran off in a different direction. Nick took in a deep breath while his unknown aide casually walked up to him. "Enjoyed your class," the stranger said, with a slight Appalachian drawl. He'd expected something darker, more clipped — not that. The noir fixation now made less sense.

"Yeah," Nick nodded. "Thanks for—"

"William Kearney," he said, extending his hand. His palm was thick and ragged with years of work. He seemed an odd mix of a man. Nick shook his hand and almost immediately they were in a coffee shop nearby with Nick's car on attentive lockdown right outside the window nearest to the exit.

Nick sat across from Kearney and took in further details to build a profile on his unexpected helper. It was a habit, established in the course of studying different types of people and their behavior, that he couldn't break even if he wanted to. The man was in his 50s and wore the signs of his age without care. Smoking lines were as obvious as the cigarette in his hand. His sense of style reached into his accessories as well. He had a gold-plated lighter for his oral fixation when any old lighter could do. He wasn't out of shape; in fact, he looked downright taut in the midsection. In a straight-up fight, he looked like he'd do anything to win — like a scrappy boxer perhaps — but he talked like a man who was smart enough to avoid fights from breaking out.

The coffee shop they picked was one of those 24-hour breakfast and non-stop coffee refill places. The kind run by people who've been there for ages and served their coffee cups on paper lace doilies. They had a miniature jukebox for their table and Nick found it interesting when Kearney popped in some coins and made several selections in quick succession. The tunes were of no consequence to him; they were simply noise to cover the conversation.

Kearney lit up and blew some smoke above their heads. "The needle thing was impressive," he said, tapping his cheek. "But can you use that technique to help someone with a fear?" He had gotten right to the point.

Nick had the feeling that deciphering the puzzle of this man might be a little more intriguing than first thought. "People process information differently," he said. Just then, a trio of elderly women passed by their table on their way to the cashier. Nick turned to them with a pleasant smile and gave them a nod to bid for their attention. "Ladies, you look lovely tonight," he said in a complimentary tone.

Kearney cocked an eyebrow.

"Thank you," one said. "Oh, you're so sweet," the second one remarked. The third woman glanced his way but didn't reply and marched ahead of the girls to hasten their steps.

Nick turned back to Kearney. "Two of them took my compliment literally. The third was trying to figure out why I made the comment. Once you figure out how a person processes information, you can help them achieve their objective. Like… removing a fear."

Kearney took a drag of his cigarette and turned up the volume on the jukebox a tad. The Beach Boys' *Sloop John B* breezed out at them. "They were right about you."

"Who's they?"

Kearney ashed his cigarette over the tray at the end of the table. "I have a proposal," he suddenly began. "Has to do with the government."

Nick's groin ached a bit, a result of a botched surgery while in the military. He flexed his foot to rein it in. "Been through this already," he said. "Some Colonel hit me up a few years back, wanted help to condition his soldiers. Never heard from him again."

"Yeah, he lost his funding," Kearney confirmed. "But that's not why I'm here. I'm looking for someone with your set of skills." Now it was Nick's turn to cock an eyebrow. Kearney blew smoke again, calmly and thoughtfully. "We might need you to help someone pass a polygraph, among other things."

"Isn't that illegal, even for the government?" asked Nick.

Kearney smiled and fidgeted with his lighter. He wasn't flicking it on; he merely turned it over in his hand, between his fingers. Despite that, he stayed totally focused on Nick. His hand moved automatically to cope with the confrontation. "A surprisingly moral standpoint," he said, "for a man who had to join the military to keep out of prison."

Nick linked the action with the reaction. Kearney was making a push, like the growl of a predator when it cornered prey. His lighter wasn't a tool; it was more of a distraction to keep him from being over-reactive. "Which might give you some insight," Nick said, strongly confirming his stance without raising it into a greater issue, "into why I have no intention of getting involved with the government again."

"So you're happy with being just an employee?" Kearney stubbed out his cigarette less than halfway to the filter in the ashtray. "You don't really think Costas is going to turn over his place to you after he retires, do you?"

That surprised Nick and left him a degree hotter than before. He was sure those matters were supposed to be private, but it seemingly spoke to the desperation that was spent on gathering dirt to force his recruitment. "Don't you have your own people for that kind of thing?"

"As you said," Kearney replied, "people process information differently." Kearney played a classic move, ending on a repeat of what was already said, robbing control of the conversation. "And if you really need to know, yeah, we have people who can do it but I don't want someone who thinks inside the box." Kearney stood up. "I need someone who doesn't even recognize the box." He left some money on the table and topped it with a business card before striding out. It was not a discreet maneuver, but an expected one.

Nick stayed in place and stared down at his coffee, which had gone cold, just like his feelings for Kearney, who had brought up the military. He reached over and picked up the business card, turning it in his fingers the way Kearney had turned his lighter. It was something that bred all sorts of hard feelings in Nick. Not simply the fact that he was forced to join the Air Force, but that once in, he had gotten a really raw deal. It started when Nick, working on jet bombers, suffered a hernia and was ordered to undergo surgery by his commanding officer. "We spent a quarter of a million dollars training you to become a mechanic. You're getting the damn surgery." The procedure was ultimately botched by an incompetent surgeon resulting in Nick's chronic pain. When Nick dared to complain, the colonel tried to cover his ass by setting Nick up with a rigged court-martial. In court, the colonel referred to Nick as "a California crumb". Nick got a kick out of that; he never really knew what a California crumb was. He lost the case. Outraged, he filed an appeal. At the age of 19, Nick was the first airman to have a court-martial overturned. He slipped the business card into his pocket and picked up his coffee. It had gone past cold into something worse, flat and stale and faintly bitter. He took a sip anyway. The livid colonel retaliated one more time by giving Nick a general discharge. No reason. Just his bullshit order.

Nick got up to leave the coffee shop. As he walked out, he passed a table and noticed an empty plate; all that remained were a few crumbs.

Later that night, Nick was lounging in the living room of the house he shared with his fiancée Kate Watson, the ultimate pretty girl-next-door who also fell into the category of "brainy". The TV volume was low. Nick didn't care what Reagan had to say about Iran, no matter how much the national news insisted that he listen to it. His chore was finding a use for his X tile on the Scrabble board. Yogi, their Siamese kitten, rested on Nick's lap while Dancer, their lab-husky pup, put his paws over Kate's leg in a pleading position.

"Well, thank God he came along," Kate said. "You could have been killed."

"Yeah, it was a strange night." Nick had only told her half of what happened; the remainder of what fedora man had to say remained hidden for now. Nick's attention then drifted elsewhere. He was holding onto his tile a bit too long and he had that far-away look in his eyes that told Kate something else was bothering him.

"Spill it," she said.

He looked up, momentarily confused, then realized what she was asking. "Ah, just something at work."

"What's going on?"

"Costas again. No more pro bono work."

"At all?" Kate asked, her voice rising.

"Not on company time."

Kate could see Nick tensing up. She shook her head. "What an asshole that guy is. Even we do some work for free."

"There's no value in goodwill to him." Nick shuffled through his other Scrabble tiles absent-mindedly.

"That's another reason why I love you." Kate paused, trying to get a better read on Nick. "I wish you could just leave the Academy and be done with that place."

"You know I'm not going to do that. It's going to be *mine* because it's *my* process, not his or his kid's. I'm not dumping out." Nick dropped his X tile in frustration.

Kate hesitated before continuing. "This is about Billy again, never giving up. I get it. But isn't it time you made your own footprints instead of following his?"

"Goddamn it Kate!"

Kate's jaw tightened, fearing the worst. She stopped playing.

"What a great fucking line!"

She was taken aback and relieved. "What?"

"The *footprints*."

"Uh, okay." Kate chuckled.

Nick reached over the table and put his hand on her cheek. "I'll think about it." He picked up his X tile and looked to make a move but came up empty.

Kate felt better about their conversation. She turned back to the game as Nick glanced down and petted Yogi. Dancer's plea for attention lost out to Kate's concentration on the board while she made her winning move. She added enough letters to bridge 'pro' and 'tor' into 'procrastinator' across a Triple Word Score slot. She threw her arms up in a celebratory move and shouted, "Score!" as if she were an announcer at a sporting event.

Nick looked at the board. The game was over and he was defeated in spectacular fashion.

"Look at that," she said, pointing to her word. "It's a Ouija board."

"How the hell did you pull that off?"

"How the hell do you think my bosses keep winning cases?" She pointed to the board, most of which was her content spread across all the available bonus tiles.

He leaned back. "You're channeling your mother, because I can definitely hear her."

Kate pouted, picked up a blank tile and threw it at him. He caught it before it flew past his face and put it with his unused letters. He looked at her word again. Aside from being impressive, it was also very telling. It wasn't a coincidence that she forced it onto the board and he knew exactly what she meant by it.

"I promise," he said, "we'll set a wedding date soon." Nick moved to the couch, causing Yogi to let out a pathetic mew as he trotted off to the corner where his cat bed was. Dancer then got up and scampered away, out of sight and out of the room.

Kate got up and gently wrapped her hands around Nick's neck. She gave him a gentle, playful throttle and bounced his body against the cushion of the couch. "You know I'll hold you to that," she insisted. He started laughing, which broke her focus and made her laugh along with him. Giggles interspersed with snorts that quieted down as she fell onto the couch next to him. Her hands drifted from their position and wrapped around him more lovingly. She curled over and her knees pushed into his thighs, up a little too close for comfort.

Nick winced and moved his hand down to stop her leg from going further. It wasn't anywhere near his groin. She was hurting him in a different way.

"Goddamn it, Nick," she said as she adjusted her legs away from his sore spot, "you really should have sued them for what they did."

"That's all I needed," Nick said as he raised his leg up once to stretch it gently. "Take on the government again."

"You're right," she said. She looked deep into his eyes and romantically protested, "Fuck the government!" He leaned up and kissed her. She kissed back, twice as hard, and guided him into a deep, reciprocating, passionate kiss. She pulled away to take a breath and give him a warning. "I hope you're not too tired." She slid her hand up his thigh, being careful of his sore spot but gave it enough pressure to tantalize him.

"You make it very hard to say no."

For a moment he just looked at her — this woman who got mad on his behalf, who fought his battles on a Scrabble board and meant every word of it. He moved on her, causing her to yelp in excitement, and scooped her up off the couch.

She held onto his neck and kicked her legs up into a princess-style carry as he walked her through the house. They arrived at the bedroom, lips still together, and got close to the bed. Their eyes were shut and all their senses were devoted to feeling the ever-increasing passion. All but their noses. Nick was the first to notice when he took a deep breath in. It caused him to stop just shy of throwing Kate onto the bed. He turned away and planted her feet on the floor. She looked confused and irritated until she also took in a breath and discovered why.

There was a perfectly placed mound of puppy poop in the center of their bed, on top of the covers, that stank up the entire room. Dancer, a new rescue and still not completely housebroken, came in, returning to the scene of the crime, and hopped up on the bed to sniff it. Nick rushed to grab Dancer and took him outside, mumbling all the way, while Kate rushed out with one hand over her nose to grab a whole roll of paper towels.

Nick kept Dancer away while Kate cleaned up the poop and removed the bedding all the way down to the sheets. It was an unfortunate end to their evening in more ways than one.

The next morning, Nick was up bright and early working on his car outside the garage, which was well stocked with an array of auto tools. He was on the ground, back on a low wheeling cart, and his prized Jag Roadster hovered above him on drive-up metal ramps for extra clearance. The manual labor combined with the precision and mechanical knowledge put him in a calm and mindful state. It was like exercise for his mind, as well as his forearms and wrists. He had already changed out the engine that came with the Jag to the more powerful Chevy V8 350. This day, Nick was fixing a leaky brake line. The fact that he could do that at all was its own reward.

Kate saw his legs poking out from under the car and gave him a gentle tap, shoe to shoe, on her way past. "May your day at the office be less exciting than last night at UCLA," she said. Nick slid out from under the car just in time to watch her hips sway as she walked to her own car, a striking blue BMW. Kate enjoyed the occasional bounce around town with Nick in his sporty Jag, but when it came to her own vehicle, nothing mattered more than safety and reliability. She didn't need a cranky car breaking down on the way to work. Too much to do at the law office where she was a top-performing legal secretary.

Kate's reminder gave Nick pause before he returned his attention back to the Jag. The prior night was indeed weird with the fedora-sporting CIA guy, the military references he spouted, and an unusual job offer Nick hadn't even begun to entertain, primarily because the idea of dealing with the government again was enough to make him bash his head against a wall. He shook his head as if he had finalized his decision, then checked his watch. Another hour to fiddle with his car before needing to clean up and head back to Costasland and all the drama of that place.

CHAPTER THREE
CHAOS

Starting his day at the Academy, Nick was nearing a conference room where he was scheduled to run a staff meeting, when —

GONG. The sound came from a small classroom. Curious, he opened the door. Not what he was expecting. Sitting cross-legged in the center of a small stage was a 60-year-old bearded hippie Gong Master with a large gong and hammer.

"Can I help you?" Nick asked politely.

"I was told to set up in here."

"For what?"

"My meditation demonstration," said the bearded one from on high. "Everything okay?"

"I'll let you know." The Gong Master's smile faded as Nick exited and closed the door behind him. "Jesus!" Nick uttered under his breath as he proceeded to the conference room.

He entered in time to hear members of his staff in their last-minute squabbling. The small group was made up of middle-agers: Darlene Morrison, a classy, sophisticated snob; Tony Alta, a former tennis player who almost made pro and was the epitome of a ladies' man; Bruce Kopek, a congenial sort who everyone liked. They were all gathered around the conference table.

"He can't make us do this. I'm barely making ends meet as it is," said Bruce.

Isis Crimms, an astrologer bordering on Gypsy with flowing gray hair and an array of gaudy new-age jewelry, pounded on a malfunctioning coffee machine. "Fuck this! And fuck him!"

Dr. George Rayle, the staid token psychiatrist, sat in a corner on his own. He sighed loudly as he looked embarrassed by the lot of them.

"Must you always curse like that?" scolded Darlene.

"How would you like me to curse?" Isis huffed.

Nick pulled up a seat. "Hey, guys."

Dr. Rayle looked relieved, while Bruce, now effervescent, chimed in. "Good morning, Nick."

"It's noon," Nick reminded him.

Bruce checked his watch. Noon on the dot. "Oh."

Isis now joined them at the table with half a cup of coffee, the only amount she could squeeze out of the crappy machine. "We were talking about the new lousy idea," she said, "Now we're all supposed to teach a free intro class at night to bring in new clients? I got a kid at home."

"Yeah," admitted Nick, "I just got the memo."

"I won't get home till midnight," said Tony. "I hate to admit I can't hack the hours anymore, but, well, I can't."

Dr. Rayle humorously offered, "I'll be dispensing Valium in my office later if anyone's interested."

"Thanks, George," said Nick, "that's very helpful. Don't worry, guys. It's not sustainable. The cost of running free classes every night will outweigh what Costas thinks will come of it."

"Damn straight," said Isis.

"I'll talk to him about that," Nick continued, "and increasing your salaries. It's been a long time coming and you guys are worth it."

Darlene scowled at Isis as she beefed about something else. "You know, I really don't think it's appropriate to have astrology posters in the classroom."

There was momentary silence except for Dr. Rayle's loud chair adjustment. It creaked as he swiveled in it. All eyes shifted between Darlene and Isis, waiting for the shit to hit the fan before Dr. Rayle came to the rescue. "You know, Nick, I think she's right. We are trying to enhance our image of professionalism."

GONG. It was louder than before. Most of them laughed, except for Isis, who was fingering her amethyst necklace in a meditative state. She snapped out of it, checked her watch, grabbed her stuff, and headed to the door. "Got a client."

"Me too," said Dr. Rayle, who also headed out in a rush.

Stevie almost bumped into him as he rushed in. "Sorry, I'm late. I was really—"

"Well, I guess that's it," Nick interrupted, causing the trio to grab their belongings and filter out. "Thanks, everyone. Remember to stop by Dr. Rayle's before the end of the day," Nick joked. He glanced over at the coffee station. "Hey, there's a donut left," he said, and exited as Stevie looked over to where half a donut and some crumbs remained in a collapsed box.

While the rest of Nick's day continued with clients, classes, and thoughts of having another run-in with Costas, Kate was having her own special day across town at her Beverly Hills law firm. Ordinarily, she'd be reviewing voluminous legal documents looking for inconsistencies, checking case law, setting depositions and doing whatever else the associates needed while other staffers were assigned to the firm's investment arm with its even higher class of clients. Kate never thought too much about the dual role taking place under the same roof. She was simply happy to be working at such a prestigious company.

But this day found Kate strangely leading a line of zombies with outstretched hands out of the conference room, where they had just signed up for the firm's Halloween event. She ushered the wacky assemblage to the elevator and said, "You all look great. See you on Halloween." Before he stepped into the elevator, one of the zombie's ears fell off and when he reached for it, his nose fell off and landed on her shoe. The zombies moaned in unison.

Back at her office, her young co-worker Cindi was stacking the contracts that the zombies had signed on her desk. "Did you tell Nick yet?"

"That we've been reduced to party planners?"

"No, that we have to dress up too."

"What?!"

That night, at the dinner table, a stream of water flew out of Nick's mouth, he was laughing so hard. Half of it landed on Kate's blouse.

"Oh, no!" she lamented, as she grabbed a napkin and dabbed at her blouse, also laughing.

"Sorry honey, but you wanted to wait until dinner to tell me the funny thing that happened at the office." He was still laughing as he tried to wipe his mouth. "We don't really have to go to this thing, do we?"

"I don't have a choice. You'll have fun, trust me."

The weekend rolled around and the dreaded party day was upon them. Kate had already gathered several pieces of old clothes that she worked to turn into zombie costumes. A shred here, a tear there, and lots of fake blood everywhere. Nick spent the day cleaning out the garage and doing his best to avoid costuming, trusting that Kate would do all the dirty work — and with pleasure.

That afternoon, she was tidying up her work and laying out the costumes. When Nick saw the too-short, stained and tattered red pants she had lined up for him, he protested. "Oh, come on, I'm gonna look like some hick from—"

"No, you'll be the zombie you were always meant to have been."

"I hope all the shit you do for that guy is gonna pay off one day."

Kate added a few extra scissor cuts along the edge of an old emerald green dress. "It will. I've just added zombie coordinator to my résumé. I can always get a job in the film industry if anything goes sideways."

"Just steer clear of the finance side of the firm. You know how those things can do a fast turnaround."

"I have no interest in stocks or bonds and certainly no aptitude in any of that, as you well know. Now go away and let me finish." As Nick walked off, Kate called out, "Oh, don't bother showering. All that dirt will make for a very authentic zombie."

It's not like kids ever went door-to-door trick-or-treating in Beverly Hills on Halloween but some houses did put on elaborate displays just for the fun of it. Then there was Kate's boss' place. *"Tucker Mnuchin's Halloween-O-Rama"* blazed the sky-high-flying banner at the entrance to the long gated driveway.

The extravaganza was underway on the lavish grounds of Tucker's mansion, with costumed guests and servers and the zombies from Kate's office milling about. Drink, food and candy stations, loud music, carnival games, smoke and scare machines, the whole works.

On a bench were Kate and Nick, as the tattered zombies they were meant to be, along with Cindi as a witch wearing a large pointy hat. Poor Nick, exceedingly uncomfortable, had an axe seemingly embedded in his skull while Kate had a fake eyeball on a spring bouncing down her cheek. They had had a few refreshments of the alcoholic kind. Kate and Cindi broke into their rendition of "The Banana Song" in honor of their boss, whom they both not so secretly resented. "Tucker,

Tucker, bo-fucker... Banana-fana fo sucker... Fee-Fi-blood-sucker... Tucker!"

Cindi smacked Nick's arm and pointed to owners Tucker Mnuchin, a 60-year-old Napoleon-esque financial hotshot, and his wife Madeleine who were dressed as an elegant Frankenstein and his Bride. They were chatting up rich prospects. Cindi declared, "Oh, let's do his wife now! Madeleine, Madeleine, bo- ... bo... Madeleine ... shit, nothing rhymes!"

Nick took in the absurdity of the whole scene.

"This is why the rich don't deserve all their money," Cindi whimpered.

Kate rose. "I'm going to get more candy." Nick hoisted his beer in a toast as he watched Kate walk off.

"My mother thinks I do real work," said Cindi. "All those years studying. I still don't even know what a junk bond is. Do you?" Cindi started crying as she laid her head on Nick's shoulder. He patted her hand in comfort.

"I don't know, Cindi... perhaps if you sing a few bars..."

Cindi snorted a laugh through her tears.

As Kate made her way back to Nick and Cindi, carrying a bowl of candy and a bottle of wine, Tucker Mnuchin waved her over. He took a step away from his guests to speak with her. "Yes, Mr. Mnuchin?"

"Kate, make sure the investor packets are in the swag bags and that everyone gets one on the way out." Tucker immediately turned back to his guests without so much as an acknowledgment from Kate who was about to tell him she had already instructed the hospitality staff to do just that. She waited a moment, then walked back to Nick. Cindi was now licking one of those giant swirl lollipops.

"What did the Munchkin want?" Nick asked as Kate took her seat.

Cindi laughed hard and slapped her knee with the lollipop, which caused it to stick to her witch's costume. "Fucker!" she exclaimed.

"He was ensuring his next meal ticket," said Kate.

Nick grabbed a handful of candy corn from Kate's bowl and they watched the guests as if it were some absurd TV comedy, while Cindi still tried to unstick her lollipop. The Bride of Frankenstein, Madeleine, walked away from her group and one zombie accidentally stepped on the overly-long train of her gown. It half-ripped off. She turned and smacked the zombie's face. The poor actor was further humiliated when Tucker himself rushed over to ream him out.

Nick sobered up fast. "I think we should leave." Kate nodded in agreement and they sneaked off, dragging Cindi with them. "Tucker, Tucker, bo-fucker…" Cindi repeated the refrain as she stumbled along. Kate chuckled.

"What a night! Thanks for the memory," Nick said facetiously.

The next day, at Nick's job, he expected things to be more sedate. He was booked with clients and had a class to teach. As he walked toward one classroom, Tony exited Costas' office. "Hey Nick, quick question?"

"Sure."

"I was just talking to John about one of my clients who believes she's seeing strange things and he told me to get rid of her, that I should turn her over to a psychiatrist."

"How old is she and what things is she seeing?" Nick asked.

"She calls them little shadow people that keep moving around. In her sixties."

"First have her see an ophthalmologist."

"Why?"

"A hunch."

At that moment, Bruce passed the two with his next client and continued down the hall.

Tony was in disbelief. "Wasn't that Hank Aaron?"

"Yep. He's looking to break Babe Ruth's record, so, besides practicing like hell on the field, he needs to boost his focus and confidence. That *is* what we do."

Nick continued on his way to class. As Chief-of-Staff, it was his job to not only field issues of office politics as well as develop course work and teaching, but also to be a sounding board for other therapists calling the Academy home. Costas, on the other hand, had few interests outside of the business end of things and sponging off his therapists' outside jobs, like Nick's special arrangement with the King of Morocco for therapy sessions — an arrangement courtesy of a personal connection through one of his students at the Academy. It was a prestigious job and ego boost for Nick and another income source for Costas, who piggybacked on the arrangement. The Academy scrooge insisted on taking 75% of the charged fee even when Nick had to do all the work. Nick knew he could change the atmosphere for the better with his hands-on approach once he took control after Costas' retirement. That was the deal they struck when Costas bargained for exclusivity of Nick's therapy process and his becoming Chief-of-Staff. However, William Kearney's words of warning about the Costas family arrangement hadn't yet embedded itself in Nick's brain.

Right now, though, it was Nick's job to be the face of the Academy to the local media. A small film crew and an eager female reporter were at the back of Nick's classroom, watching him navigate a delicate subject. Scrawled on a chalkboard behind Nick was 'Advanced Sexuality', with explicit and sexually charged bullet points underneath. Two dozen students were in attendance as Stevie watched from just inside the door.

"That covers it for today. Any questions?"

The reporter was looking at a line of astrology posters on the walls, one for each sign. She waved her microphone. "I was wondering, have nontraditional therapies, such as yours, elevated themselves from being considered just a con game? Psychologists I talk to don't seem to think so."

Stevie, always feeling far more superior than he had any right to be, scowled at the reporter. Nick thought of the many times psychologists had ridiculed him for saying therapy sessions didn't need to go on for decades, as well as his not having college degrees and a license to practice hanging on a wall. But now that he had those things, he was still plagued by naysayers because his process didn't fit neatly into the standard psychology playbook of lobotomies, debilitating medication, and the belief that homosexuality was a disease, to name a few.

"Con game." Nick paused for good effect. "Maybe they're right."

Stevie's jaw dropped dramatically and he huffed away from his position at the door. Students shifted uncomfortably in their seats, unsure what Nick's intent was in conceding the point but they sure didn't expect unfriendly fire from what they viewed as an invited guest.

Nick continued, "But, if a con game means helping someone believe in themselves, getting rid of debilitating anxiety and depression, helping them take control of their lives, then I don't give a damn what you call it."

The students broke into applause and the reporter acknowledged her approval of Nick's save with a sly smile and nod.

After the event, Nick was forced to defend himself in Costas' office. "A con game?" Costas barked. "Have you lost your mind?"

"Stevie should have stayed," countered Nick.

"This isn't about Stevie, it's about you trashing my company's reputation."

"I'm telling you, Dad, he doesn't know how hard—"

"You mean the reputation after I got here," Nick corrected.

"That's bullshit!" said Costas.

"You wanted my process. I gave it to you... with the understanding that—"

"This is *my* business," interrupted Costas, who was now a shade of cherry red.

"So don't screw it up," Stevie finished his father's thought.

Nick's eyes narrowed on Stevie. He then looked back at Costas, who was now fumbling with his lighter as he tried to light a cigarette. Nick zeroed in on the lighter. It was the second time that week he had taken notice of such an ordinary tool — in the hands of two entirely different kinds of men. Nick turned and exited, closing the door behind him hard enough to cause Costas' yacht picture to crash to the floor.

That evening, Nick's Jag was parked outside of a mundane legal office. Inside, Nick sat across from Ted Patts. The poor old man was tired from his long day in his stuffy office. Right now he reminded Nick of Bob Cratchit, the hard-toiling soul under Ebenezer Scrooge's thumb in *A Christmas Carol*. Nick was his last appointment for the day and it showed. Ted knew he was on the last leg of his career and was prone to minor mistakes that could balloon into major errors. So he was being extra careful and didn't want to let down an old friend, especially one who was doing so much to help his adopted son, Luis, the tattooed badass, who Nick helped at the correctional center.

"I really appreciate you seeing me so late," said Nick.

Ted smiled and took a sticky note and laid it on the middle page of the contract between Nick and Costas. He drew a red arrow on the note, pointing to a paragraph. "You can take him to court," Ted explained, "to get the money he owes you, but with this loophole, he can drag it out forever." Nick looked at the wording the red arrow pointed to. It was so dense it was like his eyes were pushing through visual oatmeal. Ted leaned back in his chair, which caught his weight with a creak. "Kate would have caught it."

"Except I didn't know her back then." Nick rubbed his hand across his forehead and felt the pressure beneath his skin. "All that money," he muttered. He sat up a bit and readjusted himself in the seat, taking a more confident posture to approach the matter with assurance instead of restraint or regret. "What about him taking my process and calling it his?"

"Well, we have the letter he originally sent you about your process, but Nick, you never copyrighted anything. And a handshake deal isn't going to cut it." Ted took the contract, removed the sticky note and moved over to his copy machine. The whir of the old machine deafened the room as it pressed copies of each page one at a time, complete with the crease where the staples in the spine had to be folded away. "Let me sit with it for a while and see if I can work some magic. But, I have to tell you, Nick, I think you're screwed."

Nick sighed and picked up his original copy. He slapped it against his hand and felt the weight of the flimsy paper push against him. So much headache in such little mass. It was like a bullet, something small and seemingly insignificant, that could take a life and change the world of one person for the worse.

He left and threw the document into the glove box so it wouldn't blow away. It was no time to drive with the roof up. He needed to feel speed and the wind blowing against his face. Nick's drive home was spent in keeping his emotions in check. He had a pleasant evening lined up, initially to celebrate whatever good news Kate was expecting, so turning it into a therapeutic retreat with his fiancée was definitely not on the menu.

They had planned a night out at their favorite restaurant, a small and charming Italian place that had an intentionally limited floor space. The rest was dedicated to family memorabilia like old-time photos, an old olive hand press, and ornate lace fabrics. Some of it dated back a century. Kate always loved perusing the antiques before being seated, no matter how many times she had seen them.

Tonight, Nick and Kate were garbed far better than the last time they played dress up. She was enjoying their night out but could tell he was still thinking about the contract. "Hey, I'll look it over again tomorrow, okay? I just didn't want to miss our reservation," she said.

The waiter came by with their plates and gently placed them on the table. "No, she's the eggplant," Nick said. He was polite and quiet about the mistake, but Kate could tell him pointing it out in the first place came from a place of frustration. Nick knew that as well and acknowledged it. The waiter corrected his mistake and replaced the food. Her eggplant Parmesan over angel hair pasta with a wine reduction red sauce looked and smelled incredible. His plate was stacked thick with pasta in a creamy Alfredo sauce, also made with a wine reduction of a different kind, and had freshly cut and cooked carrots and zucchini slivers layered across the top.

"Fresh pepper?" the waiter asked. Kate waited for Nick to decide first. He shook his head.

Kate responded, "Just a little. Thank you."

The waiter obliged and then stepped back to retreat to the next set of customers. Kate got her fork ready and was about to dig in when she inspected Nick. He was looking down, but she couldn't tell if he was contemplating his food or the table underneath his plate. He then looked through the scenery with an occupied stare.

"I think," she spoke up, "you should get a second opinion. I know he's good, but I'm sure I can get someone from my office to look it over."

"It would be a waste of time," Nick said. "He was pretty adamant."

"You're so pig-headed sometimes. Never hurts to have a second pair of eyes."

Nick stabbed his fork into the pasta and curled it around. He occasionally heard and felt the screech of metal against the thick dish that held the greasy nest of deliciousness.

"How's your pasta?" she asked.

His distraction caused her to stop eating as well. "Sorry, honey," he said. "We're supposed to be celebrating your promotion."

"It's okay."

"No, it's not okay," Nick insisted. "You worked hard for it." He gripped his wineglass and hoisted it up at her. "To the best… what was it again?"

Kate opened her mouth to protest, but seeing Nick's flip-flopping between self-reflective worries and a sincere drive to be pleasant was refreshing. Like a teenage boy trying desperately to do right on his first date. Nick laughed when he saw her reaction and suddenly remembered it. "Best executive legal secretary in all of Los Angeles. See? I do pay attention."

"Thank you for that," she said. "Of course, now you'll need to catch up. And with that… oh, oh, too much wine." Kate stood, didn't meet his toast, and pushed her chair to the side to retreat to the restroom. "Be right back."

Nick sank back into his seat and threw back the whole glass of wine in one go. He tried to eat but the dense flavor of the pasta felt muted in his mouth. Not quite numb, but his own frustration over his lack of foresight regarding the contract, blocked the full palette from reaching his brain. As he glanced to the side, he spotted a glint of a golden lighter. *What is it with gold cigarette lighters,* he thought. The man holding it looked familiar, but it wasn't Kearney. Although it could have been his brother. They smoked the same cigarettes with the same kind of lighter and seemed to have the same build, slender.

Nick realized he was noticing one too many coincidences. Just another annoyance in a long queue of strange incidents that were stacked up higher than Nick's mound of pasta. After a moment, Nick's brain shouted — *Enough. Get over it! This is Kate's time.*

CHAPTER FOUR

ONE MAN, TWO WOLVES

Canoga Park was a bit away from Nick's home at the other end of the valley and even further from his stomping ground at the UCLA campus. Some parts of the town were deteriorating, but not where this little gem of a house stood. It was indeed small but, in this neighborhood, they all were. Still, none was as pristine as Billy's and Ruthie's place.

Old Ruthie was obsessed with keeping her house in tip-top shape inside and out. She was a strong woman, strong enough to last longer than most would expect. All she wanted to do was take care of her husband Billy and garden every day. That's where Nick would find his grandmother pruning plants in her English-style garden. He brought her a gift, a beautiful flowering potted peony plant. So he assumed she would welcome it.

He hooked his sunglasses on the sun visor of his Jag. Something fell down from the unseen hinge on the other side. It was Kearney's business card. That meeting felt so much closer than it was. Nearly a week had passed, but signs of Kearney's presence kept coming up. Nick wondered whether they were simply steering him toward an inevitable situation where refusal wouldn't be an option.

He tossed it onto the dashboard, picked up the plant, and hopped out of the car to round the home and greet Ruthie in the garden where he sneaked up on her. She turned, trowel in hand, but smiled when she saw it was Nick. He kissed her on the cheek and handed over the plant.

"What the hell is this?" she said. Nick's self-pleased smile dropped into an awkward smirk. "You should be saving your money for the wedding."

"Okay," he said as he reached to take it back. Her arms, old as they were, held surprising strength for a septuagenarian.

"All right, but this is the last time. I'll give it a good home; clearly it's needy." As she gave the plant a good look-over, she said, "You'll find him in the shop… where else."

Nick chuckled as she coveted the plant. Then he stopped dead and crouched over.

"Oh, honey, is it bad today?" she asked.

Nick shut his eyes and focused on his pain. "It's all good," he said as he triggered his process. The pain dipped away and left him gently reeling from it, like a hard pinch beneath his groin. He walked into the garage with a more controlled step and saw Billy working with an electric sander. His gray ponytail fluttered from the breeze as he sanded a dolphin carving from a sawdust-covered loveseat.

Billy, a member of the Cherokee Nation, was a woodworking hobbyist to where there was no room for a car. He had an entire area in the corner that contained intricate and detailed woodworking projects. Various Indian-inspired spirit animals, kaleidoscopes, and other types of carvings were arranged along the many shelves that surrounded a much larger structure — two battling wolves, each over a foot tall, made from the same thick cut of an old stump and stained differently. One was bright, the natural color of the wood itself, representing good. The other was stained darker, representing evil, as if it were taken from a different tree. At the base of the stand were burned in words: '*The One You Feed is the One Who Wins*'.

Next to all the woodworking projects was an old picture of Billy hanging on the wall, with hair much shorter, in front of a Stealth Nighthawk fighter-bomber. He was receiving an award as captioned by the Lockheed Corporation.

Nick's own garage echoed Billy's in the amount but different types of tools. The major difference was the purpose.

Nick did his best to sneak up on the distracted old man as Billy was blowing off a bit of wood dust from the carving. "Hi, Nick," he shouted.

"How on earth did you hear me over the noise of that sander?" Nick asked.

Billy switched the sander off and set it down. "Didn't I teach you that everything is connected?"

"Yeah," Nick admitted.

"Well, you're connected to that earth-shaking muscle car of yours."

"And I thought it was some kind of Indian magic," Nick said.

They both chuckled it off. Billy's laugh lasted longer but sounded weaker, more tired. He tapped his hand on the wooden loveseat and brushed some of the stray sawdust off of it. "So, what do you think?"

"Kate's going to love it," Nick said as he ran his hand along the top of the loveseat where Billy had carved a beautiful dolphin arcing out of the waves. The wood was smooth as silk, aside from the flakes of dust all over it that he carefully removed. Nick's eyes wandered to the battling wolves' sculpture which instantly transported him back to his preteen years when Ruthie and Billy took him on a trip to Lubbock, Texas to meet Billy's family.

The family of Native Americans were ancestral left-overs from the great forced migrations of earlier centuries when other Indians: men, women, and children had been slaughtered. Billy's family ended up in the far outskirts of Lubbock, the furthest Nick had been from his home and culture. The house was modest, with a large backyard with only a chicken coop and a couple of trees. The kitchen was the early morning meeting place for Billy's father and mother to host their extended family with what amounted to breakfast banquets to nourish everyone before they left for their various jobs.

Nick thought it strange to have to get up when it was still dark. He remembered walking to the kitchen, still half-asleep, and when he approached the door, he was shocked awake by the aroma of scores of freshly cooked food. His eyes widened when he saw the long table set with every kind of breakfast food you could imagine. It was a friendly and boisterous family sit-down, unlike at Nick's house, where it was breakfast on the run on some days or nothing at all on others.

A few stayed after the meal to help clean up but Nick wasn't one of them. He was sent off to inspect and clean the chicken coops, a novelty to a boy from the California suburbs. He tackled the chore with enthusiasm and even tried to make friends with some of the chickens.

When Billy was ready to meet the day, it entailed a trip into town to the Sears Roebuck which was a tool lover's delight. One day, while Billy was on a search to find something exceptional, Nick went looking for a water fountain. He came upon a white wall with two attached water fountains and above the fountains were two signs taped to the wall, one printed "Colored" and the other marked "White". Nick stood contemplating the two signs. After a few moments, he cautiously turned the knob on the fountain marked Colored, expecting the water to come out like a rainbow. Nope, nothing different about the water, just the color of the skin of the people forced to use it. Suddenly, a voice shot out from behind him, "Use the other one, stupid!" The man who was shouting wore a sheriff's badge. Texas was indeed becoming a unique education for Nick.

Dinner that night wasn't as elaborate as breakfast. It was only the five of them — Nick, Ruthie, Billy, and Billy's parents — Koda and Sarah. Still, Sarah knew how to fill bellies, while Koda knew how to fill imaginations with his stories of ancient times and peoples.

After dinner, Nick wandered into the living room where Koda sat in an old chair by a fire with a coffee can in his lap. Handwoven Indian blankets and pictures of different Indian themes surrounded him. But the one thing Nick couldn't take his eyes off was the painting of wolves up in the mountains on a frosty night, howling. The remoteness and camaraderie of the wolves intrigued him as they engaged in their nightly ritual.

The old man rocked and spat a couple of times into the coffee can to rid himself of the build-up from his chewing tobacco. "Do you like animals?" he asked Nick as he caught him staring at the painting.

"Yes. We have some cats and two horses. I've never seen a wolf in real life, though."

"Dogs," the old man said, as he pointed up to the painting, "all evolved from wolves." Nick nodded as if it were common knowledge to him, but of course, it wasn't. He tried to imagine how a tiny chihuahua somehow came from the formidable figures depicted in the painting.

"Little dogs, big dogs, funny looking dogs. They all came from wolves. Many, many years of evolution and breeding. But wolves have a much more powerful bite and lots of cunning."

Ruthie, Billy and Sarah came into the room with steaming mugs of hot chocolate for all to enjoy. The old man took his eagerly and pointed up to the painting as an explanation of what they'd been discussing. "Wolves and dogs," he said simply.

Billy looked up at the painting and told his father. "He needs to hear about the wolves within."

Ruthie handed Nick his hot chocolate, then settled down near the fire with Billy and everyone turned their attention to the old man who sat and rocked and related the story of the two wolves.

"A battle between two wolves goes on inside all of us. One is evil, and it's filled with darkness, anger, greed, and lies. The other is good, peace, love, kindness, and truth. They fight and fight until one wins out."

The fire crackled as Nick's imagination went wild. He saw and heard the battling wolves as each ravaged the other in its fight for superiority. Seeing no end in sight, as each wolf seemed equally strong, Nick asked Koda. "Who wins?"

The old man spat into the can, then looked Nick dead in the eyes. "The one you feed."

Nick stood in Billy's garage with the wolves' inscription burning in his eyes, the old man's words still ringing in his ears.

Billy put the sander back in its place among the wall of tools. "So what's on your mind?" he asked.

Nick snapped back to the present and after a moment said, "Oh yeah… what would you do if you had to make a choice that would involve working for an organization you despise?"

Thoughts spun in Billy's head. He was all too familiar with the concept because when he started at Lockheed, he was a mere floor worker doing grunge work. He busted his ass amid long hours and racial discrimination and, while it was unheard of at the time, rose through the ranks to become part of management.

"Working with the government again," Nick continued.

Billy's eyes narrowed. "It depends on what you can get out of them versus what they can take from you." He walked over to the sink to wash his hands. "I don't see a problem. You had the court-martial overturned. You beat them at their own game! Stop fighting old battles."

Nick tossed a dry towel to Billy. "Turns out well, everyone's happy," he concluded. "If it doesn't, you're that much wiser. The only bad decision is…"

"No decision at all," Nick said alongside Billy. Billy nodded and looked out of the garage at the Jag.

"After lunch, we both need to make a decision," Billy said.

"What's that?"

Billy pointed past him. "How do we get this loveseat into your car?"

From outside, Ruthie called, "It's lunchtime." When she entered, she warned Nick, "And don't tell me you don't have enough time."

Nick walked over, smiled, and put his arm around her. "For you, I have all the time in the world."

"You never said anything about the fruitcake. How the hell was it?"

"Considering that Kate and I got drunk on it again, that should tell you something."

"Goddamned babies, can't hold your liquor! Well, I'm not changing my recipe. You'll have to just deal with it the way Billy does, eat it then fall asleep in front of the TV."

They all shared a chuckle as they made their way to the house. Nick was about to say something else when his pager buzzed. He thought something came up at the Academy or the prison. It was neither. He couldn't recognize the number at first, so the message CALL ME didn't click. A moment later, he realized the number matched Kearney's business card. He knew he had to make a decision. Denying it felt like the decision he wanted to make, but accepting the offer could lead him and Kate to the possibility of a more secure future.

"Sorry, I have to get this," Nick said. He made the call.

That evening when he got home, Nick started packing because the answer he had given to Kearney was taking him out of the country.

"What if something happens to you?" Kate asked.

Nick pushed a folded pair of pants to join the other items in his luggage. He was packing light, a single bag for what he expected to be a quick round trip of an uncomplicated job. "Honey," he said, "nothing's going to happen. It's just like when I go to Morocco for work."

"Obviously not," she protested. "With Morocco, I know exactly where you're going and when you're coming back."

"Trust me," Nick said. He pressed his luggage closed and zipped the top.

"Yeah, well," she began, "I trusted you to give me some wedding date options."

"So that's what this is about," he said with a sigh. He saw her discomfort and realized he was wrong. The wedding date was simply a front. He could tell she used that frustration, a minor one, to hide the more major fear she couldn't reveal to him. He moved away from his luggage and gave her a hug to assure her he was there, listening and that everything would be okay.

"I just don't like secrets," she said.

"It's not about secrets, it's about confidentiality. I gave my word." He tried to provoke a smile from her with his own confident grin, but she wasn't having it. He continued packing in silence, only to be interrupted by Dancer, who came in to bother him for a walk. A good opportunity for a break, he thought.

CHAPTER FIVE
GERMANY

The flight would take nearly a day, including transfers. Nick spotted a magazine in the pouch on the backside of the seat in front of him. The main line read: *Dangerous U.S. Foreign Policy Exposed*. It seemed like old news to him, but he gave it a read anyway.

At the end of his journey, he landed in Munich. Despite leaving early in the day, it was already night. He lost several hours of his life as his plane raced its way through time zones. It was 6 o'clock, but it was also autumn and he realized he was not fully prepared for European weather. His sweater and jacket weren't the best for Germany's deep chill.

Nick got his luggage and headed out of the terminal. A minute or so later, a car pulled up. A man exited and locked eyes with him. "Mr. Bryant?" the German asked hopefully. Nick nodded. "I'm Klaus." He held his hand out and engaged in a solid greeting, then picked up Nick's bag and carried it to the trunk of the car.

"Thank you," Nick said. He moved to enter the backseat, but Klaus stopped him. "No, no," he insisted, "in front, please."

Nick saw why. A large cardboard box full of little jars occupied the back. His German was nonexistent, but he was fairly sure that it was honey. The car pulled away and Klaus had a warmer disposition than his grizzled old face seemed to let on. "Are you a beekeeper?" Nick asked, attempting to farm for information on his elderly courier.

"My wife and daughters are the beekeepers. I am just the delivery man. Go ahead, take a couple." He glanced at Nick and nodded. "I insist. You will never want to eat American honey again."

Nick reached into the back carefully and picked up a small sample jar of the amber liquid. "Thanks," he said.

"No, take another. For a friend perhaps." Nick did just that.

"I will first drop you at your hotel," Klaus explained. "Then I will bring Marie to you tonight. Nine o'clock."

Their drive was punctual and efficient through Munich's historic streets. Nick took in the sights as they sped along, although he certainly wasn't there to sight-see. He had a much more consequential purpose. They were soon upon the Hotel Bismarck, a small establishment that wore its history on its front door with pride. It was old but impeccably preserved.

Nick was ushered out and welcomed in from a distance. A light rain started and threatened to compromise his admittedly unfitting apparel for the occasion. Klaus hurried to open the trunk and handed off the luggage to Nick, who first pocketed his jars of honey, then grabbed his bag while Klaus tended to the car and took his goods to make his main delivery.

Nick rushed in alongside Klaus as the rain picked up. "Guten Abend, Friedrich," Klaus said as he passed the lobby attendant.

"Guten Abend," Friedrich said. He chased after Klaus for two steps to get his attention. "Oh, Klaus…" and then relayed something in German, which Nick overheard. Something about Mrs. Obst and der Küchenchef which sounded too close to mean anything other than kitchen chef.

"Ja, okay," Klaus said. He took his box of honey past the guests in the lobby toward the kitchen in the far back. Nick was left in the lobby with nothing to do but stare at the slightly gothic architecture while Friedrich managed the paperwork to check him in, along with taking possession of Nick's passport.

In the back, Klaus delivered his honey onto the counter and checked in with the chef who nodded to guide him over to a spice rack. Klaus silently acknowledged and walked to the rack where he picked out an unlabeled brown bottle of spice. He twisted the top open and emptied a thin note of paper rolled up several times into his hands. He skimmed it and afterward crumpled it up and threw it into the fire of a stove burner as he passed.

Klaus marched back to Nick with a renewed sense of purpose and vigor not previously present. "Change of plans," he said. "We need to leave now. Friedrich will take care of your bag."

Nick looked momentarily confused but agreed. Klaus directed Friedrich to take the bag in exchange for a room key. "Danke, Friedrich," Klaus said as he gave him a nod and bid Nick to follow him back out to the car.

The rain invited a sudden rise of fog that covered the streets and immediately blinded the windshield but Klaus pressed forward regardless. It was a tense few minutes of driving in the dark with low visibility through busy streets where Nick lost all sense of place and direction.

"Almost there," Klaus affirmed. He was confident and stoic, like a soldier following orders. Nick was sure that he was already deep in it. The decision had been made and the consequences were unfolding. They stopped in the dark in front of a small middle-class apartment complex, and Klaus pointed to the second floor. "Apartment 2B," he said.

Nick stepped out into the rain and headed to the two-story building as Klaus sped away. He ran up to Apartment 2B and knocked. To his surprise, the door opened immediately and a middle-aged man in proper business attire stood there. The man's eyes darted around in the dark as he left enough space for Nick to slide in. Time was of the essence, so Nick had been told about his new client, and by the man's demeanor, it seemed to be short.

Nick was inside. He expected a nicer welcoming, but not on a black market budget. The apartment was dimly lit with few furnishings, more like a temporary stay at best. His attendant shut and locked the door twice before turning to shake his hand.

"I'm Alex." He moved over to the kitchenette and grabbed a towel off the counter for Nick. "Marie's in the bedroom. She's scared to death of the polygraph. What do you need?"

"An update," Nick said as he dabbed his face and hair dry. Alex offered up a bottle of schnapps. "No thanks, but I could use a glass of water."

Alex filled a glass from the tap. "The bank that Marie works at," he began, "is now certain they have a mole. And Marie is at the top of their list. The information she's feeding us has been critical to... well, you don't need to know that."

He handed Nick the water, which Nick took and carried into the bedroom, closing the door behind him. Alex, meanwhile, stayed where he was and poured himself a good-sized drink from the bottle.

The bedroom was a simple little place where no one would expect to find a woman like Marie. She was nervous. Her hair was frayed and out of order. It looked like she missed an entire night of sleep and couldn't keep her clean bob cut smoothed down enough. She was still in her high-class corporate suit and knee-length skirt. Her outfit made her look older than her forty years. The heels of her shoes were stained with splashes of water.

She sat on the side of the bed as if she were waiting for a grim doctor's report. Nick came in slowly and quietly, revealing himself in the light so she wouldn't get startled by him moving in the dark. He took a chair from a corner of the room and angled it to sit across from her. "Hi, Marie, my name's Nick and I'm going to help you get through tomorrow."

"Yes, okay. What do I do?"

Nick put the glass of water down on the nightstand. He positioned it so there wasn't a harsh glare from the light reflecting off the glass. He reached into his pocket and took out a small, thin pillbox. Nick rattled one pill into her hand. "Here, this will help you relax." She inspected it suspiciously. "It's okay. It's safe," Nick assured her.

She hesitated a bit but then asked, "Now?"

"Yes, please."

Marie remained confused but was compliant. The method behind Nick's practice didn't matter to her because she was so desperate and out of options. She seemed willing enough to consider suicide as a fairer escape than what could happen to her if she ended up failing without Nick's help. But she trusted Alex and he had others whom he trusted. So she put the pill in her mouth and swallowed the whole glass of water to chase it down.

"It'll take a few minutes," Nick explained, "to take effect. I'll be in the next room." Nick stood and leaned over the back of the chair while Marie looked up at him helplessly. "As you relax, picture yourself walking out after the exam tomorrow… smiling. Deal?"

Marie nodded. Her eyes darted. She wasn't sure if he was helping her or not yet. He could tell there was that contention but left her to it. His method was already underway. He left the room as quietly as he entered and found Alex at the table finishing his drink. Alex looked at him curiously, wondering how he was done so fast. Nick gave him a plaintive gesture, signaling that it was still underway.

"I'm sorry," Alex said, as he fished something out of his pocket. He produced a small black box and pushed it across the table. "This needs to get to Mr. Kearney."

"What's in it?" Nick asked.

"It's not my business. Keep it safe."

Some secret, off-book government-adjacent thing, Nick suspected as he picked up the box, expecting it to be hotter than fire. Whatever was inside couldn't be safe if it was only meant for Kearney's hands. He stuffed it into the breast pocket of his jacket, then checked a table clock as he slipped off his wristwatch to match up the time.

"Just a few more minutes." Nick got his watch set and hooked it back on. As he did so, he heard the honey jars lightly clanking against one another in his pocket. He took one out and placed it on the table. Alex saw it and immediately grinned.

"Ah," he said, "you will never want to eat American honey again."

Nick smiled. If so many strangers had that to say about it, it had to be true. But he was working with spies. It sounded more like a code phrase that he wasn't aware of. A trigger of some kind with the honey acting as a catalyst inspiring action… which gave him an idea. "Got a spoon?" Nick asked.

Alex headed back to the kitchenette and returned after a clatter of silverware with a small teaspoon that was small enough to match the size of the jar. Nick took it thankfully and placed it on top of the jar, balanced so the back of the spoon and the top part of the handle were steady against the lid. Alex waited with disappointment as Nick didn't eat it.

They waited in silence while Nick watched the clock. He seemed to go out of focus for a moment like his attention completely faded away to somewhere else. Alex was tempted to say something to break the mood but the silence was good. They had an important task to coordinate. Friendly distractions were unnecessary. After enough time passed, Nick picked up the honey and spoon and gave Alex a reassuring nod as he headed back into the bedroom.

Inside, Marie looked far more relaxed than before. Her movements were smooth; her eyes weren't as desperate and she seemed more lucid. Nick sat once more and opened the jar with a tiny clinking of the lid against the glass and the spoon that he held in his off-hand. He smelled it and felt convinced that the code phrase was just a compliment. It smelled fresh and herbaceous, more so than any honey he had back home.

"Oh, just smell this." He brought it up close to Marie's nose. She sniffed it cautiously at first, then breathed it in more deeply. "Smells delicious, doesn't it?"

"It's lovely," she agreed.

Nick dipped the spoon in. The honey stirred with a satisfying smoothness. It wasn't a solid block of cold caramel or gelatin like the cheap store brands. This one spread itself beautifully and stuck to the tiny silver spoon. It reminded him of clean, high-grade motor oil, glistening amber as it entered the engine of his Jag. "Here, please," he offered.

Marie took it in her mouth. She was very pleased by the honey but was getting confused. She looked Nick over awkwardly. "Now close your eyes," Nick instructed. Marie leaned back against the pillows and shut her eyes as she swallowed it, savoring the flavor so that it created a vivid and appealing memory.

"Remember," Nick calmly said in a guiding tone, "the sweet, delicious smell... and the sweet, smooth taste. Honey. Think of that word. Breathe in ... thinking of honey." She did. Unlike before, her breath went in smoothly and came out in a long, relaxed sigh. Her shoulders rolled down, her posture became even more relaxed. "Tomorrow," Nick said, "during the questioning, the memory of the wonderful smell and taste of honey will keep you relaxed. All the answers you prepared to keep yourself safe will ring true. Now just relax."

Marie let so much tension escape that she started to smile faintly. From what Nick observed, he felt confident that things were going well.

A phone rang in the other room. Alex picked it up before the second ring. Whatever he heard caused him to break the peaceful concentration that was underway as he entered the bedroom, quiet save for his panting breath. He waved Nick over. Nick obliged and huddled next to the door, as far from the bedside as possible within the small room.

"You have to leave now!" Alex whispered in a panic.

"I need a few more minutes," Nick whispered back.

"There's no time."

Nick could tell that it wasn't a simple scheduling conflict. Something was coming that Nick couldn't get caught up in. He looked back into the bedroom and his eyes caught the curtains drawn over the window. "Then think of something," he insisted. He gently pushed Alex back then moved back to finish with Marie. Alex closed the door and returned to the main room in a fluster.

Alex heard noises outside almost immediately. The sound of screeching tires in the dead of night. He glanced out the window to the street below. Two cars veered up to the curb and two men exited each car. One pointed and spoke in quick, rough German to instruct the others. Two went around the back while he and his partner marched straight up to the apartment.

Alex, in a panic, reached out for the bedroom doorknob but kept himself from opening it. Another distraction could end the whole operation. But it was already about to end, regardless. The floor was shaking from the stampeding feet that ran up the stairs. He tried to think fast and could only reach one idea in time. He prepared himself as the footsteps reached the door and a fist pounded on the other side.

"Open the door!" the man demanded in German. Alex didn't comply. He didn't move. It was so loud he was sure Nick and Marie heard it in the other room. He had to give them every second he could without risking his own life. The men, however, didn't want to wait. They had their orders. It was apartment 2B.

They kicked the door open and the lock broke. Two thugs armed with guns marched in and were immediately greeted by a red-nosed older man in his underwear standing aghast in the living room. "What is this?" Alex demanded. One thug held him and pushed him back to the wall while the other searched the kitchenette. The second thug moved to the next room, a bathroom. It was cramped enough that there was nothing inside to see.

He forced himself into the bedroom. What he saw was simply a woman under the covers who screamed like hell when she saw him. "Raus hier!" — "Get out of here!" she shouted, "Alex!" The thug shoved a gun near her face to quiet her. His partner joined him and threw open the closet door and looked under the bed, then tried to tear off Marie's covers for the fun of it. She yanked them back and cursed the man, using every foul German word she could think of. Surprising coming from the matronly businesswoman who only moments ago was timid and frightened. "Fahr zur Hölle!" — go to hell, she screamed in one last assault before slapping the man's face in total disregard of the gun pointing at hers. So, they looked elsewhere — through the curtains, out into the alley.

Nothing. They didn't see Nick, already outside, hands raw from scaling the gutter pipe that was slick with mist and rainwater. Nick crouched behind some garbage cans and waited until the light from the window was shuttered again. Once they moved away, he got up and made a hurried walk to the open street. He understood completely what was going on and whom they were looking for. No murderous sounds from the apartment. Alex and Marie were alive, safety not assured. If it was a hit job, they missed their target. Or so Nick thought. As he neared the end of the alley, two thugs made their way around the building in his direction. Nick had his collar up against the rain and turned to retrace his steps, forming a new retreat.

"Hey you," the thug called out in German. Nick could certainly figure out when someone was calling to him, particularly with that angered tone. He kept walking. Then he heard them run. "Come here!" the thug demanded. "HALT!"

Nick had the lead on them and he sprinted to widen it out. He was gone from the apartment into the unknown streets of a foreign city. He put all his power into his legs, into not being caught. Nick grit his teeth and ignored the chronic pain radiating down into his leg. The cold rainy air in his lungs, the burning in his feet and thighs, the fear — he had no time for any of that. So he shut it all off.

Nick was on a tear through the streets. He stuck to the narrow alleys out of sight and wove through the district one old lot at a time. Some were pitch black and required him to react to the obstacles as he reached them. He called upon all of his physical prowess as he threw himself over fences and ran around trashcans and through gates to the other side. No amount of distance seemed long enough and if he could surmount the obstacles, the thugs certainly would in time.

The only thing that stopped him, a pain he absolutely couldn't ignore anymore, was the old one in his groin. The pivot of all the movements he had to continue making was slowing him down. He paused and assumed a recovery stance, hands on hips and feet firm, while he moved through his process. He turned and saw the thugs gaining ground on him a street away.

Nick huffed to prepare himself and kept going. Through one more alley and he was out onto a major street with significant traffic. He nearly ran into the side of a car but stopped himself just shy of rolling across the hood, then gave the driver a quick look of apology.

Running through an unfamiliar area wasn't working so he switched tactics. Once he crossed the main street, he ran for a darkened house. Not a single light shone on any floor. It was either abandoned or its owners took their sleep seriously. He ducked behind a bush and waited in a side yard for the thugs to pass. He saw them looking around, confused as to which way to go. They didn't see Nick up or down the street, which meant he had most likely crossed it.

The thugs split up and hid their guns inside their long coats as they moved to Nick's side of the street. They were ready to kill on sight; no need to debate the issue. One rushed farther up the street to inspect the houses Nick avoided and the other came straight toward the dark house where he was hiding. Nick stayed low and retreated through the shadows to the back of the lot where he found something he could use to defend himself. The thug advanced cautiously, not even knowing if he was on the right track. He turned a corner but failed to see Nick in time. Nick swung a kid's tricycle into the side of the man's head. He was stunned and fell backward, cracking his head against some pottery. While the thug reeled, Nick made a run for it, hearing a few easy-to-understand German curse words as he fled.

He was back onto the busy street but ran in the direction opposite from the other thug. He soon found himself right next to a bus stop. His luck finally took a turn. The bus was there and accepting its last passenger.

Nick ran up, his groin pulling his right leg back, and slapped his hand on the door just as the bus slowly listed away. The driver saw him and stopped to open the door. One more fare and a few seconds late wouldn't hurt. Nick scanned the bus for any suspicious characters and glanced back at the street. For the moment, he was safe.

"Fahr," the German driver said. He pointed to a collection box full of Deutchmarks and coins. Nick swiped his hands over his pockets, from top to bottom, and yanked out a dollar. The driver waved his hand to stop Nick before he slipped it into the box. "Nein. Deutsche."

The second thing Nick hadn't prepared for was German money. It was supposed to be a quick round trip for the day with a client. They didn't give him any proper money, nor did he have time to acquire any through a proper exchange. When Nick turned abruptly to check what was going on outside the bus, he spotted thugs closing in, and—

CLANK. The remaining honey jar in his pocket hit the metal of the fare box. He quickly yanked it out and offered it to the driver with a gesture — *that's all I got.*

Startled, the driver returned a look of confusion. Nick pulled it back, then held it, label out, to the driver with a desperate, apologetic shrug. The driver read the label and turned to his dashboard with a timer ticking down. He rolled his head and motioned for Nick to head into the back, but didn't take the jar from his hand, probably figuring Nick might need it more than he.

The door closed as the thugs ran up and the bus pulled away into traffic. They continued to run until one of them peered through the door. He didn't spot Nick hiding behind a seat. The goons were out of luck and Nick was safe for the moment.

He rode the bus for a distance, then remembered to show his hotel room key to the driver, who looked at it and gave him a nod. Nick was soon at the familiar grounds of his hotel where he quickly gathered up his belongings. Friedrich hailed him a cab to the airport where Nick could stay behind several layers of security at all times. The next flight back to the States was a two-hour wait, something he did with eyes wide open.

With that part of his sketchy business trip over, he welcomed his return to the States. All he had to show for it were wrinkled clothes, muddy shoes, and a foreign substance packaged in a handmade glass container. The customs agent spent a good minute looking it over as if he was expecting to find a secret compartment or a trigger. "It's honey," although Nick was fairly sure it was liquid gold from everyone else's reaction. "You'll never want…" Nick began. But the joke was already lost on a stranger. "Never mind." That, and if the man believed him, he might keep it for himself.

The agent then pulled out the small black box Nick was to deliver to Kearney. He looked it over once and couldn't find an opening. "It's a puzzle box for my kid. I still haven't figured out how to open it," Nick said.

The agent returned it to Nick's bag. "If he's anything like my four-year-old, he'll have it open before you can blink."

Nick smiled amicably. He had nearly forgotten about it, but once he saw it a second time in the daylight, he pondered if it were the whole reason he went overseas in the first place. For a split second, he wondered if Marie's polygraph was a front but quickly dismissed the idea. She and Alex had been terrified of the repercussions if she failed. Whatever had been worth killing him over belonged to William Kearney.

One incredibly long day, a sore groin, battered feet, a rainy cold, and the sheer confusion over the many mysteries he was involved in made him want to lay low, even if it were in a cold grave. He felt an unusual flow of paranoia like the thugs were still chasing him. As if they could pop out from behind any corner. Nick took a few deep breaths, calming himself, and purposely thought about tasting the legendary edible gold as a reward for his work well done.

CHAPTER SIX

POOL COUP

Soon after his return, Nick was given a meet-up place. A neighborhood joint called the Rack 'Em Pool Hall in North Hollywood, where all sorts gathered to drink, bullshit and play the game. For bucks or a beer, it didn't matter, just so they could get out of the house or away from their jobs and pass the time, away from whatever ailed them. You could tell who were the would-be hustlers from the neighborhood regulars.

The clatter of balls echoed across the ceiling. Nick still had a bit of a limp from his jump out the window in Germany when he entered. He spotted Kearney in the back, a long walk from the entrance. He passed through the smoke-filled room and reached the back corner as Kearney was lining up his shot. A nondescript chubby man in a plaid shirt and blue jeans sat on a barstool, half-hidden in the smoke, and watched Kearney play. Nick guessed he figured that Kearney, the only one wearing a suit, had to be a better player than the rest of the folks in attendance that day.

"You're holding too high," said Nick just as Kearney smacked the cue ball, sending the 9-ball into the corner pocket. Kearney immediately looked up with a satisfied smile plastered on his face. Nick smiled too, more a smirk, as he nodded at the table, causing Kearney to turn back around in time to see the cue ball follow the 9-ball into the pocket. Disappointed, Kearney shook his head.

Nick asked, "How's Marie?"

"She did great," Kearney reported, as he pulled out an envelope and handed it over. Nick flipped through the contents of hundred-dollar bills. Twenty-five crisp ones, as promised. Not exactly easy money, he thought, but between this and what the King was paying him, maybe he could get out of his mess with Costas. Nick slid his hand into his pocket to exchange the envelope for the black box Alex gave him. Kearney quickly pocketed it. "By the way, we'd really like some of those special pills you gave Marie."

"Oh, the pills… you can get them across the street at the drugstore." A look of puzzlement crossed Kearney's face. "Fingernail strengtheners," Nick added.

Kearney thought for a moment then burst into a hearty laugh. "You gotta be kidding."

"I'm glad it worked out okay for Marie," Nick said and turned to leave.

"Where you going?" Kearney asked. He grabbed the pool cue as if to start another game.

Nick walked back to the table and leaned on it to get closer to Kearney. In a quiet voice, he said, "You put me in a situation without telling me all the possible ramifications. That's not acceptable."

Kearney's face returned to its usual stoic expression. "You're right. It's not acceptable. And I guarantee it won't happen next time."

"What makes you think there'll be a next time?" Nick pushed himself off the table and walked away.

"What if I could get you a government contract?" Kearney said. "That could guarantee you having your own academy."

Nick stopped and turned, not yet committed to walk back but enough to listen.

"Maybe that colonel's funding ran out..." Kearney pointed to Nick's breast pocket with the envelope he had just given him. "... but mine won't."

Nick tried to rein in his enthusiasm and tamp down his concerns about getting more deeply involved with a government that's proved dishonorable. But there was a spark of interest in his eyes that Kearney caught. He held out the cue for Nick to take.

"Nine ball?" he offered.

"I'll break."

"Of course."

Nick took the cue and hoped it was a lifeline leading him to salvation rather than a hook that would yank him out of freedom into slavery. He remembered what Billy taught him about decision-making. He racked the balls and lined up his break shot. Their trust was shaky and a simple game of pool wasn't going to build a bridge that could cross the gap that Kearney made between them over Germany. That would take time and promises kept.

Nick's chronic pain flared up from time to time, although he could suppress it using his process. But this night, the physical exertion complicated what he experienced in Germany. He was about to hand the cue back and excuse himself from play, but Nick thought for a moment, could acknowledging the pain cause Kearney to rethink using him for any future work, or could it also disqualify him from a government contract? So Nick bit the bullet and performed a quick application of his process.

Nick was no Fast Eddy, as depicted by Paul Newman in *The Hustler*, but he did have some experience of making a little side money while in the military. He knew how to make a solid break. The balls scattered, leaving him in an excellent position for his next shot. "One ball," he declared, "side pocket." The one ball rolled into the pocket and left the cue ball in line with the next target.

"Dicey there in Morocco these days," Kearney suddenly declared, "with the King being involved in Middle East peace talks."

"I don't deal with politics," Nick said as he took his next position. "Two ball, corner pocket." He aimed and struck. Kearney observed Nick's precise game with interest, while Nick eyed the state of the table for another maneuver. "Nine ball in the corner, off the three." Kearney knew pool hall etiquette and shifted his position away from Nick's intended pocket. He executed the shot, causing Kearney to raise his eyebrow ever so slightly.

After a moment, Kearney produced another small black box and placed it on the felt. "I hear you have an upcoming trip," he said. "Perhaps you could drop this off for me."

Nick put the cue on the table. "I'll think about it. Right now, I gotta get back."

"Fair enough." Kearney extended a friendly hand to Nick then took back the box before gathering the balls up for another solo game.

Nick glanced over to the man in plaid who still hadn't moved from his perch and departed. Kearney and his mystery guest exchanged a look. "What do you think?" Kearney asked.

"Good eye-hand coordination. He should do well."

On Nick's drive home, his head swirled with the nuances surrounding his conversation with Kearney at the pool hall. He wasn't much better when he got into the house. Kate had been rushing around gathering up pet toys and bedding for a new laundry load when he passed the laundry room. "Hi, honey," she said and promptly scowled at him when she noticed nothing in his arms. "Where are the groceries?"

What Kate said didn't register. Nick was distracted, wondering whether Kearney could be trusted to get him the government contract and if he could, how long would it take. He walked past, on his way to the den, and simply replied, "Hi, honey," as his brain was trying to calculate how long he could put up with Costas and the Academy in the meantime.

Kate dropped what she was doing. "Hey, where are the groceries?" she said louder.

He doubled back a few steps. "Huh?"

"Oh, come on, Nick. Where the hell are the groceries? What's wrong with you?"

"Oh my God, I forgot."

"Did you remember to at least get paid?" she asked as she started the washing machine.

Nick patted the hefty envelope in his pocket. "That I did."

"At least part of your brain is still working," she said as she tossed items into the wash. "I don't like you going out of town like that if it's going to turn you into a vegetable. Now, what are we going to do for dinner?"

"Take out. Whatever you want."

Kate's scowl became a smile as she ran to the kitchen and made her selection from the accumulated menus they saved. Dancer and Yogi suddenly appeared as if they too wanted in on the action. She turned to them and simply said, "Pizza?" The dog's front paws tapped the floor in a little dance. Hence the name Dancer.

As Nick walked into his den, he wondered if he was cut out for a life of subterfuge, even if it was only temporary. He put Kearney's envelope in his desk drawer then glimpsed his calendar with upcoming dates marked off with the word Morocco and a line extending from one Monday to the next. He looked toward the kitchen and smiled at the thought of adding Kate to the itinerary, so he extended the line another four days. Nick also made a mental note to arrange for Dancer and Yogi to stay with Billy and Ruthie for the duration. His illustrious client, the King, had already paid for the trip. He may as well give Kate the vacation he always promised. If and when Kearney's contract came through, he knew he'd have that thing scrutinized by the best lawyers he could afford, even if it had to be just Ted Patts and the best executive legal secretary he knew. But that time was not yet here.

The next day, Kate sat alone in the Academy's waiting room as Lynn organized files and schedules at the counter. Inside Costas' office, Nick and his boss were going at it over the problems Nick and the staff thought needed to be addressed.

"Some of our people are really pissed off having to donate their time to bring in new clients," Nick said. "They think you should be able to afford more advertising considering you're taking the majority of what they make."

As Stevie sauntered in with lunch, he gave Nick his usual shitty grin and was about to set it up on the desk when his father interrupted. "Grab some newspaper," Costas said. "I don't want this to get all over my new desk." He then addressed Nick. "Well, if that's the way they feel, maybe they should try to find another place that gives them all the benefits that I do."

Stevie took a newspaper off a side table and noticed something funny in the comics section. He laughed. Costas scowled at him, thinking Stevie was laughing at what he just said, so Stevie quickly smiled and pointed to the newspaper.

Nick countered Costas. "That's exactly what's going to happen if we don't at least try to address their concerns." Nick was now forced to step back from the desk as Stevie fussed with lunch plates before laying out the sushi buffet.

"They can give up some of their time now to benefit from the Academy getting new clients in the future," Costas admonished. "I don't see the downside and neither should you. We all have to make sacrifices."

Nick eyed the sushi. "Some more so than others."

The door to Costas' office opened and Kate and Lynn heard Nick's steps approach the waiting room. They both stiffened.

"Ready for lunch?" Kate asked, trying to be cheery.

"After listening to that bullshit, I'm ready for anything but sushi. Let's go."

Meanwhile, in Washington D.C., William Kearney had been sitting outside a conference room in the depths of a federal building. It was a humorless place with minimal effects indicating personality or individuality. A place of the strictest business the US government could enact. He was joined shortly after by a familiar face who handed him a coffee. Kearney gave him a coy smile and the man returned it. They'd worked closely together before, many times, most recently in the UCLA parking lot where he feigned trying to force open the door to Nick's car. He was one of Kearney's go-to fixers.

The man sat next to Kearney and drank his own coffee as the two waited and watched the clock. He eventually got bored and rose. "Well, it's been fun. You can tell me all about it later. I'm sure they'll be some choice words."

"Yep," Kearney said as the man moved on down the hall.

Inside the conference room were six suits that just happened to have human parts attached. They comprised various covert teams that supported spy missions and paramilitary actions by the rebels in Latin America. The only one who stood out was Emma, a sophisticated tomboy from the Vietnam War era who insisted on barely contained long hair and a stylish navy silk pantsuit to differentiate herself from the other lady who was present. That one was dressed like a secretary — a-line skirt, buttoned-up shirt and sensible pumps — but held the same unshakeable presence as the men across from her.

One man at the end of the table, who headed the meeting, stood up and worked a projector that was positioned on the table edge. The wall it faced had a screen that pulled down from the ceiling. He spoke loud and clear over the whir of the projector's fan. The images displayed a series of newsreels from international papers and English equivalent publications all reporting on the same two things: cartel and rebel conflict in Latin America.

Projector Guy stopped at a frame featuring a long-distance photo that depicted a few men walking with a flank of armed guards down an empty street. The image had the title *Nicaraguan President Daniel Ortega*, who was featured dead center of the framed shot, an affluent-looking man who walked with his hands folded behind his back. At his side was another man in tailored clothes and a manicured goatee, also high-end retail, and caught looking sternly in the camera's direction. The entourage included several others, but the Projector Guy tapped his finger on the goatee guy specifically. "Victor Espinoza. He's the one we think is really running the show. Not Ortega. But no one's willing to move without further proof."

He turned to the rest of the group and caught one of the suits with an unfolded newspaper smirking at *The Far Side* cartoon for the day, of two smiling pigeons looking down at people who walked with targets on their heads. He deliberately paused long enough for Mr. Far Side to catch up to the discussion. The guy noticed the silence and looked up. He quickly pushed the paper off to the side.

The suit next to Mr. Far Side spoke up. "They obviously don't want another Chilean coup fiasco."

"Goddammit, Project Fubelt is old news," Projector Guy said.

The suits knew all too well the workings of administrations and how they could end up in the middle of a blame game if they weren't careful. First would come government authority to do something and, if things didn't go as expected, top officials, the media and everyone else would point their fingers at the CIA as if it had been the agency that came up with the whole concept in the first place. In this instance, the Reagan administration had directed the CIA to support a force of Nicaraguan rebels, dubbed Contras, to conduct covert actions against the Soviet-backed Sandinista regime — and no one in that room wanted to be left holding the bag if it went sideways.

Projector Guy walked over to a window, frustrated, and glared out at the streets below, then without facing the group, said, "I need something and I need it today. The top floor is on my fucking back."

"Our Latin America Intel," Mr. Far Side piped up, "is bullshit. They'll come up with anything in order to get paid."

Ms. Secretary countered in no uncertain terms, "You have my people in charge down there and you'll get all the info you want."

Projector Guy turned back to the room, skeptically. "Well, thank you for your enthusiasm but that didn't work so well last time."

The third suit, more wiry and older than the rest, spoke up "I got a couple of shrinks who have some techniques that might work."

"I hate fucking shrinks," Mr. Far Side said. "Worse than that idiot who says he could kill goats by staring at them." Everyone ignored the comment.

"Okay, let's stay on track here," the lead guy scolded. "We're tasked with boots-on-the-ground intel."

"What about Kearney?" The last suit asked. "With his background in the mob, he could get anybody to talk."

"Kennedy never had a chance," the one next to him muttered with disdain, prompting others around him to stiffen and Projector Guy to give him a look to can it.

"Their expertise was shutting people up," the catty female agent interjected, "not getting them to talk." Everyone shared a dark chuckle over that except Emma in the back who sat silently seething and stiff as a rod.

Mr. Far Side asked, "When did we start having anything to do with the mob?"

"World War Two," Emma answered. "We needed to protect our shipping docks. Guess who controlled them."

"Kearney's helped us ever since the Bay of Pigs," one of them said, "and he did a great job recently in Germany. With what he brought us, we now know for sure that the bank our asset works for is funneling money to Ortega."

"The same bank," the wiry guy offered, "that funded the Nazi concentration camps." The older agent leaned back with a smile. "By the way, isn't the guy who Kearney sent over to Germany a shrink?"

Emma stood, placed her hands on the table and leaned into it. "Strictly speaking as an advisor, what the fuck does it matter? He's pulled off a small miracle helping one of our assets. That keeps our information flowing. And, he'll be in Morocco soon, working with his client, the King, by the way. A guy who's that trusted holds a lot of weight in my book."

Projector Guy nodded and turned to the group. "When he gets back, we should see what else he can do."

Emma got in the last word. "If you have any further concerns about Bill's judgment or methods, he's right outside."

Not a peep from anyone. Although, everyone thought privately that they each had a leg up on the other one. They were working together factually but rewards for their achievements were not unlimited. Each wanted to get as much credit as possible in order to position the team they were associated with in order to capture the next plum assignment. Emma believed that as long as Nick did what he was good at, the lion's share of credit would go to her, and by extension, Kearney for setting it all up. All she had to do was wait and rake in the information. She knew Kearney's team would ultimately be tasked with following the money.

After the conference room cleared out, Emma walked over to Kearney. "You're the lead team on Central America. Nick's involvement brought up some questions but they couldn't argue with results."

"Lunch?" Kearney asked.

"After listening to some of those mealy mouths, I'm ready for real meat. Let's go."

CHAPTER SEVEN

MOROCCO

Nick's presence at the Royal Palace in Rabat, Morocco was something that never got old. He wasn't there to take in the immense history and proud culture of the nation or make friends with the elites of the palace grounds. He was there on business, something more in his wheelhouse, a high-level therapy session, while the last business trip he had been on had him running for his life.

Although here, if someone wanted him dead, they could do it in front of a crowd and bury him in the desert within an hour, as had happened once to the royal photographer. The guy was doing more than just photographing one of the King's many wives. Here today, gone the same.

The palace grounds alone were enough to make a man recalibrate his sense of scale. The walls were ancient and thick, the kind built to outlast empires, and the tile work on every surface — thousands of hand-cut geometric pieces in blue and gold — was so intricate and precisely fitted it looked less like construction and more like fine art. Guards in ceremonial dress stood at intervals that made it clear where a guest was and was not expected to wander. Nick had learned early on to read a room, but reading a palace required a different set of instincts entirely — who to nod to, where to stand, how long to hold eye contact with a man whose authority you couldn't quite measure. He figured it out the same way he figured out most things. He watched, he listened, and he kept his mouth shut until he had something worth saying.

The latest therapy sessions took place over a week and had all gone smoothly. He was tasked with not only helping the King maintain the lowest levels of stress but this time around, he was also asked to help the King's general quit smoking.

Nick wasn't alone in having to navigate the intricacies of high-level palace functions. He had Henri, a former student of his and a native interpreter for esteemed and important guests, so he could communicate.

As it turned out, the smoking-addicted general was a formidable presence — stern-faced, upright, projecting authority the way men do when they're nervous and don't want anyone to know it. Of all the problems a man of that bearing might bring to a session, this was not the one Nick would have anticipated. Smoking cessation wasn't beneath him — it just wasn't interesting anymore. He preferred the complex stuff, the behavioral tangles that took real work to unravel. But what the King wanted, the King got — even though it was something, he found out, the general was reluctant to do.

The general motioned for them to sit, then said nothing. He simply stared at Nick, waiting. Nick waited back for a moment, then decided to move things along. Nick told Henri to explain that he'd like the general to take a short assessment to determine the best approach.

Before he could begin, the general asked a question. Through Henri, he wanted to know — could Nick actually control his mind using this special process?

Nick leaned forward, held the general's eyes, and told Henri exactly what to say: *"If I could control your mind, you'd be working for me and not the King."*

Then Nick leaned back and let a smile do the rest of the work. The general looked at him for a long moment, then smiled back. Nick went to work.

From what he heard later, the general was pleased with the results. Which meant the King was pleased. Which meant Nick could finally exhale.

And now Nick was being rewarded by being asked to join in celebrations for the King's birthday, a prestigious event for which he had initially been unprepared. But the King had seen to it that he wouldn't arrive that way.

Nick and Henri were dressed to match the mood in rented tuxedos made by local tailors who knew what tastes were preferred at royal events. Nick also had two security guards who escorted them inside the main hall for the festivities. Once there, the guards peeled away and moved to a different part of their patrol as soon as they were past the doors. Nick looked relieved, especially when he saw Kate standing near the long, luxurious banquet table. She was a calming presence and, tonight, a beacon of elegance in her silky full-length gown. Clearly, she had taken the week to do some serious shopping on her own, even without knowing about the party. Perhaps it was simply in anticipation of bigger events in their lives back home.

Nick led Henri over to join Kate at the elaborate feast. There were exotic dishes not only of Moroccan fame but world cuisine from far and wide. No expense was spared to make every guest feel at home. Nick caught Kate eating an intricate veggie kabob with a fine cloth napkin in her hand to catch the tangy middle eastern dip from, God forbid, dripping onto her swanky dress.

"How did it go?" she asked as he dabbed at a crumb stuck on the side of her pretty lipsticked lips.

"The King and I had a very fruitful session," Nick said. He turned to Henri. "Please thank your father again for the introduction."

"It was his pleasure," Henri said with a polite nod.

"I can't believe I finally got to visit Morocco," Kate said with awe. "And, who would have thought we'd be at the King's birthday party!"

"You deserve it, honey."

Kate smiled. "Ah, you're just saying that."

"I wouldn't even be here if it weren't for you at my side," Nick said earnestly.

Kate leaned in and gave him a discreet kiss. She then caught sight of some passing royals and her excitement was renewed. "And, at a King's birthday party!" She could barely contain herself.

"Didn't I read there was a coup attempt at one of his shindigs?" Nick recalled.

"Exactly," Henri said matter-of-factly. "A hundred dignitaries got their heads chopped off at one of his birthday parties a couple of years ago."

Kate gasped and her eyes went wide. Nick smirked. "Ah, he's just kidding." Kate didn't seem convinced. She looked at Henri but he just smiled shyly. He either had a wicked sense of humor or was very polite about terrifying truths.

Nick scanned the room. The party would continue on at its pace for quite a while. The King's celebration was not to be trifled with. It was a national holiday, although Nick doubted the common people got to have as much of a celebration as the King's upper-crust friends and business partners did. He locked eyes with a waiter carrying glasses of champagne. They exchanged a simple, knowing look with one another. Nick had something else he had to do that neither Kate nor Henri could fathom. "I'll get us some of that expensive champagne." He strode off while Kate and Henri stayed behind to chat. It seemed like Kearney was making good on his promise. His *next time* was definitely different, almost the stark opposite of Germany.

The waiter extended his tray toward Nick. "His Majesty loves billiards," he said. Nick pulled out the black box that Kearney showed him at the pool hall as he reached for a glass. He slipped the box under a napkin in the center of the tray and grabbed a glass by its stem. It was a smooth maneuver that only he and the waiter could see. The napkin was even arranged and folded in a way that it didn't lay flat but created a sort of tent on the flat tray. Nick nodded in thanks and the waiter walked off to complete the hidden transaction and service the party. Easy, he thought, now this is more like it. Nick took a tiny victory sip of his champagne. It was the good stuff and well-earned. He returned to Kate and Henri, looking mighty pleased with himself, but she looked flustered.

"Where's ours?" she asked. Nick handed her the glass and she took it with a smug grin. Henri waved his hand in a manner suggesting to Nick that it wasn't a problem that he had been so absentminded as to forget him.

Thereafter, Nick and Kate stuck close to the banquet table. They didn't know anyone else to mingle with. The King was not a man who could simply be approached at a common foreigner's leisure. Besides, he was busy mingling with his political echelon and other prestigious guests. Although Nick was technically an employee, he was a valued one. Thus, he received the invitation. And being able to see the King, in his elegant robes and waltzing around his own palace, was a treat.

At one point, a locally dressed couple of recognizable affluence approached Nick and Kate. All four talked through Henri, who switched from his friendly, chatting demeanor to a strictly business, almost mechanical, live translation mode.

"Pardon the intrusion," the man said in Arabic, which Henri translated into English. "I am Nasir Harrak and this is my wife, Alia." She gave a polite bow in response.

"Nick Bryant," Nick said. Henri didn't need to translate that part, but he did, adding requisite formalities. Nick had been instructed well ahead of time not to reach out to shake hands and only to be on the receiving end of such a gesture. Nasir nodded, so Nick nodded back.

"Yes," Nasir said, "we have heard much about you."

Nick acknowledged the compliment with a slight smile. "A pleasure to meet you." While remembering his manners, he turned to his own companions. "This is my fiancée, Kate and Henri."

"Please," Nasir began, "I am sorry for asking, but my wife for 25 years hasn't had a full night of sleep. It makes her very depressed." Alia looked ashamed to be the subject of discussion and she held onto her husband's arm from behind.

Nick immediately studied Alia by focusing on her posture and facial expressions. She was very good at hiding her discomfort, a refined woman with high society training who wouldn't scowl even if rotten food was put under her mouth. But this discussion was too much for her. It almost felt taboo, like a massive insecurity that strangers shouldn't know. Nick could see that she was closing off rapidly while latching onto her husband with the only amount of force she felt safe to give to make him stop.

"Forgive my husband," she said. "We should not be bothering you on such a special occasion." Nick went off of Henri's precise, unemotional translation, but relating that to how she talked gave him even more insight.

"Please," Nasir said, "she has tried everything."

"Nothing can help me," Alia politely interjected. "Sorry to have bothered you."

"If you don't mind, may I ask you a couple of quick questions?" said Nick.

Alia looked back at her husband as if seeking final approval, then nodded to Nick.

"Do you ever find your mind wandering from what you're doing, but you don't realize it until your mind snaps back?"

"Yes."

"And after that happens, do you ever feel emotional, like depressed or sad, maybe even angry?"

Alia blinked, trying to understand the question. Afterward, she said with surprise, "Yes, it does happen sometimes." With her acknowledgment, Nick noticed her signs of discomfort were still increasing.

"You're right," Nick said, attempting to be apologetic through his tone and motions. "You shouldn't go through any more disappointment. It was very nice meeting you." He bowed politely and turned to Kate, who looked confused. Henri was also shocked as he exited his translation stance into a more casual demeanor again. Nasir looked disappointed but Nick saw Alia show signs of relief. He took a few steps away from them, then stopped and turned back while glancing at Henri to continue for him as he did. "Although," he began, "on the plane over here, I read about an exciting new medical cure for insomnia without the use of medication. It's extremely successful."

Alia listened and stepped back from her husband to return to Nick and Henri. "Oh, please tell me about it." She sounded thankful and now as desperate as her husband.

Nick turned to two chairs that were nearby in a corner, separated from the rest of the hall, almost in their own private area. "Please," he offered.

He turned to Kate with a confident smile. "I'll be back in a few minutes." While Alia walked over to the chair and her husband Nasir observed from a distance, Kate leaned into Nick and held him up for a second. "An article you read?" she whispered. He gave her a sly grin she'd seen plenty of times before. Just his way of getting what he wanted. Denying a heartfelt request only to come up with a sudden solution at the last second. He'd already begun his process even before Alia sat on the chair.

After Nick was done with his mid-party therapy session, he left with Kate for their hotel, while Henri left for his family's home. The party carried on late into the night, with many guests retiring and going their own ways to their illustrious and expensive hotels. The hotel Nick was staying at wasn't as extravagant and famous as the ones the other guests stayed at but it was a far better one this time than he expected. It seemed like no expense was spared to give them a warm welcome, and they still had plenty of time left to see more. It was supposed to be work as usual for Nick, but for Kate, it was an exceptional break from the norm.

The next morning, they all met in the lobby for a quiet, last breakfast. Their time with Henri, as an official guide under the service and contract of the King, was at an end till next time. Kate was sitting, staring into what was left of her coffee as Nick noticed her rubbing her index figure along her jawline.

"You're thinking about those questions I asked the lady last night, aren't you?" asked Nick.

She snapped out of it. "Stop doing that!" She looked over at Henri and said, "He does that all the time!" Henri acknowledged the truth of her statement with a nod and then chuckled.

"I was gathering more information from her in order to construct what I was going to say in the session."

"Interesting," replied Henri. "I didn't pick up on it… but of course, that makes sense. I think I've been away from your classes too long." He offered to pour Kate another cup of coffee from the elaborate urn that had been placed on the table. When she declined, he poured one for himself and relished the deep aroma before taking a sip.

"She may not think she sleeps, but her brain, in some ways, has figured a workaround," said Nick.

"A workaround, what do you mean by that?" asked Kate.

"She's not insane," said Nick with a smile.

Henri added, "Nick teaches that one of the main reasons to sleep is to dream, which is to vent. If you're really sleep deprived, you'd go crazy."

They finished their meal and afterward shared a moment to shake hands and have a delightful parting. "Kate," Henri said, "it was wonderful to finally meet you. Have a lovely vacation."

"Thank you so much." She broke formality and gave Henri a hug. He was surprised but pleased. Nick couldn't hide his own delight. He could now enjoy some free time abroad with his fiancée.

"Aintazar!" came a shout. They turned to see someone rushing through the lobby in their direction. It was Nasir with his wife Alia coming up behind in a strong walk. Henri quickly turned to translation mode. He told Nick that Nasir was asking them to "Wait." Nick stepped forward to greet his acquaintance and Nasir handed him a green ribboned medal in place of a handshake.

"I thank you," Nasir said, with tears in his eyes. "May God reward you with goodness." Nick beheld the medal with honor and slight confusion. A medal was a medal. But for a simple therapy session, it was a bit much — until Nasir, barely containing himself, reported that his wife had finally slept through the entire night.

"This," a surprised Henri explained quietly, "is something the government only awards to its citizens for bravery." Nick looked at the medal differently now.

He turned to Nasir. "I was happy to help." Alia nodded with a smile and a curt bow. Nasir offered a final thank you, then turned and walked away. Alia dutifully followed, and Nick watched them for a moment.

There was more to the medal than he'd realized. It had originally been awarded to Nasir by the King for his part in a remarkable act of defiance — he was one of 3,500 men who had walked unarmed into the Sahara Desert to demand that land taken by Spain be returned to Morocco. Every man in that group received the Green Medal for their bravery and loyalty to their country.

It struck Nick how much it meant to Nasir to have given it away. He thought about the things he took for granted without realizing it — the way most people did — and made a mental note that Kate deserved better than that from him.

The lobby had a few people in it; some were departing or just arriving and marveling at the architecture and splendid exotic flair it had. One man caught Nick's eye, though. He was acting far too discreetly to be coincidental. The man had a thick, almost face-obscuring mustache and a scar over one eye. He watched the space between Nick and Nasir as the latter walked out of the lobby. Nick tried to gauge his intentions. Once Nasir departed, the scar-eyed man also left to follow them. He could have been a secret bodyguard, dressed to deter detection and protect Nasir from the shadows. Or he could have been the opposite. An observer of contacts with Americans in the country? Nick caught himself and nearly laughed when he realized he was now acting as if he were living in a spy movie.

"Hey," Kate said. She tapped Nick on the shoulder. Her excitement and pride in seeing Nick be awarded for his efforts was waning as a curious concern took over. "You okay?"

Nick looked down at the medal in his hand. "I've never gotten a commendation this easily before."

Once more, they said their farewells to Henri and got on with their vacation — and it would be a memorable one.

Lacking an official interpreter meant they'd miss out on a lot of everyday street-going conversations, but the tourism industry of Morocco was equipped to handle English travelers. For the next few days, they enjoyed their vacation without a single thought of their duties that awaited once they made final touchdown in the States.

First, they spent their day on the water. Nick arranged for one of those glass-bottomed boat rides. They arrived by bus and followed simple English signs to the dock that stretched out over crystal-clear waters. It was nothing like the Pacific they knew so well. It was so clear they could already see nearly to the bottom of the shallows off the dock.

Their ride was peaceful as they viewed schools of fish and other coastal life along the seabed. Anemones, barnacles, and diminutive coral strands were everywhere. It was a multicolored spectacle deep in the blue, which stretched on for miles like the sky had fallen and swallowed up the land. As the boat moved further offshore, a pod of playful dolphins met them. Seeing Kate so enamored by those little jesters of the sea made him grateful for that part of his life. But Nick could never escape the reality of some things. He remembered reading reports on the use of dolphins by the U.S. Navy for a variety of things, including setting explosives, an upsetting thought. So, instead, he tried to focus on the little mammalian torpedos zooming past the boat and leaping through the air and Kate's joyful laughter.

After the boat returned to shore and they were happily exhausted by the sun and salty air, they had lunch in town at a place where they could order with simple English and even simpler Arabic from Kate's trusty phrase book. They had previously sampled the best food on offer from the highest office in the land, and they followed it up with simple street kebabs with couscous bowls.

"Oh no," Kate said.

"What?"

She looked up with a moment of incredible guilt and laughed nervously. "It's fantastic," she said.

"That sounds like a good thing," Nick said.

She took another bite and laughed to herself as she chewed. "I think I like it better than the palace food."

Nick stifled a laugh and leaned in close to her. "You need to not say stuff like that until we're home." The extra pressure made her laugh more, causing some couscous to fly across the table and spatter onto Nick's shirt. At that point, he gave into the whole absurdity of the situation and laughed louder than she.

After that long, wet day, they spent their next excursion in the opposite environment that was within Morocco's border. They took a scenic tour of the Saharan dunes, out into the wasteland where no life could survive for even a day without aid. It was hot and dry. Nick and Kate were advised to wear more than the usual amount of headgear, and they elected to dress in traditional long robes to keep themselves covered.

Once they got far out into the dunes, they were swept away by how majestic it was. Endless waves of golden ground stretched out for hundreds of miles. Tall mounds of steep sand obscured the city in the distance. If not for their camel caravan, they would have easily slid all the way down the dunes, which itself seemed like an appealing way to enjoy them. They got a picture taken with the dunes in the background, a memory they could bring back home to remind them of the beauty hiding in such desolate places.

That evening, they enjoyed a romantic candlelit dinner provided by the hotel. It was in the middle range between the King's limitless extravagance and the boardwalk food vendors Kate loved. A simple, semi-traditional meal was prepared for them. Nick had just enough time alone in the day to find a jewelry boutique while Kate was unaware and bought her a gift. To commemorate their unforgettable adventure together, he got her a turquoise and gold keychain shaped like a dolphin, a tiny statuette that she could carry with her wherever she went.

Nick took her hand and pulled it toward him. He gently opened her fingers and placed the keychain in her palm. She eyed it thoughtfully, her finger tracing the shape of the semi-precious stone. "Oh, my God, it's absolutely beautiful." Her eyes glistened as they filled with tears and she bit her lip to keep from crying.

The next day, they checked out of their hotel, drove to the airport, and boarded their plane as if they were leaving a dream.

Nick was happy that the brief assignment he was given had gone so easily and nothing out of the ordinary cropped up. But he knew he couldn't leave his safety up to chance and fate anymore.

Now back home, while Kate was off visiting her mother, Nick was in the kitchen beginning to make one of his favorites, a peanut butter and banana sandwich, when the doorbell rang. The tasty treat would have to wait. Dancer ran to the door and wagged his tail while Yogi, who was nestled in his cat tree, kept on snoozing. Nick ushered Dancer away and opened the door to find Darlene, Tony and Bruce, his Academy co-workers. From the looks on their faces, he knew there was trouble. "Come in," Nick said. But they didn't budge.

"We just wanted to tell you face to face, Nick, we're leaving and it has everything to do with Costas," Darlene said.

"Sorry, Nick," added Bruce.

"Are you sure? Why don't you come in and we'll talk."

Dancer nosed his way back to the door and Tony kept him entertained with lots of petting.

"We're on our way to the attorney now," said Darlene. "But the shit's gonna fly on Monday and we're hoping you can avoid the splatter."

"I appreciate the heads-up."

"Sorry, we'll be leaving you short-handed," Bruce said.

"I'm sorry to see you go," said Nick. "But I certainly understand. More than you know."

They all shook Nick's hand, and Tony gave him a pat on the back. "We'll miss you," Tony said.

Nick gently constrained Dancer, closed the door and walked back into the kitchen. But he had lost his appetite and just stood there. "Fuck," he muttered under his breath.

CHAPTER EIGHT
GUNS & COMPASSION

Right now, Nick was in a bad part of town — Hollywood to be exact. Most people who lived outside of Los Angeles only knew it as an almost mythical place where people came to get rich and famous. They weren't aware of just how nasty and seedy it could be, even in the daylight. It was unapologetic.

Two hookers were cruising the sidewalk for Johns. A drug dealer leaned down into the window of a car to make a sale to someone passing by. If Nick was a cop, he'd have his hands full.

It was a place he'd normally never want to be in, but today it was necessary. He had a special meeting arranged by Kearney, and felt he had already been waiting next to his Roadster a bit too long. It was fifteen minutes past the scheduled appointment time and he was about to leave when a white van skidded around a tight corner and roared up his way. The windows had iron bars fixed in place, which was a unique solution. The van stopped with a jerk right behind Nick's Jag and a man got out. He was bordering middle-aged, short, chubby, and looked like a jovial attendant at some rural road stop from long ago. Nick watched curiously as the man unlocked the gas cap door, reached in, lined up the holes in two pieces of metal, and locked them together with a padlock which prevented the van doors from being forced open.

Nick recognized him. Although he had been half-obscured by smoke, he was definitely present for the debriefing at the Rack 'Em Pool Hall with Kearney — the silent man on the barstool.

"Michael Davies?" Nick asked.

Michael warmed up immediately. "The one and only."

Nick checked his watch. "Guess I had the time wrong. I thought we had an appointment fifteen minutes ago."

"Rule number one," Michael said. "If someone's late, you wait at least thirty minutes or more. Stuff happens."

"As long as I know the rules, I know how to play the game," Nick said. Michael extended a hand and they shook.

"What you'll be learning is far from a game," he offered. That statement comforted Nick. He knew he'd be in the hands of someone who took his situation as seriously as he did. "Follow me," Michael said. They passed by Nick's car on the way to Michael's apartment building. "You got an alarm on that thing?"

Nick raised an eyebrow as if to say, *shit yeah*. He followed Michael into his apartment. It was small, even for the older parts of Hollywood, and it was dense. The door had double deadbolts and all the windows were iron-barred, despite being on the second floor. Nick took a gander at the place to see what he could assess. An entire lifetime was jammed into the small apartment.

Cardboard boxes and heavy metal ammo cans stacked up high created a maze-like hallway that wound through the apartment, reducing the already cramped space into a fortified bunker. Guns were laid out in various states of assembly. Handguns, rifles, shotguns, automatics — Nick suspected there would be a rocket launcher hiding underneath a seat somewhere if he bothered to check. He was glad he didn't see any grenades until he passed a box labeled "Grenada".

Aside from the aesthetic of warfare, Nick noticed an appreciation for a certain mistress of the dark. Michael had some scattered paraphernalia of Elvira, the famed horror movie hostess, hanging on his walls. He had a poster, a magazine spread, a calendar, and even a clock bearing her likeness. Despite all of that, he wore a wedding ring fixed on his thick finger.

One breakaway of normality was an impressive human interest piece that was framed on the wall. A cover of *Firearms*

Magazine, an obviously named enthusiast's periodical, featured Michael on the front in full combat gear, holding a gun and a flashlight. *The Davies Flashlight Technique for Self-Defense* was the featured article.

Nick noticed a crossed pair of drumsticks stuck on a far wall. He figured Michael had some history with those but wasn't getting any inkling yet of what that might be. Until Michael informed him, "Marine band," when he caught Nick looking. Michael was a former Marine, as there are no "ex-Marines" and he explained he started out as a drummer in a Marine Corps band before becoming a journalist for the camp paper and going on to train with heavy-duty weaponry and explosives. He even had a small shrine dedicated to his Marine days off in a corner with a display of not only the camp paper's masthead but photos of him posing with fellow soldiers in full military regalia at various South Pacific locations: Okinawa, the Philippines, Thailand and Vietnam. He pointed to his pin. "3rd Marine Division FMF." By his outward appearance, never in a million years would anyone think Michael was the sort of guy who would — or even could — be involved in the type of work Kearney did, although his knowledge and interest in military weaponry and tactics were quite extensive as evidenced by the books, periodicals and treasure trove of equipment that surrounded them. Nick took it all in as he peppered Michael with questions and got an earful in return.

Michael pointed out an old typewriter and a stack of papers on a coffee table and said, "You can read my book when I finish the manuscript. It's about coaching and tactics. I work with Marines, Special Forces, Navy SEALs, FBI agents, police, you name it."

"Special forces, wow… how—?"

Michael rolled right over him. "You'd be amazed by how much they don't know. Right now, I'm working on a section about the American Pistol Institute that my good friend Jeff Cooper founded."

"Jeff Cooper?"

"The godfather of modern combat shooting. Hey honey," Michael called out, "some drinks please." Nick turned to the hallway, past the boxes where Michael projected his voice. There was no response but Nick heard some movement through the walls. "Mary, my wife," Michael said as he pointed to a photo showing them together. They looked happy, but also like they waited for the photographer for too long. There were a few others of Mary ice skating and one of her standing on the ice in a too-short-for-her-age skater's outfit. Michael turned around right in front of a couch that was awkwardly shoved back up against a bookcase — as if there were no better place to put it — and motioned for Nick to sit.

The smallest sound of Mary arriving prompted the men to stall their conversation. Nick took a seat on the couch while

Michael sat in a chair across from him with a coffee table between them.

Mary looked no older than the framed picture, which itself looked at least ten years old. Yet, she had a motherly appearance, as if she looked that old her whole life, and had grown into it. High cheeks, sloping eyes, curly dark hair cut short, with a simple scarf tied around her neck like her heroine Annie Oakley sported. She carried in two hefty coffee mugs and a bowl of single-serve coffee shop half-and-half containers. Michael shoved aside the typewriter and papers so Mary could place the tray down without the coffee so much as swaying. She had honed her drink delivery skills as a years-long waitress at myriad diners across Hollywood and beyond.

"Hi," she greeted with a sugar-sweet tone. "My name is Mary."

"He knows, honey," Michael said flatly.

She smiled at him, wider than she smiled at Nick. "Of course he does." She turned back to Nick and, out of the blue, asked, "Do you skate?"

"No."

"Oh, that's too bad." Mary waltzed back to her kitchen domain to leave the men to their business then called out, "It's really fun, you know."

Nick turned and saw Michael going through container after container of the half-and-halfs that were obviously pocketed from Mary's waitressing job. Each one was slipped into his coffee until the surface rose near the rim and turned the dark brew into almost white. Michael stood up to drink and Nick, who kept his coffee black, joined him.

"So," Nick began, "how long have you known Kearney?"

Michael took a deep sip of his creamy blend and sucked it back through his teeth. "Job here and there. Have you seen his paintings? Damn good artist. Oh, and if you need your taxes done, he's great. He learned a lot from working with Meyer Lansky."

An inexplicable sound of a gothic church bell chiming followed by an erotic moan interrupted their conversation. The Elvira clock on the wall announced the hour. Nick's eyes darted to the source of the sound. It wasn't just Elvira-themed but Christmas as well, with an inscription boldly emblazoned along the panel underneath the clock face: *"Revenge is Better than Christmas."*

"Meyer Lansky," Nick said, "the Mob's accountant?"

Michael nodded and turned his back on Nick to rummage around a bookshelf as if he were looking for something, but it was half-hearted at best. Nick, now more curious, wasn't acknowledging that Kearney told him anything, only that he knew the name Lansky as it related to the mob since he was recently on the news claiming he was dying of cancer and wanted to visit Israel once more before he died.

Nick could tell from Michael's body language that the subject of Kearney and the mob was now off-limits. His eyes continued to wander around for clues and probing points. He saw a few photos of a younger Michael with servicemen and police officers. He was the only one out of uniform but seemed to take a central position in the frame.

"You train civilians?" Nick asked.

Just then, Mary sauntered back into the room carrying two more mugs of coffee and a load of half-and-halfs. "Hi, I'm Mary," she said to Nick in the same sugar-sweet tone. Nick was momentarily taken aback but, upon seeing Michael's acute embarrassment at her reappearance, he recognized that Mary was probably suffering from early stage dementia.

"Not now, honey, we're still good with these," said Michael as he held up his original mug to show her. Mary's smile vanished upon realizing her error; she crunched her face as if trying to remember who Nick was then left the room still carrying her refreshments.

Michael let out a deep sigh then turned back to Nick, quick to pick up with their prior conversation, while hoping to skirt the subject of Mary. "Germany got to you, huh?" He also circled right back to his beloved milk coffee and took another gulp.

Nick's mind raced through the events in Germany, causing him to take more than a moment to answer. "You could say that," he said as he sipped his coffee bit by bit while Michael seemed to chew his down.

"You have any experience with weapons?" Michael asked.

Before Nick could even answer, Michael said, "Ah, doesn't matter." He sifted one hand through a stack of paper publications and old newspapers until he snatched up a pamphlet. Nick off-handed his coffee as he prepared to take it. It read *Jeff Cooper's Color Code For Awareness.*

"In your work," Michael instructed, "you have to be pretty perceptive. This will give you a new spin on that." Nick flipped it open and pushed the pages apart with his fingers while he balanced the coffee in his other hand. "You can finish that on your own time. Let's get you doing some dry firing."

Nick closed the pamphlet and slid it into his pocket, then finished his coffee while Michael cleared a path to a target on a wall. He unloaded a .45 semi-automatic and motioned Nick over so he could demonstrate the finer points of aiming and shooting a weapon without actually firing a live round. It involved a steady arm and hand, controlled breathing and, most importantly, a proper grip. Without that, none of the other elements would mean anything. You may as well be doing yoga.

Michael summarized it into terms Nick enjoyed. *"The Zen Art of Killing,"* Michael said. "You know Zen?"

"I know *of* Zen Buddhism," Nick admitted. "I studied it briefly when I was—"

"Those samurai," Michael said, "were crazy sons of bitches. They believed they could stop lethal wounds from bleeding with the power of their minds. That's how they fought without fear. They weren't afraid of death because they thought they could control it along with any pain."

"They weren't afraid of death because they served a higher purpose," corrected Nick, "therefore, pain was an abstract."

"Either way," Michael warned, "if you lose your sense of pain, you lose your sense of danger. You can't survive without that." Ironic that Michael understood a tenet of Nick's numbing process without ever realizing it. It was similar to Nick's warning to students at his UCLA lecture about not numbing your emotions for too long.

That week, Nick took instruction with Michael and all of it was about gun safety, dry firing, assembling and disassembling, all the basics. It was preceded, of course, by Michael's coffee klatsch with general gossip about anything that interested him, usually guns, his obsession with the Marines, and rotten politicians everywhere, but not Mary. As a topic, she was generally off-limits. She was away at work anyway, leaving the men complete privacy, which Nick was grateful for since he was being treated like the rookie he was. It was a far cry from his position at the Academy where he was top dog, at least in the teaching department, if not the whole shebang. But this dog was now learning new tricks which would support what he was bringing to the table with Kearney: calculated insight and expertly guided, *manipulated some would say,* behavior modification. And he knew its value:

$2,500-5,000 per assignment and the government contract for his therapy process, as he was promised.

After Michael declared the last long session over, he grabbed a book off a shelf and, from a secret inside compartment, pulled out a stacked envelope. It had Nick's name on the front. He jotted something on the back of it, then handed it to Nick. "For Morocco. And be there tomorrow at seven a.m." he said as he pointed to his note. Nick felt the weight of the envelope and pocketed it as Michael moved for the front door, past the steel and cardboard hallway without waiting for Nick's approval. "Let's see if you still have a car." Nick heard that one before; it was a running joke, yet he always knew there was a possibility his car could be gone.

They stepped outside Michael's apartment. "You got lucky again," Michael said. The car was still there, although a little grimy from the bumper-to-bumper smog. The prostitutes on the corner looked bruised, like a fight broke out and settled while Nick was indoors. "Yeah, it's a garbage pit," Michael said. He shook his head in amusement. "And you're wondering, if I really loved my wife, why would we live here?" Nick neither confirmed nor denied the curiosity, but noted Michael's oh-so-willing projection onto him as his mentor returned to the apartment door. "What doesn't kill you makes you stronger." Michael left Nick with that last bit of wisdom as he stepped back inside, closed the door and engaged the deadbolts.

Nick returned to his car and checked Michael's note. Wes Thompson's Shooting Range with an address in Canyon Country. His new endeavor was really getting serious and his heartbeat hastened in anticipation.

Michael, meanwhile, returned to one of his chores. He carted out a small caliber reloader, a can of 231 gunpowder, bullets, primers, and cases, and set them on a bench to knock out a couple of hundred rounds.

It was work Michael could almost do in his sleep. He was meditative about it and although he was generally a gregarious guy, he appreciated the solitude. Mary occasionally interrupted when she dusted and cleaned around the immovable object that was Michael, always grateful for the extra cash his freelance work brought in.

Early the next morning, Nick arrived in Canyon Country, a little suburb north of Los Angeles. At first, it was a little hard to find his intended location, but he finally spotted a small sign next to a dirt road that read Wes Thompson's. It seemed an odd placement for a shooting range since the area looked residential. But after driving a few blocks up the dirt road, he found himself in the middle of multiple shooting ranges that had been carved into the hillsides long before the appearance of any homes. Still, the ranges were far enough away and protected by the hillsides that the sounds of gunfire didn't reach most of the community.

Nick stopped to figure out which way to go when he heard someone yelling at him from a small makeshift office set up in a trailer a few yards away. He walked over and, standing amid some barrels and old junk but not enough to turn it into a junkyard, was Wes Thompson himself, an old crotchety guy.

There was no welcome for the newbie, just an admonishment, "Can't ya read?"

"Read what?"

"The Goddamned signs," he said, pointing.

Nick finally spotted a dinky sign next to the road stating 5 mph and apologized for having gone over.

"You pay here," indicated Wes.

Nick paid the day rate then asked Wes if he knew Michael Davies.

"Everyone knows Michael." Wes pointed up the road. "Second range on the left."

Nick got back into his car and drove further into the facility and parked where he saw a sign for *The Equalizers* — Michael's club. He grabbed a bag with his gear and stepped over to a table to unpack, which took little time at all. Nick only had a pair of hearing protectors that Michael had given him, a notepad, and his small caliber Walther PPKS, that he brought in order to shake off the rust. He never had much experience shooting a gun except for a bit in the Air Force.

Nick was alone on Michael's range but he could hear that the other ranges were well populated. Though, it sounded as if some shooters on those ranges were using much heavier calibers that roared at their paper and steel targets.

He turned after hearing the familiar sound of Michael pulling up in his van. When Michael slid back the side door, it revealed a survivalist's dream come true. Guns, ammo, meal kits, water, a shovel and saw, extra clothes, and everything else needed to escape Armageddon. Michael strapped on his gun belt and holster. He filled his magazine pouches, loaded his .45 and holstered it while Nick waited with his measly gear at the table. When Michael saw what Nick brought, his response was, "Nice toy you got there. You can put it away now." Nick muffled a sigh and zipped his gun back into its case as Michael reached into his gun bag and pulled out a pistol case containing a Colt .45 and a couple of magazines. He handed them to Nick. "Load up." He then pointed to a target 7 yards downrange. "That's a bad guy trying to kill you. Stop him."

Nick took a preparatory stance, a deep breath and slowly squeezed the trigger. He fired once, right through the center of the target. "I think I got him," Nick said with a smile.

Michael shook his head. "You got the dry firing down but now you gotta change it up because while you were taking your time lining up the sights and squeezing off a round, he emptied his gun into you." Michael drew his .45 and shot three times in a split second at a target about 25 yards away compared to Nick's 7. Michael's shots were dead center and formed a distinctly larger hole, because they were grouped so tight, causing the cardboard to disintegrate between them. He reholstered.

Knowing Michael was a competent shooter and a trained, military expert differed from seeing him in action. His precision and control were on a scale Nick couldn't fathom. "Now, what was your mistake?" asked Michael.

"Obviously not being fast enough but I didn't want to miss."

"Exactly on the first part but don't worry about the second." Michael knew Nick had reverted to what people had seen on TV and in movies: The old pro teaching a newbie to line up the sights, take a deep breath and slowly squeeze the trigger. "Remember what I said. As long as you have a proper solid grip… did you?" Nick nodded. "Then you'll be quicker while maintaining your accuracy even at long distances. Now do it again."

Nick picked up the gun, racked a round into the chamber, fired and nailed it with the same accuracy but better speed.

The practice continued for some time and each time Nick gathered a bit more speed and comfort in his handling of a loaded weapon. At the end of the day, while packing up their gear, Michael noticed Nick lost in thought. "Something not clear?"

"I was wondering how to explain all this to Kate."

"You'll figure it out."

Nick always did. The Walther PPKS in his case was proof of that. It had been with him since the days when figuring people out meant something entirely different — like when he was a sometime bouncer and bodyguard in his mid-20s. He was living his dark side by frequenting dive bars and mingling with bikers like The Satan's Slaves. He also had a friend who, from time to time, had a job for him. The latest one paid $500 for a couple of hours' work and needed to be done that night. So, without hesitation, Nick accepted. It entailed a classy hooker named Tina with a young son who was taken by the woman's ex-boyfriend who lived up in Hollywood Hills. Tina didn't have a prayer fighting the guy in court with all of his high-priced attorneys. So she wanted somebody to "convince" the fucker that he should give the kid back and leave her the hell alone.

Nick picked Tina up at her apartment. She was a beautiful blonde who could have been a model. They drove to the ex-boyfriend's house. Nick pulled into the driveway and stopped a few yards from the man's front door. And within seconds of them getting out of the car, Tina's ex walked out of the house brandishing a baseball bat. She immediately began arguing with him, so Nick touched her on the shoulder and said, "Please let me handle this if you want your boy back." In reality, Nick was winging it, giving it his best shot.

He told the guy to stop where he was, that it was going to be simple; they were there just to get the boy and didn't want any trouble.

When the kid came out of the house and stood behind his father, the man became belligerent, as if he were trying to put on a show for the kid's sake. It was at that point that Nick unbuttoned his sports coat to reveal the Walther nestled in his waistband. It was all that was needed to get the guy to back off. Nick told him to tell the boy to get into Nick's car. That's when the therapist in him kicked in. He told him a father should be able to take part in his son's life, but it shouldn't be to the detriment of the mother. With the boy and mother safely in the car, Nick said one last thing that sealed the deal. "I can find you at any time, at any place, and there's nothing you can do about it. So be nice!"

Technically, that was Nick's first house-call therapy session. Although there were so many things that could have gone wrong, Nick rather enjoyed the fact that he had correctly calculated the prick's behavior, knowing that he would back off if a "bigger bully" confronted him. There was no kidnapping, only a grateful woman who rewarded Nick with five hundred-dollar bills.

As far as his Walther PPKS, Nick thought it was cool until he discovered Michael considered it a "mouse gun". Michael also considered a 9 mm a mouse gun, good for penetration but not as good as a .45, which is better for knockdown power — the difference between being struck with an ice pick compared to that of a bowling ball.

Nick would later learn an interesting history lesson from Michael about the military's lousy decision-making when they replaced .45s with 9 mms. It was bad enough that they gave the contract to a foreign manufacturer but their lame excuse for replacing the .45 caliber was that the 9 mm could hold more rounds. Michael always thought it would be more efficient to teach soldiers how to hit what they were aiming at instead of firing a bunch of rounds at the enemy and hoping one hits home. He called it spray and pray.

That night, while he was home, Nick spent extra time close to Kate. They cooked dinner together while the pets played around. They were playfully and harmlessly fighting over a small rubber ball before Dancer chased Yogi into the other room. Meanwhile, Kate turned the fish while Nick handled the chopping board. He thought about how she always supported him in his pursuits and goals, but those goals were never lethal by nature. Nick took a step and felt the rubber ball underfoot. He casually kicked it out of the kitchen. "Did you read about those people getting robbed?" he asked.

Kate seemed distracted but aware. "In Sherman Oaks." He nodded toward the nearby newspaper and out of the corner of his eye saw Yogi trotting into the kitchen with the ball in his mouth. "Kate!" Nick said. She turned and saw Nick pointing down at Yogi as he dropped the ball at Nick's feet. Nick picked it up and tossed it out of the kitchen. Then they both waited. A moment later Yogi reappeared with the ball. He again dropped it at Nick's feet. "Did you teach him?" Nick asked.

Kate shook her head no. "Our child is a prodigy."

"Yeah, next he'll be playing the piano."

They both got a good laugh at that. Nick picked up and pocketed the ball so they could get on with their meal preparation. "Later, little guy," he said.

Kate took a glance at the newspaper and returned to her fish. "That robbery was just down the street. Maybe we should join the neighborhood watch."

"Yeah, good idea." Nick steered the conversation back into what he needed. "I think I'll check out some other ways to protect ourselves."

Kate waved the spatula at him. "A man should always be able to protect his home and family."

Nick set his knife down and crept up behind her while she attended to the fish. He stroked his hand over her belly, just below the stomach, near the center of her abdomen. "Family?" he said. "Is there something I should know?"

She turned to him with a smug look and pointed her spatula over her shoulder right to where Yogi and Dancer now sat in the middle of the kitchen. They were looking up hopefully as the dinner was nearing its completion. Once the humans ate, the animals got to eat, too. They were like tiny, misshaped children. Nick laughed it off. He was actually relieved.

The rice timer dinged, so Kate plated the food while Nick glanced over at the newspaper one last time. He felt comfortable now with the idea that he could justify getting another gun or two and whatever other equipment was needed to satisfy their shared sense of protection. But he was going to take it slowly because he didn't want to seem too eager, too rushed to take that next big step.

He tossed the newspaper into the trash. He didn't know when his next assignment would come up, but he wanted to be as ready as he could when it did. When he turned back around, he saw the pleading eyes of the fur babies. He quickly distributed their meals and then joined Kate at the table.

They were halfway through their meal when Nick's pager beeped. He checked it: 9-1-1. "Give me a minute." Nick rushed to the phone and placed his call. Kate looked over and saw Nick jot something down as he talked. "On my way," he said.

Kate looked at him expectantly.

"Client emergency."

Kate knew the drill. As Nick dashed to the door, she gathered the rest of his meal and stored it in the fridge for later.

Nick hopped on his motorcycle and took off toward his destination in West Hollywood. Twenty-minutes later, he pulled up outside Club Love, a well-known and popular Gay Club. He entered the noisy, packed establishment. Music blasted and patrons flirted, danced and drank. Carrie, the transgender who attended Nick's UCLA lecture, rushed him, arms wrapping around his neck.

"Oh, thank God," she said.

Two transsexuals came up and stood next to her with worried looks. They half-waved awkwardly at Nick. Carrie grabbed Nick by the hand and hurriedly led him through to the back hallway, each ignoring the stares from the patrons. It wasn't them moving through the crowd so quickly that got people looking; it was that Nick, well frankly, looked too square to be there. Although a few of the guys in the mix were definitely checking him out.

She pointed down the hallway. "The employee bathroom with the pink flamingo. Her name's Amy."

Nick made his way down the hallway, past some heavy petting and more, and knocked on the door. A voice answered, "Go away, Carrie."

"Amy, my name's Nick. I drove a long way and I'd like to use the bathroom."

"Occupied! Wait ... are you UCLA Nick?"

"I guess you could say that."

The door cracked open and a petite Amy, with a wig covering half her face, peeked out to see if anyone else was with him. Coast clear. She let Nick in and quickly locked the door. Amy kept her back to him. "You can go. I won't look," she said as she opened and closed her hands, finding it hard to stand still. She pulled down a sleeve to hide bruises along one arm.

Instead of using the toilet, Nick leaned against the edge of the sink.

"I know why you're here," she said. "It's not going to work. I'm not going to put up with those assholes making me feel like a freak!... Fuck!"

Nick spotted the crumbled lipstick and makeup compact on the sink counter.

"I just want to be..." her voice cracked.

"You?" asked Nick.

"Yes, I want to be me. I'm not fucked up!"

"I don't know why you think I'm here, Amy, but I'm sure in hell not here to fix anyone."

"Then why *are* you here?!"

"Because Carrie asked me here and that's what friends do. They show up."

Amy now relaxed a bit.

"There's no way I can relate to the pain you experience. But I can relate to feeling angry and lost."

Amy interrupted, "That you have no control over your life?"

Nick agreed, "That's right."

There was a knock on the door, eliciting the same response from them both. "Occupied!"

Amy finally turned around. She was pretty except for the bruises on her neck, face and cut lip. "You're just saying that," she said in response to Nick's prior statement.

Nick hid his surprise when he realized Amy was Carrie's friend at the UCLA lecture who asked the revealing question about numbing one's emotions. He grabbed a tissue and wet it as he tried to come up with something in his life that she could relate to in order to gain rapport. He dabbed her cut lip as he spoke. "Do you remember your very first day at school?"

She was noncommittal so he continued on. "Well, I definitely do. I had no friends so I was excited about going to school and finding some. I ended up running all over the place and talking to everyone." Amy relaxed even more as she focused on Nick's story. "The teacher got so mad because I wouldn't stay put, she grabbed one of the jump ropes and tied me to a piano leg." He paused to let the image sink in. "For what seemed like forever, the other kids laughed and made fun of me. I often came home with bruises." He finished dabbing her lip. "There, that should do it."

Amy looked right at him. "And that story's supposed to make me feel better?"

"Well, it was worth a try. Now, tell me, why do you think people beat you up?"

"Because they're afraid of us?"

"You mean transsexuals… gays in general?"

"Yeah, all of us."

"I've heard that answer a lot but, Amy, does that really make sense?" She scrunched her face, confused by the question.

"Tell me… what are *you* afraid of?"

She thought about it. "Dark places, like streets, especially since…"

"It doesn't matter why at the moment. Tell me something else you're afraid of."

"Snakes… because…" She caught herself and smiled. Nick returned her smile, but hers was already gone, replaced by a look of sheer frustration. "Arrrgh," she couldn't even articulate what she was feeling.

"No one who's afraid of a dark alley deliberately walks into one," Nick said. "And no one who's afraid of snakes goes near one and certainly, no one who's *actually* afraid of gays or transsexuals goes out of their way to be near them or touch them."

"So why do they do it?" she pleaded.

"Because they're fucking bullies who need to suppress their own insecurities and failings by beating down others, which makes them feel powerful. But that also doesn't matter now."

"Well, what the hell does?"

"You. None of us can take on all the haters but we can make ourselves stronger. You ever watch Star Trek?"

"Yeah. My dad's a big fan. It's the only time he'll let me spend with him."

"He knows, doesn't he? Nick asked.

Amy nodded and began to tear up.

Nick ordered, "Okay, shields up!" confusing Amy for a moment before she realized what he was referring to.

"That's right," Nick said, "we're gonna build you some kick-ass shields."

For the first time, she saw the people who hurt her not as unbeatable monsters, but as deeply flawed individuals fueled by their own insecurities. "So, what do I do?"

"You can't change all of them, but you can change yourself so that their bullshit doesn't get to you," Nick answered.

"What about that emotional numbing thing you talked about?"

"Let's start on that right now."

She closed up the lipstick tube, stood it upright on the counter with a determined slam, and turned to Nick. "I'm ready."

Back in the club, Carrie and her friends sat staring in the direction of the hallway. "He's been in there a long time," said one of the girls. "What do you think he's doing?"

Carrie closed her eyes as if meditating and twirled her fingers around her temples. "He's doing his thing."

Another girl said, "Carrie, he's been in there too long. I think we should go and find out what's going on."

Carrie replied, "Honey, how long have we been good friends?"

"Over three years, I guess."

"And in all that time, have I ever given you bad advice?"

"No."

"So, honey, shut the fuck up."

Carrie's friend sat and waited patiently just like the rest of them.

A while later, Nick and Amy came back in. The friends jumped up and group-hugged Amy, all tears and smiles. Carrie then walked over to Nick as the others stayed in their love circle.

"She'll be fine," Nick said. "For now, make sure she has someone with her when she goes out.

"Charlie will watch over her." Carrie nodded to a tall, muscular guy in his 30s in a crop top, who moved toward them with an umbrella drink. "There's only one thing Charlie likes better than giving a blow job and that's kicking ass."

Nick shook his head and half-smiled. He got serious again. "I don't know how much you talk to Amy about what I do, but she wants me to help her with the physical part of her transition. How old is she?"

"21."

"Carrie, come on… she can't be over 18, if that."

"Okay, she's 17."

"She's a good kid but still a kid. I'll work with her to make sure she's mature enough to know she's making the right decision. Now, I gotta get going. Be good."

"Always." Carrie gave Nick a hug then took his hand and put a crumpled-up wad of money in it. "We took up a collection."

"Carrie, it's not necessary."

"Don't argue with me," she said with a smile.

Nick headed for the door and spotted a small table near the exit with a donation box labeled *Aids Research*. He dropped the wad of money in it and left.

CHAPTER NINE

QUIT, TRAIN, WIN

At the Academy, Nick had put in a full day of teaching and seeing clients. It was now late and Lynn and everyone else had gone for the day. Or so Nick thought. The lights in the hallway outside Nick's office were off and it was illuminated only by a single source coming from the waiting room. He bid his last client, Morgan, who was now better dressed, a goodnight. As Morgan walked out, Nick turned to go back to his office and saw Costas standing in the hall. "We need to talk," Costas said in a stern voice.

"Just a minute." Nick went back into his office and quickly scribbled something on a piece of paper. He came back out and handed it to Costas.

"What's this?"

"The last straw."

Costas scanned the paper. "You can't do this."

"Really?"

Costas wasn't prepared for that. "I was going to turn the place over to you."

Nick smiled and shook his head… *more bullshit.*

"Don't think you're taking your clients with you," Costas crowed.

"I don't own them and neither do you. They'll do what they want. I'll be back in the morning for my—"

"You get out right now and don't come back."

"Fine." Nick continued to the door and a calming feeling surged through his body. He felt renewed.

Even with the Academy in his rearview mirror, Nick's time was still being stretched thin between promoting himself by lecturing, seeing clients, working with Kearney, and training with Michael. But now, the choices he made were completely his own and gave him more satisfaction.

Because of the combination of mental and physical challenges, Nick became more thoroughly immersed in his weapons training that it even crept into his dreams. His hands jittered and vibrated as if they were feeling the recoil in his sleep. As instructed, he kept count of every shot so his gun would never run dry. As for Kate, she was a sound sleeper and never noticed his movements. He didn't tell Michael about it, but he knew if he did, his instructor would have been proud.

Months passed at that level of training, followed by a complete paradigm shift. Nick was upgraded to heavier weaponry and a whole new shooting range, located up at Angeles Crest Highway, in the boondocks. It was the home of Desert Marksmen Shooting Range which was Michael's more private domain for special clients and had a 1,000-yard range for snipers and sniper-wannabees.

Over the next couple of months, Nick was on his way to becoming as competent with long guns as he had proved himself to be with handguns. Soon, Michael had Nick begin night training. The specific area they used, although still part of Desert Marksmen, was a private reserve co-managed by a friend of Michael's from the Marines. It was primarily used as a training ground for paramilitary soldiers operating outside of the traditional branches. These private security forces and counter-guerillas would go on to Central American conflict zones as trainers and recruiters. Other times, they contracted work in South Africa to work with ranchers who wanted to stop the government from taking over their land. But that wasn't Michael's thing. He was a natural-born teacher who preferred the interactions with his students who were eager to learn of his and Jeff Cooper's innovative techniques regarding weapons and tactics.

Michael introduced Nick to his famous Flashlight Technique for scenarios that might take place in low light to complete darkness. He explained to Nick that it gave the shooter not only ease of operation of the flashlight but also stability in maintaining a good sight picture during recoil.

Nick was eating up the physicality of shooting. It also fit well into his persona. Even though most of his energy had always been spent on analyzing human behavior, he loved physical pursuits. It fed his adrenaline junkie profile. In high school, because of his speed and strength, he was on his way to becoming a formidable athlete. But that was derailed by teacher misconduct, which led him down the path to trouble with the law and his involuntary involvement with the military.

What was happening now, however, was not something he could have ever foreseen. It was not even anything that Nick understood consciously. He was learning to kill. And because of Germany, it was as if Kearney had sent him into the forest with the wolves, with one wolf inside Nick feeding off his fresh energy. Not that Kate was oblivious to any change in Nick, it was just that she was happy that he found something he enjoyed, especially while facing obstacles he needed to overcome to get his own academy.

During one practice session, Michael said, "Let's add something to the mix." He tossed a piece of paper onto Nick's shooting bag. It floated into place just under Nick's eye level. He glanced down at it, then back up to the cocksure Michael.

"Shooting competition?" Nick's eyes lit up. Another adventure, another challenge.

The summer changed to early fall and the temperature dropped quickly. It was coldest in the mornings but grew warm by noon. In Kern County, about 2 hours northeast of L.A., it was already jacket weather. Everyone came out with a new sense of fashion with jackets and long sleeve flannel.

Kearney arrived with Michael at the competition site outside of the rural side of Bakersfield. They were ushered into an area for spectators who were kept a set distance from the competitors for safety and to prevent any illicit communications with the shooters. These matches were renowned because shooters didn't know what the course entailed until they stepped up to the firing line.

There were two stages of the match that were separated by a small hill. What made the organizer's matches especially challenging was that shooters couldn't practice for them. This would somewhat level the playing field between the pros and the first-timers. If you knew the basics, you had a chance for a decent placement on the scoreboard.

"I should have worn a heavier jacket," Kearney complained. He had on a simple, lined windbreaker while Michael, who knew better from years of experience in the field, going out on assignments in the cold, had on multiple layers to keep his body warm and flexible. "What's so important that I needed to be here at this hour?" Kearney added.

"Quit bitching," Michael said dismissively as only he could to Kearney. "You need to see this for yourself."

The first stage was simple until it wasn't. Each shooter was escorted to the firing line to keep other shooters from knowing what was in store for them and afterward, they were quickly taken to the second stage. With a single target at 7 yards downrange, all a shooter had to do was draw and fire six times in an easy time span of ten seconds. But right after each shooter loaded his weapon and holstered it, the range officer, to everyone's surprise, put a cloth bag over the shooter's head and then went through the commands to fire, which could be taken as ready, aim, good luck.

Kearney and Michael watched shooter after shooter miss. But not Nick, who now sported a few months' worth of facial hair, and one other guy named Steve Lanky, aptly named since he was tall and slender.

Michael and Kearney followed Nick to the second stage which was a man-on-man contest. After all but two of the competitors had been eliminated, Nick walked up to the firing line with steely eyes of unnerved focus. Predator's eyes. He glared downrange at a man-sized steel target, like a wolf glaring at a deer for an easy meal. A few feet to his right, facing his own steel target, stood Lanky, one of the league's top competitors, who knew he could win against a newbie. He wore a pristine white baseball cap with a company logo on it. He was sponsored to be there.

"How far?" Kearney asked.

"Forty yards, one shot, two seconds," Michael said. Kearney tilted his head to the side as if he didn't quite catch the measurement with his eyes alone.

The range officer came up behind the two shooters. "Any questions?" The men shook their heads. "Load your weapons." They loaded up, then assumed the surrender position, with hands above their shoulders. "Stand by," the officer declared. "Ready...."

Their go signal was a random beep from a timer. At that sound, both men's hands dropped from their shoulders. Weapons drawn, raised, aimed, and fired. In less than two seconds, two pings sounded. The two shots sounded like one distinct ping with a mighty echo behind it. Both hit center mass.

The range officer told them to clear their weapons and re-holster before instructing them to move back twenty yards. Everyone did so, including the spectators, while the bullet hits on the targets were touched up with white paint.

The competitors kept moving back 20 yards after consistently hitting their targets. They now found themselves at

140 yards. Sensing the end of the competition, photographers took their own shots.

Nick fired on command and even though his shot wasn't dead center, it was on target. Lanky's shot was a total miss. The confidence in the pro's face waned; disappointment set in. Nick's mental process and Michael's training had given him a unique advantage. His mind was clear and command over his body was absolute. His weapon truly had become part of his body.

"Winner, Nick Bryant!"

The crowd erupted in applause. Nick turned and shook Lanky's hand then lined up for photos. Another adventure taken; another challenge met.

"And I was happy with just his process," Kearney said. He spoke loud enough to catch Nick's attention as he walked over with Michael. He gave Nick a congratulatory pat on the back. "Looks like you have a new skill set."

Nick nodded. "Could help me open a new client base of athletes." If Nick or anyone else at that moment thought he had forgotten his desire to have his own academy, they were sorely mistaken. He wanted to prove he could achieve more by using his own process than anyone could imagine. He wanted to solidify his reputation and he expected that government contract Kearney had promised. Polygraphs and other mental support? Check. Help in the field? Check.

Defend himself? Check. Whatever the government might throw at him? Double Check.

Before Kearney stepped back to let the public take over the moment, he leaned into Nick and whispered, "By the way, tell Kate to get another job. That junk bond boss of hers is going down." That left Nick surprised as the crowd converged around him, preventing him from getting any clarity. As Michael and Kearney walked to their car, Kearney asked, "Why didn't you tell me he was this good?"

"Why didn't you ask?"

It was early evening when the doorbell at Nick's house chimed. He hadn't yet returned from Bakersfield. Kate ran to the door and found Lynn from the Academy struggling to hold a cardboard box of books and binders. She quickly opened the door. "Here, let me," she said as she took the box and ushered Lynn in. "Is this it?" Kate asked. Lynn offered an apologetic look. "All the work he did there!" lamented Kate as she put the box on the coffee table.

"I had to dig most of it out of the trash," Lynn said.

"He hates Nick that much?"

"You bet. He's got this whole conspiracy thing going. He thinks Nick talked the others into leaving too."

"Oh, so they did end up leaving," Kate said.

Lynn pulled out an envelope from her purse and handed it to her. "He's so busy looking for a new chief of staff, he doesn't have time to spend with his teen bride."

Kate just about gagged. "You mean he hasn't given the job to Stevie the wonder boy?"

"Oh my God, don't even think it. Today I saw him walking back and forth between classrooms, wondering what to do. Then he told me to stop looking at him!"

"Christ, how much longer will you be able to put up with it?" Kate asked sympathetically.

"Only until Nick has his own place. I hope that's still his plan, right?"

"It's what he's been working for. He just thought it would happen by way of the Academy. This whole thing sucks."

"Agreed. So tell him to hurry. My sanity's going fast."

"Well, you are kinda in the right place." Kate chuckled then realized it wasn't so funny by the look on Lynn's face. "You'll be the first one he calls. Come on, I'll make you a cup of tea." Kate directed Lynn towards the kitchen.

"Thanks, but I can't. I gotta stop and pick up a teething ring for Mrs. Costas."

They both burst out laughing as Lynn headed to the door. "No, really, I got a ton of laundry that's been building for a week. Next time?"

"Nick will be sorry he missed you. Take care of yourself in the lion's den."

Kate locked the door behind Lynn then suspiciously eyed the envelope with Nick's name written in bold Sharpie ink on it. "Fucker Costas," she spewed.

That night, Kate watched with trepidation as Nick read the contents of Costas' missive. "He's keeping all my money."

"You said he pulls this crap, but I didn't think he'd do it to you ... after you gave him your damn process."

"That damn process is going to help us get our own place."

"Oh, stop, you know what I mean."

"Don't worry," assured Nick, "it's all gonna come out okay in the end. The new connection may be our ticket."

"I can't wait to hear more."

"Nope, can't jinx it. I'll keep you posted."

Nick tossed the letter into the box and carted it into the den. He placed the box on the desk then stood, with his arms crossed, staring down at years of hard work.

CHAPTER TEN
DESERT SHOOT OUT

The box sat in the den for three days before Nick could bring himself to open it. By the time he got around to it, something else had arrived to take up space in the garage.

Nick had ordered a gun safe that arrived soon after the competition, just in time for him to have trimmed his beard in a more presentable, late-era beatnik sort of way. His survivalist gunpowder-cologne phase was over. He was ready to be a better, more capable and skilled Nick Bryant at home. And Kate was quite relieved and thankful for it.

He stood in the back of the garage to help direct the two hefty movers who brought his new safe over. They unloaded it from their truck and wheeled it in on a heavy-duty dolly. Nick had a space cleared out in the back corner for the monster vault.

He saw Kate drive up and park behind his car. It wasn't the usual Jag, which gave her some pause. Instead, she ended up behind a yellow Ford Thunderbird. She glanced at it as she walked up carrying a plastic bag of takeout, just as the workmen set the safe in place.

"It needs to be that big?" she asked. The movers took their dolly back and let the metal lip slide out from under the foundation of the full metal closet. They waved goodbye and went back to their van.

Nick nodded toward the safe again. "With all that jewelry I'm gonna be buying you, sure."

She tittered and turned to the Thunderbird which made her stifle an honest chuckle. He rolled his head in a pitiful nod. "A rental. I'm having a hard time finding a part for the Jag."

"Why don't you just fly?" she asked.

"You know I enjoy driving at night. Gives me time to think." He walked with her out of the garage and shuttered the door before they went into the house to tackle the takeout food.

"You excited about the event?" she asked.

"Nah, I've lectured in Vegas before."

"Not under your own company banner!" she said excitedly.

He smiled back. "One man does not yet make a company."

"This man will," she said as she looped her arm around his and they disappeared into the house.

Nick felt a surge of emotion from her support and belief in him. He wasn't about to let her down. Kearney had guaranteed him a fast track to higher fields when he took on the last assignment in Morocco. While this trip to Vegas wasn't one of them, it was a golden opportunity to make his therapy process known to a wider audience. Anybody who was in the business of helping people, physically or mentally, would be at the convention. That would make him more valuable to the government because he'd get easier access to overseas clients and the government could legitimately piggyback on his travels for him to do what they needed him to do. He was glad he hadn't backed out of the event after leaving the Academy. Kearney was footing the bill this time around.

The sun set behind Nick as he drove on the eastbound road just outside Palmdale, California. The only thing he had with him besides an overnight bag was his loaner gun from Michael. A .45 was in his glovebox, secured in a holster that was easy to access. It was already loaded, which was inadvisable under legal standards, but necessary in the new world Michael and Kearney had introduced him to. Plus, he always would remember Michael's edict, "I'd rather have a gun and not need it than need a gun and not have one."

The road was long and lonely. The sun vanished and the only lights he had were attached to his car. Even streetlights stopped after a certain point. So did the trees. The hard-planted greenery in and around LA made people forget just how far into the desert they really were. Palmdale would be the last patch of green land he'd see for a while. The next trees he'd see would be in Las Vegas outside of some big-time casino that could afford to water the desert.

He decided to enjoy his alternative car for a while. The Thunderbird, although much bigger, didn't come close to the horsepower and maneuverability he was accustomed to with his Jag. Nick passed the time with the radio. It was the one thing he had to split his attention on the long, hypnotic drive. As long as the road was straight and his hands were steady, he could think about anything he wanted on his way east. He wouldn't have to actively drive until he hit the city of Barstow.

Jazz helped him settle into a tranquil state. The more he listened to its rhythms, the more it made sense and he could appreciate the artistry of it. What made little sense on such an open, barren road was traffic. A sedan came up behind him and got close. Its lights shined in the rearview and blasted his eyes. He adjusted his mirror to lessen the glare and slowed down. It was obvious they had places to get to faster than he did.

"Okay, you can pass," he said, angling his head to the side. The sedan didn't make the attempt. There was nothing ahead, no cars in sight. His lights caught nothing and neither did theirs. Nick reversed his decision and sped up again. The sedan kept pace. "What the hell are you doing, guy?" Whomever that guy was, he was acting like he wanted to own the whole road, so Nick let him. No confrontation and no racing. He just wanted to get where he was going peaceably.

After a few minutes, Nick came upon a slow 18-wheeler and passed it. He thought the other car would be stuck behind it because of oncoming traffic. But to his surprise, the sedan did a speedy swerve around the truck to come up behind him again. Using Jeff Cooper's analogy, Nick's threat assessment went up from green to yellow — *caution*.

By now Nick was getting deep into the desert, so he had a decision to make regarding the car in the rearview mirror. The only people around were in the vehicles traversing the highway. There were no homes, gas stations or other businesses around where he could turn in for safety. Just sand and cacti. He realized that all the tactics and training Michael was teaching him were now in play. That gave him some confidence that he could deal with whatever was coming. He didn't want to take a chance of trying to outrun them or pull over and stop in the middle of nowhere.

Nick noticed an entrance to a frontage road up ahead that ran alongside the highway. Taking it could be the determining factor of whether or not he was in trouble. There was no more time to think; he had to act. He wrenched the steering wheel hard toward the frontage road and, to his dismay, so did the sedan.

Yellow quickly turned to red. *Alert!* The sedan kept on his bumper. Unlike most access roads, this was a short one. "Shit." Nick had to pull a quick U-turn or force the sedan to go around him. He chose the second option because if he pulled it off, the mystery car would be forced to react to him rather than the other way around. That just might give Nick a few extra life-saving seconds.

Nick hit the brakes, forcing the sedan to brake hard and swerve around him. Nick guessed right; they weren't about to risk disabling their car in a crash. The tires squealed against the cold asphalt for a few yards as the sedan came to a stop. Intuitively, Nick had angled his car in such a way that his headlights were pointed down the road and now spotlighted the sedan.

The car now sat ominously in front of Nick. It was a dark four-door, black or navy blue. While it was coming to a stop, Nick had thrown his transmission into park, grabbed his .45, threw open his door, and took a position behind it as he saw their doors opening. He was in position and they weren't. That was his few seconds' advantage.

He saw men scrambling inside the car to get out, then two exited the rear seat with guns of their own, held and at the ready. Nick had just one obvious target, the guy coming out of the rear passenger side. Nick's first two bullets struck his target in the chest and the man collapsed back onto the rear seat. His next shot was to the head of the man in the front passenger seat. The instant the shot went off, his head disappeared from view. The man either ducked or lost it. Nick couldn't tell which. The others were shocked by Nick's speedy response. He still had the advantage.

The driver and the remaining man from the backseat started firing back. At least one of them had an automatic. Nick stayed low and retreated to the back of his car while a hail of bullets peppered the front and side of his T-Bird. The two were easily hiding behind their sedan because the car went a little horizontal when it drifted to a stop. Nick cleared his mind of everything but his training. His targets were moving but they were just targets. All he had to do was wait for the right moment and shoot before he got shot.

Nick's bullets had a chance of tearing through the sedan while the large engine block of the T-Bird would stop theirs. Nick peered up and tried to assess his targets. One was hidden too much in the shadows that the Bird's headlights cast. The other one looked familiar. He had a large, dark mustache, but also a scar over his eye. The man from Morocco. It was now obvious that Nick was up against pros.

Panic set in. Nick was stuck between fight or flight. Even with just two men remaining, they would most likely have enough ammo between them to chew up the rest of the Bird's body until they finally got to him. Nick ducked on instinct and a bullet shattered the front windshield. He used his night course training next. He picked a direction to run towards that would keep the T-Bird between him and his attackers.

Nick jumped up a berm and fired two shots from the higher ground to pin them down then slid down to the other side and zig-zagged across the dark terrain. The men caught up a few seconds later and fired at him from above but their bullets didn't reach him. They got close but Nick was faster and the bit of moonlight was being obscured by clouds. He ran off into the sandy landscape and went over another ledge in and out of a ditch. Eventually, the sound of gunfire stopped. Nick kept going.

The desert at night had a silence to it that was different from any other kind of quiet. It wasn't the silence of a room or a car or a closed door. It was absolute — the kind that made a man aware of his own breathing, his own footsteps, the blood moving through his ears. Nick had read about it but never experienced it. No one was shooting at him. No one was following him. There was just the dark and the cold and the sand giving way under his feet with every step.

He didn't let himself think yet. Thinking was for later. Right now there was only movement and the distant smudge of light that was either a town or wishful thinking. He'd find out which one when he got there.

Wearing only dress shoes, shirt and slacks, Nick had been moving for about an hour, stopping only to listen for any sounds of his assailants. His body temperature was dropping fast as the cold air replaced the warmth from the adrenaline rush created during the shootout. So he used his mental process to increase his body temperature; the strategy was a favorite with many of his female clients who had cold hands and feet.

Once he knew he wasn't being followed, he figured the best approach was to head toward a little town he had passed through while driving. From the distance he was at and the speed he was going, all he could see was a light about as bright as a firefly perched inside the petals of a wilting flower. It was the town of Little Rock, aptly named, and that was his new intended target. He needed to keep off the road because they could be looking for him, thinking he might flag down a car to get help.

It was now around one a.m., three hours since the shootout. He made sure to rest every hour. At one location, he rested in a damp river bed, collapsing onto his back. It was colder but he was well concealed. Something moved in the darkness a few feet away — a dry, papery sound against the rocks, low to the ground and unhurried. Nick went still. Whatever it was, it knew he was there and didn't care. After a moment it was gone, swallowed back into the dark. He exhaled and kept his eyes open a little wider after that.

Somewhere in the distance, a coyote started up. Then another, further away, answering the first. The sound was mournful and wild and completely indifferent to the battered man picking his way across the landscape.

The temperature continued to drop and he was getting thirsty. He was bruised and cut; his groin stabbed at him. The thought caught up with him about what he'd done. His .45 took at least two lives that night. It felt heavier in his hands now and reminded him of the first time he ever held a gun. The weight of such a small thing impressed him, both physically and the weight of responsibility it represented.

He plodded on then saw the sun coming up over the horizon and soon could feel the warmth of the sun's rays. Of course, the problem of not having water increased as the day grew hotter. After a few more hours, Nick came upon a rock quarry. After some time trekking through it, his feet felt like someone had been beating the bottoms with a hammer. Once again, he relied on his process to ease the pain and cope with the tremendous thirst.

Nick caught his breath and forced himself to keep walking. Even pro-killers might want vengeance. They might have absolute orders to hunt him down no matter what. There could even be more coming.

He half-ran, half-hobbled his way through the landscape all the way until the sun was overhead. He hid out a few times to keep his tracks light and his body nursed.

The midnight lights over the minuscule town were long gone. The morning sun cast long, red shadows across the land from over the sharp tops of the distant mountains. Nick's hand was brushed red from scrapes and scrambles over sharp rocks. The only clean thing on him was his gun, which never left his grip.

A town, if you could call it that, since it only had a few buildings, finally came into view. Nick pushed with all his might to hurry there. He slipped his gun under his shirt, into his waistband. The closest building was a simple diner with two cars at the back and none at the front. He checked the road up and down before he entered. No one was coming. No black sedans with broken windows were in sight.

Nick entered and startled the veteran waitress at the counter. He staggered up to her. "Please," he said, his voice horribly hoarse, "a pitcher of water." The lady put a large pitcher under the tap and filled it up. "Phone?" he asked. She pointed across the floor to a pay phone on a wall in the back. Nick pulled out his wallet. "Change?" he whispered.

He made his call then sat in a booth, humped over and eyes closed, next to the front window. Flashes of the night's harrowing events flooded his brain. Car screeching, muzzle flashes, bullets whizzing by, pings against his car, a body falling, his heart pounding. Nick startled awake, wondering if it were all a dream. Seeing the sheriff's car arrive indicated it wasn't.

The deputy walked in and surmised that Nick was the one who called. "Are you the owner of a yellow Thunderbird?"

"Yeah, and you should know I have a gun on me. How do you want to handle it?"

"Just take it out slow with your finger away from the trigger and put it on the table."

Nick followed the instructions and added, "It's loaded." The deputy cleared the weapon then told Nick that a trucker had reported seeing his car off the road last night and then again this morning on his way back with the lights still on. After investigating the scene, they organized a posse search on horseback for the driver. That's all the deputy was willing to share at that point. He drove Nick to the Sheriff's station to document the full story.

CHAPTER ELEVEN

AFTERMATH

Out of all the people Nick could have called or wanted to call, his first instinct was to do the proper thing and establish a legal report with the police. After all, the rental car was semi-totaled and had to be accounted for; the crime scene needed to be investigated and any reports of gunshots had to be claimed. There was also the matter of the killings that he had to attest to clearly as self-defense.

None of that seemed as relevant to the Palmdale sheriff's department as his motor skills and level of communication. A man out of the desert with a gun - registered, but also recently discharged - with a story of a gun battle had all the same trim and detail as a 60s-era crime thriller. He could feel the entire office full of side-eyes at his back while he sat and allowed Detective Carson, now in charge of the case, to shed some light on it all. Carson was just as scrutinous and judgmental as the rest, but he had enough tenure to get away with being more honest about his suspicions.

Carson returned to his desk with a folder of preliminary evidence and, as he passed Nick, he noticed his back was covered with dry mud. "Looks like you laid down out there. You're lucky, this time of year with all those green snakes." He had with him a can of soda from the vending machine and handed it to Nick. It was warm from his grip. "One bite and you're dead." He punctuated his warning by slapping the folder onto his desk between them. He sat down and leafed through the pages. "So, you have no idea, whatsoever, who they were or why they came after you?" His rotten attitude reeked.

Nick was about to answer when Carson checked his watch. He was in the presence of a potential self-defense killer, with pictures of a crime scene, of an attempted killing or kidnapping, and he thought he had something better to do. Or, he didn't believe Nick at all.

"Correct," Nick said, speaking clearly and professionally. "But what I do know is that I hit at least two or three of them." Sounding overconfident didn't mean he would be wrong. He was sure about one, unclear about two, and didn't check to see if his retreating fire landed, though he secretly hoped that it had. A few of the officers who hovered nearby made whispers of conviction or disbelief.

"I'll tell ya what we know," Carson stated plainly. "A car with twenty-six bullet holes and no bodies. That's pretty much it." He closed the folder with that line of under-spoken finality.

"Pretty much it?" Nick repeated.

"Someone will call you about picking up your car." Carson leaned back in his seat, already retiring the case in his mind while Nick was still there and a bit shell-shocked over the whole handling of the situation. "And we'll be keeping your gun for a while."

"What about the shell casings?" Nick asked, sticking to the facts of the case. He had more interest in the potential oversight than the obnoxious police procedures.

Carson shrugged. "None," he said. "Not even yours." Nick looked distraught. That tidbit of info confirmed Nick's suspicions. Obviously cleaning up a crime scene, especially with at least one of their own dead or wounded, indicated that the guys were pros. Carson leaned forward to assuage Nick's rising irritation. "Listen, the only thing we got here is a car full of holes. Most likely from a bunch of kids using it for target practice."

That wasn't true, of course, but Nick recognized the stench of bullshit and gross negligence. He had anecdotes and a bleary-eyed recollection of a midnight roadside duel with a group of shooters, one of whom may have been from another country. It was a coordinated attack. He just couldn't prove it. "Kids would look for all the shell casings in the dark? Yeah, right." Nick glanced back and caught a few cops looking his way. They immediately turned around and pretended to be too busy to listen.

"Like I said," Carson repeated, "you'll get a call."

Nick stood to leave. He locked eyes with the paper stack on the desk. It was pitifully thin. It would be processed in a day and filed away forever as a strange, unprovoked misdemeanor made by some phantom teens for old folks to pin the blame on. He turned and left the office then waited outside the sheriff's station for his one phone call ride to show and pick him up — the only person he trusted to be with him that soon after a life-threatening episode.

Michael's mobile armory rolled in and picked Nick up out of the shade of a roadside tree. He had a can of soda at the ready to offer Nick before he even got in his seat. Nick put the can against his forehead and felt the icy cool touch calm his reddened skin. He no longer questioned the need for Michael to have a cooler in place of a center console. Michael bombarded him with questions. "How many were there? How many did you put down?"

"Jesus, Michael! Give me a minute." Michael kept driving while he leaned eagerly to hear the report. "About four or five of them. I think I got three. Two for sure."

Michael nodded and started talking, but Nick couldn't hear it. He fell fast asleep before Michael finished his first sentence and didn't wake until a little over an hour later when Michael shook him from outside the passenger's seat. They were in a Denny's restaurant parking lot.

"You're too dirty even for Denny's," Michael said. Nick got out while Michael opened the side of the van where he had, among other things, extra clothes for his travels. He threw Nick a shirt who set it down next to him and used both hands to peel his sweat and dirt-caked shirt off. It pulled hard against the middle of his back. His groin injury was also acting up again. Michael walked around back when he saw Nick twist around awkwardly and inspected him.

"Jesus, Nick! You've been shot!"

"Michael, I'm too tired," Nick slurred. Michael grabbed Nick by the arm and turned him around so he could see in the side-view mirror for himself. He had a bright red welt that was surrounded by dry, brown blood close to his spine. Because of Nick tugging on his shirt, it had bled a little. "I thought I felt something," Nick admitted. "But just blocked it out."

Michael grabbed his first-aid kit, squirted some saline over the wound until it ran clear, then slapped a large bandage over it. "I'll make a call," he said, then hurried into the restaurant. Nick, meanwhile, closed his eyes and prepared his mind to focus on controlling the bleeding.

They drove a few minutes to Northridge, which was right down the road from their current location. Nick relaxed and kept his eyes closed, trusting Michael was headed toward someone other than a veterinarian.

Once there, Nick got out and tried not to use his arms too much. Any movement would flex his back and work the wound open again. What was most worrying was that there was no visible exit wound. Whatever hit him was still in there.

Michael and Nick walked up to the side door of a humble-looking private practice. "This is one of our guys," Michael explained. That meant he was part of the fraternity that Kearney led. One of *their* guys. Nick looked forward to meeting another character that the agency surely recruited to keep their matters secret.

A man answered the door just a few seconds after Michael knocked. He was a grim and imposing figure. He had no name tag; no one inside did. The doc had one of those awkward names that was deliberately shortened to just one letter so people could easily remember it — Dr. T. He led them into a small examination room where he asked Nick to sit on a stool. Dr. T then cleaned the wound as Nick prepared himself to feel nothing, not the icy cold of the antiseptic or the rough squeezing of the doctor's fingers.

"I'm told you can deal with pain," Dr. T droned. He plunged ahead with his instrument. Nick winced as he felt his body contort. He felt no pain, but he felt something happening. In his mind's eye, his whole back was being twisted open, numb and baggy, like a Christmas turkey being pried open and dressed. With the aid of forceps, Dr. T pulled out a flattened slug and held it up while Nick controlled his breathing.

"From its shape," Dr. T said, "a ricochet."

Nick tried to explain. "The car had a lot of—"

"Don't need to know the details," Dr. T insisted. He dropped the slug into a metal bowl, then applied a basic suture to the wound then closed it out with a metallic strip of cloth.

"What's that?" Michael asked.

"Silver particle cloth," Dr. T explained. He applied it with a gentle touch over the wound. "Helps prevent infection." He then explained how the country's first settlers tossed silver coins into their water barrels to keep the water fresh from bacterial growth. The adhesive clung fast to Nick's back. Dr. T gave him a reassuring, or a condolent, pat on the back and left the room. Michael followed up with a congratulatory pat of his own. Now that Nick had taken a bullet, it was like he was finally a real part of the team.

Michael drove Nick home, back to Kate. The ride there was a bit stiff. Nick was already exhausted, forced to control his emotions as best he could, and he didn't even know the whole time he had a slug embedded in his back that helped sap his strength away. The added frustration over the sheriff's attitude worked itself under his skin like a second wound.

Once they got to Nick's house, Nick slumped out of the van. He tried to hurry to the door but his legs wobbled. Nick tried to get his key in the lock but the door opened before he could get to the handle. Kate had seen Michael's van pull up and just caught it as it left.

"Oh my God," she gasped, "what happened?" Nick moved past her and she shut the door behind him. It felt good to be home, but at the moment, nothing in Nick's life felt good at all. "Where have you been?" she asked. "You didn't call. I was worried sick."

Nick looked at her with careful concern. He wanted to keep her out of things as much as possible. "The car broke down in the middle of the desert," he said. He shifted himself so his injured side was far away from her. He rolled his shoulders back and tried to stand with mock confidence like he'd overcome the hurdle after seeing her relieved face.

"Oh baby," she said, "I'm so sorry." She reached in to hug him. Nick almost stepped out of it but braced himself and stood firm. Her hands went up, away from the patched wound. "I would have picked you up."

"I thought you said you'd be out with your mother," Nick said, excusing his lack of connection.

"Is there anything I can get you?"

Nick sighed. "I could really use a shower." He rubbed his hand through his hair and could feel the dust that stuck to the grease of his panic-sweat-soaked head. He moved past her, as naturally as he could, which meant leading his body by twisting his back, which summoned up a twinge of pain. Kate saw the stutter in his movements. She always noticed when his old wound acted up and it was the same then but from a different place.

Nick went to the bathroom and ran the water. He leaned over the sink and stared at the mirror for a bit until it fogged up. He didn't want a hot shower, although even hot water would have felt refreshing after a stint in the desert. Regardless, he turned down the heat and undressed.

"You must be starved," Kate called from the hallway. "Chicken or tuna?" She intruded just as Nick's shirt hit the floor and she saw the patched-up state of his back. "What the fuck happened to your back?"

All of Nick's initial brainpower went to thinking of how to wash around his bandages, so he wasn't ready to answer her. He raced to figure something out. "I got stuck," he claimed, "by a cactus. No big deal."

Kate's eyebrow arched considerably. He could tell that she was trying to picture how he went from waiting at the roadside for a passing car to rolling around in a cactus patch out in the California desert. Nick had no follow-up, so he ended her speculation by smiling at her as he closed the door.

"I'll have tuna," he said. "Thanks, honey." He kissed the air between them. Kate didn't move an inch, even as the door was gently shut in her face. For the first time in their relationship, Kate knew Nick wasn't being honest with her. She just didn't know why. She hoped he would come clean, not just in the shower, but with an alternative explanation.

The warm water was soothing, which helped Nick relax his body and mind for a few precious moments before it would force him to think about how he would justify himself to Kate. But the heavy thinking brought him to the brink of falling asleep under the water as it coursed down his torso. Nick shut off the faucet so he wouldn't end up in a heap on the floor. As he stepped out of the bathroom, he could smell the heavenly mix of olive oil, herbs and spices and the thick scent of fish fill the air as it wafted up from the kitchen. He filled himself on the smell alone and drifted into the bedroom wearing nothing but his robe. As if sensing his plight, Dancer surrounded Nick's legs and Yogi hopped up on the bed, mewling for attention.

"Honey, come and get it," Kate called. She waited by the table for a minute, assuming Nick would come running for the food once it was ready. Filthy or not, he had to be hungry after a long night like that. Even if he got something to eat in the interim, nothing beat her home cooking. She went back to check on him and see if he made it out of the bathroom. The small size of the patch over his wound looked odd, she thought, for his having backed up into a cactus. After all, the spiky plants would have caused multiple punctures over a larger surface. But that was just her investigative, legal mind kicking in.

She went into the bathroom and spotted that the door to the bedroom was ajar. She heard the jangle of a collar tag and saw what the fur babies were doing. There she found Nick curled up on the bed with Dancer laying at his feet and Yogi curled up near his stomach. He had one hand up that was stroking the cat before he passed out and let his hand lazily flop over for Yogi to rub against. A full night and day of activity left him completely drained and he collapsed before he could finish it right. Kate stood watching him, feeling left out, that Nick's life was developing out of sight. Tears welled in her eyes for him, for herself, and for their relationship. She shivered as a feeling of dread crept over her that somehow she wouldn't get as many opportunities to be with him for much longer. But she was still determined to fight for him.

Kate gathered Nick's dirty clothes and took them to the laundry room. She ran the water and checked the pockets before putting them in the machine. In one of the pockets was a metal object. She pulled it out, and in her palm was an empty gun magazine. Her mind raced.

The next day, Nick was still in his bathrobe when he walked out of the kitchen with a cup of coffee in one hand and Yogi in the other. He went into his den and put Yogi down on his desk near the box that Lynn had brought over from the Academy. Just as he set his coffee cup down, he saw a neat stack of his freshly washed clothes on his desk chair. He smiled then noticed the dark outline of something on top of them. It was the gun magazine.

He closed his eyes against the churning of his stomach then took the magazine and threw it into a desk drawer. As long as it was out of sight for now, he thought he could erase any thoughts about Kate and what she must have been thinking when she found it.

He now had a complete picture. The hard start in Germany was a signal of a greater danger than he knew. All his paranoia was justified, which was an awful feeling. One thing he always tried to teach his military veteran clients was that they were safe at home and no one was trying to harm them anymore. His "Charlie" really was in the bushes, though, out and about on the roads and in the desert, waiting for him to take one wrong step in their direction, where his handlers couldn't protect him.

By now, Yogi was nosing into the box and trying to pull out a small paperweight but it wasn't budging. Nick stared down into the box, at his carefully labeled binders and the letter from Costas front and center. Frustrated with his efforts,

Yogi sat back and looked up at him. Nick piled the binders on the desk in no particular order, without noticing that the Costas letter dropped to the floor. All he could think about was time. The time spent developing his process. The time spent at the Academy developing a curriculum and promoting the place. The time it would take to get his new practice operating. And how much time he had left to fix it with Kate now that she knew he'd been lying to her.

Before, his stomach was churning. Now it was bubbling up in angry turmoil. He slammed his hand on the desktop which caused Yogi to scatter and knock the now-empty box to the floor. Nick then spotted Costas' letter next to it. He picked up the letter, tossed it on the desk, then picked up the phone and dialed.

"This is Kearney," came the response.

"That government contract… it better be fucking real." Nick hung up.

He was still in the den when Kate returned home with a bottle of wine, then heard her opening and banging drawers closed. Nick entered the kitchen.

"Oh good, you're up," she said. "Where's the fucking corkscrew?"

Without a word, Nick opened a drawer and produced the corkscrew. He opened his hand, offering to take the bottle.

"I'll open it myself." She grabbed the corkscrew from him and proceeded to open the bottle.

"I'm sorry. I'm really sorry," Nick said.

"I'm just curious, when did it start?"

Nick looked confused.

"You know, when lying became part of our relationship." Nick watched as Kate grabbed a wineglass from the cupboard and fill it.

"I should have been honest with you."

"Then why weren't you?"

Nick couldn't get another word out before Kate jumped back in. "It's this new contact of yours and don't bullshit me."

"All I can say is that he's part of the government and there are people who need my help. And in return, I get a government contract. And you know what that's worth."

Kate laughed. "You're going to trust those fuckers who caused all that pain of yours…" She pointed to his crotch. "then tried to court-martial you to shut you up? Those are the people you're going to trust?"

"No. I grant you it's the same government but different people."

Kate took a gulp of her wine and thought about it. "So what actually happened in the desert?"

"Some guys attacked me on the road."

"What?!"

"I think it has something to do with my working with the King."

Kate was stunned, "Jesus, Nick… did they catch them? Are they still after you?"

"I've told you everything I know. I'm waiting to hear back. The last thing I want is for you to worry about anything. Trust me."

"Just don't keep me completely in the dark."

CHAPTER TWELVE

DARK WOLF RISING

It was a quiet day at the Kearney household, at least at the start of what seemed like a routine and pleasant Sunday. The only thing Kearney wanted to do was keep his brain calm and his hands occupied, so he went to the window in his den where an easel, a full set of paints and a half-finished landscape awaited him. Two grazing horses, the subjects of his painting, moseyed in the pasture just a short distance from the house. They were his and wife Emma's horses. Yes, the same elegantly dressed Emma from the CIA conference room.

Their house was a full but not too large ranch down San Diego way, complete with an ample backyard and barn. It was an old house, yet something prestigious and well furnished with collections of rarities gained through a diverse life few men could handle. The home certainly had space enough for a family but it was just occupied by the two of them.

Kearney's interest in art came in different forms: landscapes, portraits, some minor sculpturing, and something less ordinary, like forging documents. A work table in the back corner of the room was set for the latter. It held a Lightbox, magnifier, papers, a variety of colors and types of pens and a paper cutter, with organized stacks of passports, drivers' licenses, FBI and Secret Service I.D.s and badges. All in different stages of completion. All for different assignments, some of which had nothing to do with his immediate team.

Emma, now wearing jeans and a simple blue pullover, stood looking over the documents. She smiled and shook her head. "You just can't help yourself."

Kearney, his sleeves rolled to his elbows, was deep in painting mode. Fingers delicately held a brush in one hand while the other clutched a palette. "What?" he asked as he glanced over to the table where she was standing. He then admitted, "I know." His forgeries were so precise, Emma had to counsel him more than a few times to scale back the workmanship. The documents he was producing were better than the real thing. "There's something seriously wrong with the agency if they can't see true genius in my work," he said jokingly.

"They don't want genius. They want the same garbage they used to produce before you came along."

"Okay, I'll give them the same crooked lines and out-of-focus logos that were on the originals."

"I got a better idea. Just run them through a copy machine!"

That gave them both a good laugh until Emma's phone rang. She left to answer it and was gone for only a few moments before half-storming back in. Kearney didn't even have to turn around. From the sound of her footsteps, he could tell something was wrong. "Okay, what?"

"Michael…" she said with annoyance.

"Turned it down, didn't he?" Kearney kept painting. He heard it all before and wasn't concerned.

Emma was always on the lookout for freelance weapons training jobs Michael could grab between assignments because of his financial needs of keeping Mary's condition in check. Michael couldn't tolerate being away from Mary for too long, so he had to turn down some lucrative jobs. Emma always had to gauge which would fit the assignment schedule for Kearney's team. It was something that occasionally created unnecessary conflicts. But more important, Michael's excuses, no matter how valid, had now become a source of frustration and brewing anger in Emma who had used her contacts and their goodwill one time too many. "I keep getting him these sweet deals with good pay."

"Mary not doing so well again?" Kearney asked.

Emma grunted an acknowledgment then added, "Meds overdose," as she made her way over to the painting to check Kearney's progress.

"Well, I'm sure he really appreciates your efforts."

Emma recognized Kearney's glib tone. She imagined the wheels turning in his head, calculating that Michael's loss was to her husband's benefit. She had been fighting so hard for Michael because she genuinely cared for him and Mary. Now she felt her own husband was not only devaluing Michael but also devaluing her to an even greater extent. Her frustration with the situation tipped into genuine anger. "You really don't give a damn, do you? As long as he's on your team and your team makes you look good."

"I look good, you look good, honey."

Emma knew Kearney would never be totally trusted in the agency, because many believed he was connected to JFK's assassination. "Bullshit," she said. "They'll never see you as anything other than a mob guy."

Kearney repeated his well-practiced line. "They know I was there working for the agency."

"Yeah, sure you were there for the agency, but you rolled into Dallas just after doing work for Nicoletti." Emma glanced out at the horses then added, "It's a good thing you coughed up Nick Bryant or you and Michael would be back testing silencers in Goleta."

Kearney turned to her but his face was as placid as it was the moment before. Trying to live down his mob days was the story of his life and it's been rinse and repeat for decades. "See, that's another reason why I love you," he said.

That barely tamped down Emma's fuming or the nick to Kearney's ego. She pointed to the out-of-place glop of paint that had dropped onto the bottom of the canvas, then stepped away. She grabbed a bottle of whiskey before leaving the room, disgusted. "You feed the horses tonight!"

Kearney stabbed at the glop until his brush bristles splayed against the canvas.

The following day dawned gray and dreary over parts of Southern California, a rare curtain of rain sweeping across the landscape. Kearney and Michael had weathered far worse conditions and took to the road with unwavering confidence. Kearney gripped the steering wheel, his eyes focused on the slick asphalt ahead, while Michael sat restlessly in the passenger seat, his fingers tapping a nervous rhythm against his knee, clearly uncomfortable with not being the one to drive.

"That guy yesterday," Kearney said, "didn't work out?"

"Nah," said Michael. "I'll find somebody." He positioned his elbow on the paneling of the door and rested his face on his fist for about half a mile. The first bump they hit in the road made him nudge his knuckles against his cheek, so he stopped and crossed his arms. "Did Emma's contacts come up with anything about who was behind the attack on Nick?"

"Not yet," Kearney answered. "But something interesting happened in Morocco the very same day. A dignitary and his wife, who Nick previously worked with, disappeared." Michael took in the information, but before he could say anything, Kearney interrupted. "Where's Nick now?"

"Probably where he's been spending a lot of time lately, at the range."

Kearney nodded and waited for a clear road ahead. He made a sharp U-turn to head back to Canyon Country's back roads that led toward the shooting range. Michael got pushed around in his seat by the sudden whiplash.

When they got to Wes Thompson's, the rain picked up along with a light fog that provided an extra layer of difficulty to the obstacle course Nick had set up. The fog wasn't too thick or widespread, but it formed thin carpets of gray over the muddy grounds. Kearney pulled up to the range, cut the engine and let the sound of rain tapping against the window take over. They sat and watched Nick run the course in the rain, moving from target to target without missing a beat. He took each corner at sufficient speed and adjusted his movements to the slick surfaces as naturally as if he were skating on a frozen lake. "What do you see?" Kearney asked.

Michael looked out. The sound of rain was punctuated by occasional gunshots along with pings off steel targets. "A dedicated shooter," Michael answered. He was honest but short-sighted. To him, anyone who put time behind a gun was the same kind of soldier.

Kearney smirked. "I see a guy who'll do anything to get what he wants." He then lifted a steel thermos of black coffee, unscrewed the top and poured himself a cup then took a deep sip. He sighed once his mouth was free from the rim. "The desert shootout was the best thing that could have happened for us."

Michael examined Kearney's expression, now at a complete loss for words, something he was not accustomed to, because Michael was the kind of guy who, when asked what time it was, would tell you how to build a watch. He looked back at Nick. What he saw was a struggle of desperation to cut down every action to an instinctual reaction. He saw a man trying to become a machine. It was an old sight to his experienced eyes and not one he expected to see Nick undertake.

Once Nick reached the end of the course, he holstered his gun and ran to a bench under an awning to save himself from further saturation. His shoulders and hips were soaked but he kept moving so swiftly that parts of him were still dry. He shook his head to clear his hair and beard of water then looked up when he felt someone approaching. He should have been relieved to see it was Kearney and Michael but they just made him on guard in a different way.

Kearney came under the awning first and immediately lit up a cigarette while Nick grabbed some ammo and began loading his magazines. Kearney doffed his hat and tapped it against the side of his leg to flick off the rain. He stood in front of Nick, like a sergeant addressing his resting private. "They think you could be right. It could have been something to do with Morocco."

"Of course it did since I saw that guy there."

"Yes, but we need a lot more than someone you think you recognized. After all, you were in the middle of a fucking gunfight," said Kearney.

"Yeah, but I slowed it down."

Kearney and Michael had no idea what Nick meant and didn't know how to respond. They just looked at one another. Nick was referring to a neurological condition that he activated in clients called 'tachypsychia' that distorts the perception of time, appearing to make events slow down or speed up. This would help some clients disassociate the emotional pain from a traumatic event.

"We should know more by this weekend." Kearney then added, "The desert thing was quite a deal." He blew smoke out of the corner of a proud smile. "So, how are you doing? You okay?"

Nick was still affected by what had happened and what he did, justified or not. He took a moment before answering. "Yeah, I'm okay."

"Bit of an adrenaline rush, huh?" Michael asked as he swept back the hood of his jacket. Nick looked away evasively and seemed to shrug off his own response. He really didn't know what he felt but knew that kind of answer wouldn't fly. Nick was still between answers. He didn't feel good, but he had to try.

Kearney seemed to notice his indecision and decided for him. "You really held it together. Impressed some important people."

Nick grabbed another magazine to be loaded.

"People who give out assignments to the teams," Kearney said.

Nick stopped and looked up. "There are others out there?" he asked.

"A few," Kearney replied. "This will give you a chance to get some more work. If you want it."

Nick looked out into the rain and thought about it. It sounded like an offer but he wondered if it really was. Was it a test? He was working towards a therapy institute, and to do that, he had a loaded gun at his side and a sweaty back from shooting at fake targets in a mock urban environment. He thought back to the polygraph assignment and how simple that was supposed to have been. But then again, he had asked for this. "Sure," he found himself saying. "Any chance to demonstrate my process, let me know." The reality was that it was getting harder and harder for him to focus on finding clients on his own. A combination of his own psychological needs and the growing self-help landscape where more and more newbies were entering the field, no matter how ill-equipped they were. Nick now needed Kearney, more than ever, to come through with paid assignments and fulfilled promises.

Kearney flicked his cigarette into a puddle. "The wife and I are having a little get-together on the fifteenth," he announced. "Bring Kate."

That caught Nick a bit off guard. "All right," he replied. He said it pleasantly but he felt as if he were answering the call to an assignment. Kearney donned his hat and Michael his hood and they ran back to their car. The sparse conversation about business left Nick feeling like a distorted reflection of himself.

The day's relentless push had taken its toll, so he made a quick check of his body's aches and pains. Not too bad, he thought. He reloaded his gun and ventured back into the rain. He had to improve, he reasoned, for Kate's sake. Yet, doubt nagged at him — was he really on the right path? He had promised her a stable life, and his therapy institute was a crucial part of that promise — no matter the means he used to achieve it.

Across the county, Kate worked hard at her job for similar reasons. She worked, not knowing what kind of pain Nick was putting himself through but her suspicions were mounting. Fortunately, she had a break from her worries during the day when the pain of others took up all of her concentration. The new law firm she worked at dealt with more cases than the small staff could handle. Now all the paperwork passed through her and cluttered her office with stacks of folders and orphan documents.

Today, Kate received an unexpected visitor. An older woman with permed hair and a mid-western accent poked her head into Kate's office with a paper bag of Chinese takeout in one hand and shaking off her wet umbrella in the other. "Ding, dong," she announced.

"Mom!" Kate exclaimed. Sheila Watson, Kate's mother, walked in and started assessing the room as she looked around. "Well, at least you still recognize me. That's good," she said as she propped the umbrella against a chair.

"Oh stop," Kate replied. She sat up from her work and smiled.

Sheila stepped up to the desk. "Your other office was a lot nicer and much bigger. I still don't know why you had to downgrade to this."

She lifted her package up as Kate cleared some space for the white paper bag and took in the smell of fresh, hot lunch wafting her way.

"Chicken for you," Sheila said as she took out the containers. "Different chicken for me. Let's eat. Your new boss does let you eat lunch, doesn't he? If not, you're certainly in the right place to file a lawsuit." She handed Kate a pair of chopsticks as they both settled their meals on the clean corners of Kate's desk.

"I've been very patient with you two," Sheila said just before Kate opened her container of rice, "but weddings don't plan themselves. So what dates did Nick give you?"

Kate paused and pressed her lips together. "He's been very busy with things," she explained. She could tell her mother wasn't there for more excuses. Her eyes were all business. "I'll nail him down."

"Uh-huh. Is that like code for a month from now?" she pushed. "Because I'm sure I heard that same refrain last month and the month before that. Even kings and presidents have to stop what they're doing some time. Unless there's a bigger problem?"

Kate recalled Nick's back and his obvious excuse to distract away from it. It had healed since, but the image stuck in her mind, and every day he came home he smelled more like gun smoke than before. "No, Mom," she insisted. "No bigger problem. He's just juggling a lot of things."

"Then you make sure he doesn't drop the ball on this one thing," her mom insisted, as she dug into her food. Not hearing chopsticks clicking at the other end of the table, she then noticed that Kate was distant, staring off and focused on something that wasn't her work or her concerns over marriage. "How many red flags are you going to ignore before you finally wake up?"

"Mom!" Kate went over and closed the door to make sure their conversation stayed private.

"Kate, I like him, but I've never been convinced he's the type to settle down. And on top of it, he doesn't even have a job anymore."

"Now, that's not fair," Kate said, as she hovered over her desk. "You know what happened with that."

"See, that's the problem," Sheila said pointing with the greasy tips of her chopsticks. "We only know what he tells us."

Sheila continued to eat her lo mein while Kate stood and eyed her food thoughtfully. Her mother was right, more than she realized. There was clearly a growing disconnect between the man Kate loved and the man Nick was becoming.

CHAPTER THIRTEEN
PARTY FAVORS

It was a big occasion, the kind of get-together most would save for a holiday, though for the Kearneys it sort of was. Thirty years of marriage was a landmark achievement for them. When Nick and Kate arrived, the party was already in full swing. Most people there knew Kearney only as a friend, painter and accountant who did their taxes; Emma played the role of real estate agent. Yet here they were, brashly displaying their pride with a full celebration, friends and kids included, taking advantage of the wide open space. It was a side of Kearney that Nick had never expected, let alone seen.

Emma downplayed her utilitarian seriousness for the event and dressed in a lighter, summery outfit to enjoy the outdoors with friends and family.

A sheet cake sat in the center of an open banquet table with a sentiment in frosting that read *Congratulations Bill & Emma, 30 Years and Still Going Strong.*

Kearney stood near the house, overlooking the yard, with his arm around Emma, who seemed especially happy. "Another One Bites the Dust" by Queen blasted out at them, courtesy of the hired disc jockey. Everyone laughed, especially the happy couple. But in Nick's eyes, Kearney didn't seem like the type to wear an honest smile. He knew him only as a cut-out for some larger organization that he thought was unchecked in its power. Nick didn't exactly trust him when he grinned. He assumed Emma, never having seen her until now, had some connection as well. She certainly didn't seem like a wife who was out of the loop of her husband's work. A man like him could only hide so much — which gave Nick a twinge as he reflected upon his relationship with Kate.

Nick's suspicions aside, it was a perfectly friendly, ordinary get-together with a barbecue going and plenty of food to go around. Kate seemed to be enjoying herself as well, as she introduced herself, and complimented the other ladies' outfits. Flowery capris pants and in particular, culottes, were all the rage that year along with espadrilles, ribbon-laced or plain. Although, Kate's choice that day was a print sundress and sandals. For the men, it was mostly neat Bermuda shorts or simple khaki trousers and loafers. But Nick wore jeans while Kearney sported khakis.

The music switched from Queen to the Olivia Newton-John and Kenny Rogers variety, which was more to the crowd's liking. Most of the kids in attendance, though, were young enough not to care, one way or another.

Nick brought Kate over to meet Kearney and Michael. Dressing up in any manner wasn't Michael's strong suit — he didn't even own one — he just had on a neater shirt that a newly, clean-shaven Nick hadn't seen before. As Nick and Kate got closer, he realized Mary was there too; she was now using a cane and struggling a bit to stay in the moment. Nick looked quizzically at Michael, who simply shook his head to ward off any discussion then helped Mary to a nearby bench to sit.

Kate smiled and shook hands as she was introduced around, with the last one being Kearney. "It's so nice to meet you," she said, shaking Kearney's hand more strongly than the others. "I want to thank you for the heads-up you gave Nick about my ex-boss."

"Happy to help," Kearney said. He glanced at Nick, almost as if to say, *I told you so.*

"And a government contract for Nick would be absolutely amazing," she said, to Nick's surprise. "You'll never find a better process than Nick's!"

"It looks very promising," Kearney agreed. "But the wheels of government do tend to turn slowly."

"Just as long as they keep on turning," she said. They all laughed. Kate's laugh was innocent, a little wry and impersonal. Nick laughed for her sake, but couldn't help but judge the others on their reactions — Michael's cynical, dry chuckle and Kearney's even more restrained wry smile.

Just then, a friendly French Bulldog ran up to the four of them, wagging its tail for attention and barking. Emma bent to pick him up. "This is Hercule, as in Poirot. My daughter had a thing for Agatha Christie when we got him."

A daughter? Nick wasn't expecting that either. He glanced around, hoping to spot a child that matched the Kearneys' looks.

"Oh, is she here?" Kate asked hopefully.

"No," said Emma with no further explanation. A story for another time, Nick guessed. He made a mental note to ask Michael about it. Emma then said, "Be right back." She returned the dog to a little playpen area from which he had obviously escaped.

"So Nick," Kearney began his small talk routine for Kate's sake, "Michael's been telling me you're his prized student." Michael hoisted a glass toward Nick as in celebratory recognition and took a sip.

"Oh, so I've been replaced, have I, Michael?" Emma asked as she helped Mary rejoin the group. Michael smirked from behind his drink.

"Oh, Michael," Mary interrupted, "they have a dog. Did you know?" Michael nodded.

Emma turned to look Nick over but noticed Kate's surprise. Like it was the first time she'd heard of Nick being associated with the gun instructor before. "Well," Emma said as she turned to Kate, "it was the only chance to spend time with Bill between work, the animals and everything else. Besides, I'm a sucker for a good man with a big gun."

Whatever doubts Kate harbored were replaced immediately with a bit of surprised embarrassment. Michael nearly choked on his drink. The joke was completely lost on Mary. She thought Emma was strictly talking about guns as she nudged Michael's arm and smiled proudly, almost sickeningly so.

"Emma," Michael started once his throat was clear, "uh… never mind. I won't say a thing. Except, no one could replace you."

Kearney leaned over and kissed Emma on the cheek. "That's why 30 years and still going strong," he said.

The air evened out from the awkward moment before. Kate smiled sweetly at their commitment. "Congratulations," she said.

"Thank you, dear," Emma replied. "Now, all of you, shoo, go mingle. Bill, the barbecue needs tending and I've got lemonade to make." But before she left, Emma took Michael aside and asked, "How are you two coping?"

Michael replied, "It was worse than last time but she's doing much better."

"Obviously, if there's anything I can do, I will. Be strong." Emma squeezed Michael's arm then went off to attend to her party chores.

Kearney nodded to Kate and Nick. "We'll chat again a bit later." It sounded friendly, but Nick knew it was more of an order than a suggestion. They weren't there for business, but Nick knew that their business had no days off.

"Let's get something to eat," Nick said to Kate as the group began to disperse.

"Hold that thought," said Michael, whose eyes locked onto a guest across the way, an eccentric loner who stood out from the crowd. He was tall and sharp looking and his mouth was constantly moving in an audible mutter. He moved away from small groups and stayed on the fringes of the party like he was trying to look for a way out. "There's someone you have to meet." Michael called out, "Hey, Jim!"

Jim Bowen, a rough, bearded guy in his mid-forties, whose reputation definitely preceded him, wandered over like his body heard his name but his face still didn't acknowledge it. He kept talking, even as he walked up to the small group.

"Jim, this is Nick and his fiancée Kate. Nick just got into the sport."

Jim nodded and said simply, "Did good in Bakersfield. A hundred forty yards. Impressive. Just think what you could do with a real gun." Before anyone could comment, he spun on his heels and walked off, leaving everyone but Michael a bit surprised.

"That's why they call him the mad scientist. But he's the world's best gunsmith." Michael turned to Nick. "You'll be paying him a visit before too long." He then took Mary's arm and helped her toward the food table. "Okay, I got dibs on the ribs."

Nick and Kate stared after Jim a moment longer until he reached a unique steel garden sculpture and ran his fingers along the welded joints as he commented to himself about the skill of the welder. Kate turned slowly back to Nick. "Interesting friends you've been making lately." Her tone iced into him. She then walked off to help a woman who was struggling to free her shawl from being stuck on a rose bush.

After having met Jim, Nick was now wondering how many of the other guests might be part of the intrigue surrounding the Kearneys. They seemed like everyday folks — most were chatting about sports, politics, family, mundane jobs, and food — but if they weren't, they were doing a helluva job pretending. At least sixty people filled the backyard space. Nick listened and watched for any break in routine to glean the answer. He then collected Kate and headed to the food table.

Kearney worked the barbecue until there was a sizable amount of food to offer, then he turned the rest over to an oversized friend, wearing a gaudy Hawaiian shirt with his Bermudas, who gladly handled the second portion of meat. Kearney then caught Nick's eye and nodded toward the house. Michael and Mary ate together, and then Mary kept eating after Michael excused himself. Emma talked with some mothers who came by while Kate hovered around, admiring the dedication toward family they all showed, her thoughts totally occupied with ideas of marriage and children and the house she wanted to raise them in. She then decided to spend time with those kids at the younger mothers' table, just to be included somewhere she wanted to be.

Nick wandered into the house and found his way into the den. The items on the forgery table had been replaced by a pleasant flower arrangement. He looked at the photos that lined a row of bookshelves where most of them were of Emma and her military accomplishments. She had both an Army and Navy background, as well as several awards in long-range shooting competitions. Michael was featured in some of her pictures, younger and fresher from his training days, showing off his prize student. Her much younger pictures were of her on horses. The trophies and pictures occupied a wall of their own.

Michael entered and saw Nick perusing Emma's photo display. He chuckled. "She wanted me to train her to shoot from horseback."

"Did you?"

"Yeah, me on a horse... are you kidding?"

Kearney's pictures were far fewer like the first half of his life was just about missing from his own home. Except, for a few odd collectibles that sat apart from the rest on a side table: an old and well-used .45 semi-auto in a display case, framed photos of a young boy walking a high wire and wing-walking a bi-plane. There was also a photo of a young man piloting a plane and an old newspaper clipping of three shabby-looking men being escorted from a boxcar by the police. The date was November 22, 1963; the dateline was Dallas, Texas. Nick stood looking at the newspaper clipping, trying to read the fine print.

"So, where were *you* when Kennedy was shot?" Michael asked.

"March Air Force Base, Riverside doing hard labor after a shit court-martial." Nick peered more carefully at the third man in the newspaper photo. "Wait, is that Kearney?"

"Amazing resemblance, huh?" Michael said slyly. "Government secrets and all that."

Nick was in shock. He took a step back as if to capture the whole mini-museum in one short take.

"Hey, you two have something in common," said Michael. "Well, sort of. Kearney was in the Army Air Corps. Got sent to prison for assaulting a non-com. He did a two-year stint in Leavenworth Penitentiary."

"And I thought my court-martial was a big deal."

"Leavenworth was where he met some mob guys and got into bookkeeping. Sweet deal going from mob bookie to the dark side."

Prison and the legal system. That was about as close as Nick's and Kearney's lives intersected, until now. Michael then pointed to the wing-walking photo. "That's what he traded for flying lessons during his circus days." Nick was seriously impressed by how colorful and multi-faceted Kearney's life had been. All he could do was shake his head in amazement.

The room was of two different worlds, that of Emma and the mysterious Kearney whose life story was revealed to Nick in time but only in bits and pieces, just as in that old adage about "need to know."

Nick turned toward voices coming into the den. It was Kearney with Emma, to his surprise, joining them. Kearney locked the door. Despite whatever suspicions Nick had about Emma's general knowledge of Kearney's work, he hadn't realized that she was so intimately involved — until now. They all sat in a round of chairs and everyone's mood swung from pleasant and easy-going to a sort of pressure Nick could only internalize as Federal.

Emma took command of the room. "We don't have all day, so let me get right to it. There's a lot of shit going on behind closed doors over Nick's client…" All eyes swung to Nick, as Emma continued, "… the King now getting involved with what's going on in the Middle East between Iran and Iraq."

"Does that have anything to do with what happened in the desert?" Nick asked.

"Certain people don't want peace in the Middle East," she answered, "and your King can screw things up. Peace doesn't make money, conflict does."

Kearney saw Nick shift in his chair and, about to say something, so he put him on hold by raising a finger to stop him. "That's why," Kearney added, "the White House is going around Congress to sell weapons to Iran through Israel despite the embargo."

"The guys in the desert," Emma explained, "they couldn't care less about overthrowing him."

"They were just trying to throw him off kilter by taking me out," Nick figured.

"That's the consensus," Emma said.

Nick looked over at the window. They were having their discussion in broad daylight, with the curtains undone, visible to the outside world. He saw Kate playing tag with some kids, running gingerly at them and then full-speed away, smiling while the kids laughed behind her. She spotted Nick through the window and waved to him. He smiled and waved then turned back to the conversation.

"The money from the sales through Israel," Kearney explained, "will be backing rebels in Nicaragua. So sharpen up your Spanish."

Emma took out a photo that she and her husband were familiar with, the newsreel image of President Ortega and the mysterious goatee-wearing Espinoza, who was the subject of conversation in the conference room with the suits. Nick leaned in to check it out as Emma tapped her finger on Espinoza. "We now know because of Marie's intel…" Emma smiled at Nick. "…that this guy is using his German banking connections and drugs and arms network to help keep Ortega in power. The more we can disrupt his business, the more we cripple Ortega. We grabbed one of his guys, so Nick, if you're interested, you'll be interrogating him."

Nick looked up in surprise — not at the mission, but once again, at the choice on offer. It seemed like everything they went over led up to his agreement before he had a chance to think it over. There was really no choice because he definitely needed the money. But more importantly, he wanted to continue to prove the value of his process in order to secure the government contract. So he nodded.

Emma looked to Kearney who turned to Nick. "Thanks to you," he said, "our team got first pick of the assignment."

"What is it with these assignments?" Nick asked. "They're a competition?"

Michael waved his hand to hold Nick off. "Everyone's trying to protect this country, but—"

"Nah," Nick insisted, "government… business… they're one and the same. A few think they can do a better job, the majority just want to cash in." Nick looked back out the window and pushed himself up off the seat. "It's all bullshit."

"I thought you were Mr. Positive," Michael said.

Nick looked at him and stopped himself from speaking again. He checked Kearney and Emma's reactions as well, but they seemed unfazed by his cynical comment. "I'd better get back out there," he said. He straightened his shirt and passed by the happy couple in their lavish den. He felt their eyes on him as he left.

Once outside, Nick pasted on a smile, grabbed a drink and rejoined Kate. It was the best acting he'd done all day.

CHAPTER FOURTEEN

SPECIAL INTERROGATION

Kate spread herself longways on the dolphin loveseat and looked out at her barely there, fenced-in yard. She always felt the desire to fantasize about what she could do with her own backyard after having seen the lovely rural estate of the Kearneys. There wasn't space to run around or play with kids like there was at the party. That would come in time and with greater stability in both their careers, though Kate knew it was really Nick's career that was more in flux. So for now, this would have to do. Their place was enough for now, especially for its proximity to the main drag of Studio City, just two blocks away. Lots of show biz people in the area, which meant quaint places to eat, coffee shops galore and people-watching.

Nick came out to join her with a glass of wine in each hand. He could guess what she was thinking. He handed her the wine after she sat up to clear some space for him to sit.

Kate snuggled up close and he draped his arm around her shoulders as she stared out at her yellow roses and dreamed of what else could be there and how much more complete her yard could become with a family. Her yearning only deepened with Nick by her side. The anniversary party reminded her of just how long they'd been together and what celebrations they missed from not seriously settling down. Nick, on the other hand, thought inward, about darker things. All he saw in the evening were shadowy corners and places to hide. Places he could only reach with a gun. It was an interesting dance he was doing, advising clients to relax in order to cope with their daily lives, while Nick was almost doing the opposite.

"I keep thinking," Kate said, "how happy Emma and Bill are after thirty years. What do you think we'd be like after that much time?"

"Bored?" Nick responded with a hint of casual humor. Inside, he longed for the stability of a lasting marriage and a loving family. However, the specters of his tumultuous childhood lingered — his parents' fiery arguments and his siblings' frequent fights. Calling him conflicted would be an understatement; his heart was at times a war zone, torn between yearning and fear.

Kate had been in a dreamy, romantic state and Nick's flippant response pulled her right out of it. "Christ, there you go again," she said as she turned sideways to face him. "I'm being serious and all you do is make a joke."

"I was just—"

"I bet Emma wouldn't put up with that kind of dumbass answer. Guess nothing about their life even sunk in with you."

"That's not true. You'd be—"

"I want a life with you and I need to know that you want one with me."

"You know I do."

"Yeah? How long do you think I'm going to wait for that life to actually get started?"

"Kate, I've been having to deal with a lot of shit since leaving the Academy."

"Well, don't lump me in with your shit. Even my mother doesn't buy all your delays and excuses. They never end."

"What do you want—"

"A bona fide commitment. That's what I want. You didn't even want to spend time with me at their goddamned party. Who does that?"

"I had to talk to him about the contract."

"The contract, the contract. Well, it better be real." It still stung that she'd had to leave her old firm on Kearney's word alone, trading her salary for a smaller desk at a place that was still figuring out what to do with her. Kate got up and took a step to go back into the house but Nick grabbed her hand to stop her. He stood up and pulled her in close.

"There's no one else I want to be with and there's no one else I want to spend the rest of my life with. You're the best thing that ever happened to me. I don't want to fuck this up. I give you my word, we'll skate circles around the Kearneys' relationship."

"I want to trust you."

"You can." He said it straight, no performance in it. He pulled her close and kissed her, and she kissed him back like the argument was finally, actually over. He walked her inside, his hand at the small of her back, and she let him.

The days that followed settled into a grinding kind of routine. The few therapy clients Nick still had came and went. Training filled the gaps. The desert hadn't left him the way he'd expected it to — Michael had called that one right. The adrenaline was still there, quieter now, but present, like a low hum he'd stopped trying to tune out.

The next week, Nick made time to stop by Jim Bowen's Gun shop. It wasn't the first time, as right after the Kearney anniversary party, he did exactly as Michael suggested. He went to visit the mad scientist to get himself a 'better' gun. Nick wanted something he could bet his life on rather than the relics the government offered. He had seen and envied Michael's armory. Although for Michael, it was a lifetime's worth of collection. Nick knew he'd have to start out slow since money was a big issue. He wanted Kearney to come through with an assignment, but most of all, the promised contract. The assignment money was so-so, considering it wasn't steady work, but it helped keep the lights on, or as Michael would say, keep the wolves from the door.

Jim's business was in an old industrial unit in Panorama City, a rather uninspired town that could never rise to its goal of middle-class status.

Nick hit the buzzer and waited until he heard the door unlock. He entered with a six-pack of beer in one hand and his leather gun case in the other. The door slammed shut behind him. The shop was filled with the sound of a lathe spinning and occasionally a sheering away of a layer of metal. Housed at the front was a cabinet full of guns and ammo for sale covered with a metal-wire grate. He noticed a magazine hung on a wall, just the cover, with him on the front holding his custom .45. The headline: *Nick Bryant Wins Northwest Championship With a Jim Bowen .45*. That's how far Nick had come in his competitive shooting gigs since the Bakersfield match. Seeing himself and the way he held the gun while shooting gave him pause. He wondered, in that moment, if he looked that professional and efficient when he killed his pursuers on the side of the highway. He shook off the thought and continued into the back where the real guts of the shop were, Jim's workshop. There was so much scrap and metal for adjustments and customizations that it looked like an indoor junkyard. The smell of hot metal was second only to the smell of gunpowder and machine and gun oil.

Jim was hunched in front of a lathe wearing shades for safety glasses, a Los Angeles Raiders ball cap, shorts and an old Grateful Dead T-shirt. He looked like he was relaxing, not working with dangerous machinery but he did it so smoothly that he seemed calm. Nick set his goods down on a bench. "Hey, Jim," he called just over the sound of the lathe.

Jim rocked his foot off the pedal, and the lathe powered down slowly. He nodded and stood up, favoring his left leg. Once he turned, Nick saw why. There was a hole in the flesh of Jim's right shin the size of a nickel that went down to the bone. It was red but dry, and his bone was off-white.

"What the fuck?!" Nick exclaimed. He calmed himself and assessed the situation. Jim was walking like he barely noticed it. "Jim, what's with your leg?"

Jim walked past Nick and yanked a beer out of the six-pack. He droned out an answer like he was bored with explaining it. "Got messed up in a car accident and the doc put back a piece of bone upside down."

He calmly uncapped his beer, prompting Nick to insist, "I'm calling my doctor." He picked up the phone behind the counter. "Yours is obviously a moron." He got the first two numbers out before Jim clicked the receiver to stop the call in progress.

"It's my leg," Jim said. "I'll deal with it! Now, why the hell are you here?"

Nick shook his head and left his trusted gunsmith to reckon with his own injury. He opened his gun case and took out his familiar .45. It was unloaded but Nick treated it like it was and handed it off to Jim. "You said you had an idea to convert this so it can take large capacity mags."

Jim moved back to his workbench with the gun in hand. He sat on a stool and entered one of his famous spaced-out modes. When he snapped out of it, he set the gun on top of his scuffed workbench and sorted through a stack of boxes of different kinds. He had some larger parcel packages and a few shoe boxes mixed in, but all of them had a purpose and a proper placement. He went through them like he was working a Rubik's Cube and ended by picking one out from the back of the stack. Inside was a folder filled with drawings and blueprints. He held up a few and waited for Nick to inspect them. "How 'bout," Jim began, "instead of a .45, I build you a large capacity nine-millimeter with the knockdown power of a .45?"

Nick was immediately enthused. He looked over a few of the schematics with intrigue and a bit of confusion. He wasn't the gun expert Jim was, or Michael for that matter, but he learned as much as he could to know that a design like that was a higher concept than what he was used to. "What do you need," Nick asked, "and how soon can—"

Jim held up Nick's gun. "I'll use this. But it might take me a while." He looked down at his leg past his deeply bent knee. "I have to go see a moron." He set the gun back on the bench and went over to his lathe to continue his previous work. Nick returned the papers to the folder in the box and became distracted by a beeping sound that was just barely audible under the sound of the spinning lathe.

It was his beeper. He checked the message. "It's a Go." Kearney's call was perfectly timed for new needed funds especially since Kate's job had been recently downgraded.

As Nick headed for the door, he heard Jim buzz in a new customer. It was actually three of them — big guys standing in the front office. They looked military; from the tattoos, maybe ex-military. And from the equipment they were carrying, they were there for some serious business. Nick put two and two together and got mercenaries.

Nick left his home country once again on a mission that required the cover of dark and international secrecy. The difference this time was that he didn't go alone. He and Michael met at a military base and training grounds to hitch their first ride. They were working with the Army, at home and abroad.

They flew from a military airfield to a landing strip in Honduras in Central America. No papers to check, no passports to clean. They were both listed as cargo for the journey, while Michael served as the primary contact between them and the soldiers onboard the plane. They disembarked from one bright afternoon to a dark evening and were inside another militarized vehicle in no time. There were no formalities, just quick movement from point to point. It felt like another training exercise across an obstacle course, except all the walls and ramps were men with automatic rifles.

They made their way out of the major city's thoroughfare of controlled territory to an outskirt region surrounded by dense forests. Their destination was unlisted. Nick rode in the back with Michael beside him, and sat opposite Brent Johnson, a decorated officer who was strict and serious like he never took an at-ease order in his life. He was dressed in fatigues like the two soldiers beside him who knew they weren't on any official clock.

The ride was rough; the heavy-duty transport's suspension was made to overcome and surmount obstacles, not necessarily provide a smooth and comfy ride. Roads were underdeveloped as they got away from the city. Soon they were on freshly carved paths over forest growth.

While Nick was looking out the window, trying to gauge anything about their surroundings, one soldier leaned forward between rough bumps as if trying to get his attention. "We've

water-boarded him so many times, my fingers are wrinkled."
He snickered then sat back as Johnson looked him down with
disapproval. There was no admonishment though. The
statement was true enough that it didn't bear correcting.

"We have to confirm the intel," Johnson explained. "All
I needed was a little more time."

"If that were true," Nick said, "I wouldn't be here."

The other soldier fought back a smirk and hid his failure
away from Johnson, who remained in the same state of stoic
discipline for the rest of the trip. Nick again looked out the
window to see all the nothing they passed by. All the light was
up at the front of the vehicle. They were out in the woods, lost
except for the driver's sense of direction.

Then they stopped. Nick turned, peered out through the
windshield, and saw a massive solid gate with iron bars. It was
alarmingly out of place. Johnson took out a walkie-talkie and
muttered into it. The gate clacked audibly and rolled away.
The transport rumbled off onto a smooth stretch of a
compound and they entered the black site.

The driver brought them up a few more yards to a main
building that looked like an old concrete shell of a school.
Johnson got out after the soldiers and signaled for Nick and
Michael to follow close. They didn't speak while outside.
There were few sounds except for the idle of the vehicle's
engine and the chirping of various jungle critters. They were
in the dead of night, off the radar physically and audibly.

Johnson led the group through the building, past the ground floor hallways, into a recently reclaimed portion in the back. The real black site was past a layer of armed guards. Several soldiers stood out of cover and at attention as Johnson passed by. Their lines of sight were locked all the way down the hall and alternated from room to room where the soldiers laid in wait for a possible ambush or deployment. No one could sneak in or out.

The group arrived at a more technically driven area that was lit by portable floodlights and stocked with various pieces of equipment. Nick saw just how comprehensive the security was. Multiple small CRT monitors were stacked together to form a small wall of vision from unseen cameras that caught all angles of the facility, even outside the walls. A few cameras also showed the exterior of nearby sheet-metal-siding houses in the miserable town the troops were quartered in. Some even had headphones jacked into the monitors that were shared between three different soldiers on surveillance duty. In the far corner of the room, Teletype machines clacked with information from who knows where. They were covered over with heavy cardboard to keep the racket down.

Finally, the group came to their destination, an interrogation room viewing station. Michael and Nick followed Johnson in, where he introduced them to a younger-looking Hispanic fellow with smoothed-back hair and a thin frame. He was not a soldier or a captive.

"This is Ernesto," Johnson said.

"Nice to meet you," Nick said, while Michael gave him a quick nod.

Ernesto wasn't one to talk. Instead, he held out a tape recorder, which Nick took. It was bulkier than he expected, with multiple compartments for different cassettes to fit into and a swivel-arm microphone built into the bottom. The interrogation room itself clearly had been converted from what was once a latrine. Along the walls were outlines of missing urinals, toilets and a sink. It now consisted of one small metal table and chair both bolted down to the floor in front of a viewing window. Seated was a man in a jumpsuit handcuffed to the chair.

"That," Johnson said, pointing at the prisoner, "is Miguel Rojas, distributor for our man behind the man. He's our only living lead to the movements of the armed cartel."

Nick asked, "Anything else?"

Johnson thrust a folder at him that contained a few images of Ortega and Espinoza and a whole lot of paperwork that amounted to virtually nothing useful. Nick scanned the contents of the folder and thought back to what the soldier in the transport had said about his wrinkled fingers. Johnson waited but nothing further was forthcoming from Nick who turned his attention to Rojas.

"Can I get a coffee?" he asked. "And what do you guys do for breakfast out here? You got donuts?"

Johnson stared Nick down hard and tried to snuff out the request with nothing but a smoldering dismissal. Nick politely insisted with a lean-in look and a slight smile.

"Ernesto," Johnson said without breaking eye contact with Nick. "Get Mr. Bryant a coffee and a donut from the kitchen." Ernesto nodded and walked out. Nick switched his attention back to the prisoner. He started making mental notes while he waited for his requests to arrive. Rojas was static. He knew the situation he was in and still seemed strong. He wasn't glancing around either. The room couldn't have been perfectly soundproof; even closing a door would have made enough noise to indicate a change of guard outside. He seemed focused and grounded, a hard man to reach through and manipulate. The kind of man who could count his own breaths to pass the time.

Nick grinned. Johnson noticed, but before he could launch into a lecture, the smell of fresh, hot coffee filled the room. Nick lugged his folder and recorder under one arm and held the coffee and donut in his free hands. "Great," he said. "I'm ready."

"This man has resisted considerable amounts of forceful information extraction," Johnson warned. "He failed to respond to coercion or bribery. We've deprived him of food, sleep and exposed him to every other kind of stress. So what the fuck are—"

"Thank you, sir," Nick said. "I think I have a clear understanding of what didn't work. I'll be using my own method from here on out."

Johnson's jaw tightened as Nick headed to the interrogation room door. A soldier on guard opened it for him. Johnson turned to the window and ordered Ernesto to start the recording. Nick's new assignment began with a captive audience who had no more tolerance for failure.

The prisoner stared at the window as Nick entered and set up. Nick knew he was being ignored and worked at a modest pace. He positioned the recorder and the folder on the table, then put the coffee and donut down.

"Mr. Rojas," Nick spoke loudly, his voice filling the entire room with positive energy. "How are you?" The man glared at Nick in response. "They tell me you're a tough nut to crack." Rojas leaned back and put his chin up. It was scarred recently and left unstitched. It was like he was waiting for his introductory punch from yet another stiff-handed trooper. Nick noted his behavior and slid out a photo to put between them.

"I've never been much of a coffee drinker," Nick lied as he took in a deep breath, "but this stuff smells absolutely delicious." He moved the cup one inch closer to Rojas, then walked around and stood behind him. Nick put his hand on the man's shoulder and leaned in. "Between you and me, I don't believe in torture. My only purpose here is to help you."

He then moved to Rojas' side. "But I'd appreciate a little favor." Nick reached across Rojas, right through his personal bubble, and tapped on the photograph. "I'd like to meet this gentleman. Do you know how I can find him?"

Rojas looked blankly at the photo, then at Nick, who expected dejection, but was met with a demented, evil look before Rojas' face instantly morphed into something more human. He looked at Nick like it was insane to even suggest that a chained prisoner would have any interest in helping anyone associated with his abusers.

Nick took out his own personal tape recorder, lined it up with the military device, and switched them both on at once. "The date is July 19, 1982. My name is Nick Bryant and I can verify that all of Mr. Miguel Rojas' statements will be true and correct."

Nick looked over at the window. From their side, it was a mirrored slab on the wall. He also spotted the camera that was anchored high in the concrete above the window. Nick moved in front of Rojas. Both the window and the camera could only get a view of Nick's back and virtually nothing of Rojas.

Johnson and the observers in the viewing room were confused. "What the fuck is he doing?" Johnson said. The soldiers were ready to rush in and contain the situation when so ordered. Not being able to see was, to them, an early sign of a potential problem, but nothing to move on.

"Are you ready?" Nick asked.

"Fuck you, puto."

Nick quickly thrust his hand toward Rojas. All the viewers could see, through the camera or the window, was Rojas shaking while Nick stood still with his arm stretched toward him.

Johnson leaned forward to get a better angle. "Now what's he doing? I can't see a thing. Ernesto, is the camera showing anything?"

"No, sir. He's in the way." Ernesto tried to get a better view through the window. "Sir, I think he just hit him but I'm not sure."

Johnson grumbled and moved to the door. "I'm going in there."

Michael blocked him. "No, you're not." Johnson looked to his soldiers. Just for a moment, they didn't know whom to follow. "We didn't come all this way for you to… just give him a minute."

Johnson turned back just in time to see Nick's process come to a head. Nick stood off to Rojas' side as the captive was slumped over in his seat, completely lethargic, in a state the previous interrogators couldn't put him into unless he was fully unconscious.

"What's your true name?" said Nick.

"What the fuck just happened?" Johnson asked.

Michael stepped up closer to the window, also intrigued by what Nick had done. They all watched and listened.

"Francisco Perez," Rojas answered. The viewing room was in shock. Michael couldn't hide his grin while Johnson sat, elbows on the armrests and curled his fingers together under his nose.

"What do you do for Mr. Espinoza?" Nick asked. He waited. His fingers lightly touched Perez's neck, right over his carotid artery. He wasn't pressing them hard; he just took the pulse and measured it, then tapped his free finger against the table in the same rhythm as what he felt. Then he started slowing his tapping down and the pulse followed.

"I protect his distribution," Perez answered. Nick smiled. He used one finger to tap and pivoted his hand to leaf through the documents until they were spread out further across the table. Maps, road networks, boat paths along the Pacific, and lists of contraband with missing allotments were all arranged, all questions to be filled in.

"You like Mr. Espinoza?" Nick asked.

There was no answer. Nick could feel Rojas' pulse increasing.

"You don't have to be afraid. Everything's going to be fine." Nick focused back on the photo. "We're going to keep you safe but you need to tell us where we can find Mr. Espinoza."

It took another twenty minutes. Nick worked quietly and methodically, the same way he worked with any client — following the thread of what the man gave him, reading the pulse under his fingers, adjusting the tempo. The difference was that no client had ever sat across from him in handcuffs. No client had ever been kept in a converted latrine in a jungle. He didn't let himself think about that distinction for long. There was a man across from him who knew where Espinoza was.

When Nick got all he needed to get out of the man, he exited the interrogation room and Michael greeted him with an approving nod. Johnson, who had been working with his tech crew to verify each piece of information that was coming out of Perez, walked in at the same time Nick put Rojas' folder down on a nearby desk. Michael looked at Johnson expectantly.

"They just missed Espinoza," Johnson reported, "and his warehouse was empty. They must have moved their operation right after we grabbed Rojas or Perez, whatever the fuck his name is."

"Well, that's too bad," said Nick.

Michael said, "What, you're surprised?" He then turned to Johnson. "We're done here."

"Not quite," Johnson said. "What if we have more questions?"

"Well," Nick answered, "you could try waterboarding."

Michael chuckled, causing Johnson to scowl. He then shrugged and silenced himself with a smug grin. Fed up, Johnson sighed and turned back to Nick, who remained observant of his client through the window. "It must feel good to be so self-righteous," said Johnson.

"That's the problem with you guys," Nick said. "You can't see the forest for the trees."

Johnson didn't know what to make of the analogy but he knew he didn't like it. Nick saw he was treading the line too close and turned his attention back to the window. "You want more answers, just put a cup of coffee in front of him, put your hand on his shoulder, and tell him word for word — a donut is coming. He'll be happy to cooperate." Johnson peered past Nick to their captive. The man they took in as Rojas was drinking the coffee and eating the donut as if it were the first meal he'd had in weeks.

Nick walked out with Michael and left his handiwork in the hands of the soldiers. His job was done and cleanly at that. Moreover, his secretive process remained protected. What little was observed of his session didn't relay the true nature of his technique. A secret that could unlock other secrets, something that the government would be desperate to replicate, and their only sane way to do so would be through him.

As they were being escorted back through the secure hallways, Nick whispered to Michael, "Is it you can't see the forest *for* the trees or *through* the trees?"

"And you're the smart one?" Michael retorted.

The remark was good for a laugh between friends as neither wanted to speak the obvious — why the hell hadn't Johnson called for help sooner — before Espinoza could run? Why have a person like Nick if the decision-makers were going to waste time with old, unproven techniques? Perez hadn't spilled the beans despite multiple tortures and deprivations. While Michael and Nick each had widely different experiences in the military, they both couldn't hide the bad taste left in their mouths from not only Johnson's ineptness but from the stalling by the suits at their end. It was like swimming upstream.

When they got back to the military vehicle and the driver attempted to start the engine, it spun for a few cycles before crapping out entirely. Par for the course.

CHAPTER FIFTEEN
KATE'S SHOT

Nick got back home in the dim early morning hours. Kate was fast asleep because she knew he was due back late. He ate for the first time since taking off and went to sleep on the living room couch so he wouldn't wake her. Nick knew her job required as much focus as his. He got a few hours of rest in before Kate got up at her normal time and found him with a note he'd written for her on the coffee table — *Work went well. Love you, my honey!*

She woke him up with a steaming mug of coffee and helped him get ready for his day, whatever that was going to turn out to be. Kate never really knew, but everything was back to normal at least for the moment, relatively speaking. She served up a hearty breakfast and made small talk about the goings-on at her job and her mother's latest dating escapades. Kate wasn't expecting much back from Nick because talking about his clients was expressly forbidden. Right now, they had each other against the world and nothing seemed wrong.

Kate checked her briefcase, offered a peck on the cheek and rushed off to work, giving over the house to Nick and their pets. He felt like he could finally relax, like the weight he carried was no longer about to crush him. Nick left a conflict zone behind him in a literal sense. An unhidden war, where death happened every day in firefights across a wide landscape while a hidden war, with who knows how many deaths, was ongoing behind closed doors. Nick's part in the larger picture was so small that he failed to see how his efforts would affect the overall balance of powers, but that was what his services were ultimately meant to do. Bloodless, painless control over the uncontrollable.

He tried to call Jim to check on the status of his gun, but predictably, there was no answer. He'd keep trying.

In the meantime, he spent the next several hours on much-needed time organizing and developing his business plan and course structure for his new institute. He got to work on the thick binders of course materials he had developed at his former job. Nick knew he'd have to redo them to take out the junk science that Costas forced him to include. He wanted to get back to the pure essence of his process and the way he could use it in Honduras, albeit not in the extreme sense like with that Rojas-Perez character. He hadn't gotten the assignment out of his mind because it was, in its purest form, precisely what he wanted to accomplish in this world. Simple, effective, needed changes to behavior done proficiently and in a fraction of the time. He never took notes on any other assignment but this time he did. Not the kind of specifics that would get him into any trouble but just enough to guide him into a tweak of his process for the public. Change the environment. Change the tempo.

He was ready for a break. He noticed the time. Noon. The precise time the working folk longed for, aside from quitting time. Lunchtime. That's it! His face lit up. People could come into his new institute during their lunch break and spend twenty minutes going through his process to rid themselves of stress and reinforce their goals. The room would be full of recliners with attached headsets. Nick saw himself sitting at a control board in front of the room with a microphone and recorder that fed music and positive suggestions to the group. And the beauty of it was that he could flip a switch and give direct suggestions to any individual. Personalized and affordable and a lot more than what he could make in an hour therapy session with a single client. Everyone wins.

He went over to the open window. It was such a beautiful day. He took in a deep breath of fresh air, excited and eager to tell Kate about his idea. When she got home, they celebrated with a glass of wine on their new favorite sitting area, the loveseat.

"Nooners? Now that is so funny but I think it will work," she said. "The control board sounds tricky but I think my brother has an electrician friend who works at the studios."

"That'd be great. I'll sketch out a layout of the room."

Kate leaned back and looked at him. "You know what I love about this idea? It's pure you. No government. Just your process doing what it's supposed to do." She raised her glass. "To Nooners." Nick clinked his against hers. For a moment it felt like the life they'd always talked about was actually within reach.

They sat enjoying their wine and looked out at the yard. Kate then turned back to Nick. "Actually, I had been thinking about what Emma said at the party. With all these guns around, I should at least know how to use them. You know... just to be safe." From a practical standpoint, Nick thought it might be a good idea but knowing Kate, he also thought there was something else going on with her. "The family that shoots together stays together," she said. Nick was dubious and just smiled.

But the next morning, she brought it up again. She saw it as both practical and as a means to be close to her man, just like Emma said. So Nick gave in and said, "I'll ask Michael to fit you in on the weekend. How's that?" Kate beamed and then finished up her morning chores before heading off for work. Her job was less glitzy and profitable than her previous one, as even her mother had noted, but ultimately it was more satisfying because she got to work more on people problems rather than corporate ones. Plus, it allowed her to steer clear of any involvement with junk bond sellers and sketchy investment deals as was going on at Tucker Mnuchin's firm.

As she drove away from the house, she had a satisfied grin plastered on her face. She was now safe at her job and on her way to being safer at home, not just by being able to protect herself but being able to protect her relationship with Nick. She firmly believed that the deeper she fit into Nick's world, the more valuable she would be to him as a life partner. Just like Emma and Kearney.

The next day, Nick called Michael and asked if he'd take on Kate as a new student. Even Michael was more than a little surprised. It's not as if he had many female shooters under his wing. Emma was years ago and that was after her having an extensive military background. But, as a favor to Nick, he agreed to find a spot in his schedule. Even Michael was trying to make ends meet financially while awaiting Kearney's assignments to come through. As a waitress, Mary was bringing in the minimum plus tips which paid the utility bills. She also took care of the groceries and a few other household needs, unless she was too ill to work, but Michael was tasked with the bigger expenditures, like rent and insurance. He was always on the edge of having those wolves show up at his door to collect his debts.

It was a long holding pattern that Kearney's team was in as the leads to Espinoza had gone cold and the U. S. political scene was in disarray because of the Reagan administration being at loggerheads with Congress over funding certain foreign projects. Nick was still working with a few private clients and looking for more. Michael was working with his own set of clients, teaching at either Wes Thompson's or Desert Marksman. Kearney was doing accounting jobs as he could find them. The recession was causing everyone but Kate, who had a steady job, to take a hit to their usual sources of income.

Still, it did give Kate the opportunity to enjoy her new hobby. She took eagerly to her lessons with Michael and, just like Nick, got into the whole paraphernalia thing — shooting rig, ear protectors, shatterproof glasses.

One Saturday, as Nick was in the garage doing bench presses, Kate entered with her shooting bag. "How did it go?" he asked.

"This is so much fun and Michael's great." She put her bag on the workbench and removed her gear then placed her gun in the safe.

Nick caught sight of her holster, a plastic one that Michael had designed. He walked over and picked it up. "Michael wants you to use this?" he said, a bit surprised.

"Michael said it would give me a faster draw. Why?"

"Because normally it's for advanced shooters."

"Well, I guess I'm advanced then, and it only took me a few weeks," she said proudly. "Now, I've got to wash up while *you* start lunch." Kate sauntered toward the house, leaving Nick still a bit concerned about the holster.

Before too long, Nick got to witness for himself Kate's newfound skill. He and Michael watched Kate, who was wearing shorts and her shooting gear, stand in front of three targets. They were back at Wes Thompson's. Michael told her, "This time, two hits on each target. Load up."

Kate loaded her .45 and lined up her sights then waited for Michael's command to fire. She took two shots at each target. The hits were well-placed. Michael ordered her to re-holster. "This time," he said, "just do six slow shots on the center target. Fire when ready."

As Kate prepared, a shooter from one of the other ranges came by and watched. "Where'd she get that holster?" he said to Michael as Kate fired. "Looks pretty fast."

"Michael, I'm done," interjected Kate.

"Okay, re-holster." Michael turned back to the visiting shooter and explained, "I designed it for competition. Hey Nick, grab that Tec holster from—"

BANG! The men were surprised by a gunshot and a scream coming from Kate's direction. Nick swung around to see Kate sitting on the ground and the gun nearby. A bullet from her own gun had torn through her upper thigh and exited just above the knee. It had completed its trajectory by skidding along her calf before hitting the dirt. The wounds bled heavily. Kate looked up at Nick, then back down, and screamed again.

Nick ran to her while the other men gathered around. "You're going to be okay," he told her. But that wasn't good enough; Kate was panicking. "Stop!" Nick shouted. She looked up at him. "Use the process. Stop the pain and the bleeding. NOW!… You know what to do!" He then turned to Michael. "Grab the stuff."

"Now go through your keywords," Nick instructed Kate.

Kate shut her eyes and started the process. As she softly recited her verbal formula, she repeatedly touched her right thumb to her little finger. She entered what seemed like a trance and Nick knew she was indeed performing the ritual to control pain and bleeding.

Michael grabbed all the equipment and tossed it into his van while Kate worked on herself mentally. Once Nick saw that the pain and bleeding had subsided, he helped Kate to her feet and walked her to his car. Inside, Kate remained quiet with her head back and eyes shut as she maintained the process to stay the flow of blood completely.

What felt like minutes later, from speeding all the way with hazard lights flashing and weaving in and out of traffic, Nick arrived at the closest hospital in the town of Santa

Clarita, a neat little bedroom community in north Los Angeles. "Tell me when you're ready," he said. Kate was fully alert as Nick helped her out of the car. She took a couple of moments to check how much pressure her wounded leg could take then gave Nick a slight smile and nodded.

Then, with a slight limp, she hobbled her way with Nick into the hospital emergency room and straight up to the check-in desk. A nurse saw them coming in and helped get Kate processed and shown to a bed. Nick went through the myriad questions and insurance protocols on her behalf then, when finished, sat in a chair opposite Kate's bed waiting for the doctor. "I'm sure it got stuck on the holster," she said, "because I felt a pull." Nick thought back about the holster when he first saw that she was using it, then about Michael and the visiting shooter at the range. He seemed to get more antsy by the minute as he played the blame game. But he contained himself for Kate's sake. He wasn't pissed at her or himself at this point. Someone else was on his mind.

After a relatively short while, a male doctor, whose look and manner reeked of traditional old fart, entered the partitioned space. He saw Kate sitting up in bed, reading a magazine with her legs covered by a sheet. "Oh, sorry, wrong patient." The doctor turned to exit.

"Who are you looking for?" asked Nick.

"A gunshot patient."

"That's me," said Kate, pointing to her leg.

The doctor glanced at his clipboard. "It says here you shot yourself," he said as he looked sympathetically at Nick as if to suggest Kate was a dimwit, then added, "What'd you shoot yourself with… your little twenty-two?"

"No, my big forty-five," said Kate as she pulled back the sheet.

The doctor's smirk dissipated into shock when he saw the size of the entry and exit wounds and no bleeding. He rang for a nurse and ordered up what he needed to clean, irrigate and stitch the wound without any further misogynistic commentary.

As Kate was being attended to, Nick stepped outside. He spotted Michael standing next to his van in the parking lot and barreled toward him. "She said the gun got stuck on your holster. What the fuck's up with that?" Nick just about shouted at Michael.

"She was using it wrong."

"No, I don't think so. And what the fuck does it matter? You should've been watching her instead of selling your holster to some guy."

"Hey, hey, hey, no one else had a problem, including you."

"Don't give me that shit. She shouldn't have been using that holster in the first place. It was for advanced shooters, at least that's what you told me."

"Yeah, but—"

"What were you doing, using her as a marketing tool?"

The truth was all over Michael's face. He gulped.

"Jesus fucking Christ! I trusted you to keep her safe. Wake the fuck up. I am so done with all this shit and you." With that final blow, Nick stormed off, back towards the hospital. Michael started after him but stopped himself, realizing Nick had been on the verge of doing something they'd both regret.

At the hospital, the doctor had wrapped Kate's leg in sterile gauze surrounded by a heavy-duty elastic bandage to discourage any future contaminants. He gave her a clean bill of health, a full set of instructions for proper wound care and walking papers — provided that she not actually try to walk too much for the next few days.

By the next day, Kate's wound was healing at almost a miraculous rate, but there would be scarring on her thigh and calf.

Nick knew he was partially at fault for Kate's accident. He knew her behavior best and that she was prone to overconfidence. In any other endeavor that might be an asset, but when working around guns, a cautious and humble approach is mandatory. But there was still no way he could forgive Michael for treating Kate with such carelessness. It was the ultimate betrayal. Guilt, sorrow, anger were all in play.

In the ensuing days, Nick did everything he could to make her comfortable, including running out to bring back groceries, along with what he thought would be a slightly uplifting surprise.

One day, on his way back from the grocery store, he went through the backyard to cut a yellow rose and passed their adored dolphin loveseat. It was one of two objects that cemented their relationship. The other was the dolphin keychain from their time in Morocco. Nick entered with the rose and his arms full of snacks as well as the essentials. "I got your favorite," he called out. "Mint chocolate chip." He waited for a reply but heard nothing. "I'll fix you a bowl," he said, to the silence with as much positivity as he could summon.

"That won't be necessary," an older, harsher woman's voice insisted. Nick knew whom it belonged to, and could see her standing in the doorway with her arms crossed and face scowling in his mind before their eyes even met. It was Sheila, Kate's mother. What he didn't predict were the suitcases at her side, Kate standing behind her on her prescribed crutch, and Dancer leashed to one of the suitcases. Kate had always considered Yogi more Nick's pet so, just like in some divorces where the kids were split up, their pets would suffer the same fate.

"What's going on?" Nick's eyes darted between Kate and Dancer as his heart raced.

"We've decided," Sheila raised her voice, "that Kate would be safer with me."

Nick looked over at Kate, who tried to be understanding, but not apologetic. She'd made up her mind. "Nick, it's not just about my leg. You're all over the place. I can't keep up anymore. There are only two places I wanted you to be… with me and your career."

Nick was stunned. He didn't see this coming — a blind spot he hadn't anticipated.

"You know she's right," Sheila said. "Normal couples go to the movies, out to dinner, raise a family. They don't hang out around guns and make excuses about everything else."

Nick hung his arms at his sides. "You're right," he said. He saw no way to argue through it. Not when it was true and while his life was still in limbo, and yet — he turned to her with a regretful look, hoping she'd at least understand that he was trying his best to turn things around, something he knew her mother wouldn't believe. "I made you promises and I broke them. I'm sorry. I can do better."

"When?" she asked. "I'm still waiting on a wedding date. Government contract? I doubt that's coming. Will I ever have kids? Not with you apparently."

"Kate, please don't do this."

Kate's eyes welled with tears as she shook her head sadly. "This was never going to work. Even if things magically fell into place, you'd never have time for a family. You know why?" She tapped her heart area. "You don't have it in here... and you certainly don't have it up here," she said as she touched her temple. You're just not committed. And that's the sad, sad truth. Guess I never wanted to admit it." She turned away from him.

"I'll let you know," Sheila added, "when I'll be by to pick up the rest of her things."

"Kate…"

Dancer looked up at Nick as Kate and Sheila left while tugging the reluctant dog along. All of Nick's best hopes and thoughts seemed to fall away as Kate left. Yet he still clung to the thought that he would make things better. He held onto those hopes even as Kate entered the car and drove away. And again after her mother came to claim the rest of her things. He stayed hopeful for a few days. Then a week. Then two.

Nick could endure and push past all kinds of pains but the severe hurt he felt in his heart was something he couldn't adjust to. He neglected the things he knew were important. His life just stopped and fell apart. It wasn't one big thing; it was all the little things. The way Kate laughed at a joke before the punchline landed because she'd already figured it out. The sound of her keys in the door. The way she always checked on the pets before she took her coat off. The spatula she waved at him when she was making a point. Her not being around was the weight he couldn't carry anymore.

Weeks passed and there was no sign of things getting better. No signs of recovery. He stopped trying to call Kate when it was obvious she wasn't going to pick up or return his calls. He stopped listening to his own messages as well. They all came from the same group of people. A few about bills, about lectures, and some from Kearney and Michael. The source of all his troubles. The ones who made him lie to Kate about how deep he was getting into this cloak-and-dagger existence and who co-opted his life. Nick couldn't even stand to see that he had messages to listen to anymore. He had already turned over his clients to others, knowing that he was not in the right state of mind to help them.

Nick stumbled into his den and sifted through the clutter and disorganized mess that had only gotten worse with time. He pushed a stack of papers and folders away, uncovering the answering machine. 29 messages. He pushed down hard and long on the erase button and turned it back to zero. But the phone was still plugged in. A second later, almost in response to his machine clearing out, the phone rang. So he yanked the phone cord from the wall. No more disturbances.

During the day, Nick was like the lone scarecrow propped

in a dormant field. Purposeless. The only visitors were postal workers who left mail in his mailbox.

At night, Nick's shoulders would be hunched and his steps heavy and slow as he trudged down the street, like a man condemned. His face was gaunt and his skin pale as his eyes darted around anxiously before resting on the sidewalk in front of him. The sun had nearly set when he made it to the convenience store, where he quickly filled a basket with food for Yogi and closed his ears to the sound of chatter from nearby shoppers. Nick didn't want to hear the news of the day or cheerful talk from anyone. He walked home shrouded in shadow, safe from the piercing stares of his nosy neighbors who now whispered about the strange figure that kept to himself. There wasn't a day that went by that he didn't beat himself up over the abandonment of his relationship with Kate. He felt he deserved to be forgotten as well.

It was nearly a month on when Nick glanced out to the garden out back. Kate's beloved rose bushes were dead. At that moment, he couldn't stand the sight of death, so he dug up the large bushes and shoved them into trash bags. It cleared out a huge amount of space in the backyard. His hands stung from the pricks and lashes of the thorns and his tight grip on the roots when he forced them from the ground. Instead of numbing the pain with his process, he relished it. As far as the remaining sadness, he numbed that with alcohol, one beer at a time, until he could feel nothing.

Then one day, Nick heard a pitiful cry come from the bathroom and saw Yogi straining to defecate in the litter box. There was a glop of blood and then Yogi vomited. Panic set in. Nick rushed him to the vet and waited anxiously for the X-rays and other tests to determine what he was up against. He waited for hours, along with other pet parents, and watched while still others came in with their pets. Some animals were on leashes, some were wrapped in towels, others were in cages, all held by concerned and caring owners. Nick recognized he was one of them.

Yogi's diagnosis was an intestinal blockage and Nick had to leave him overnight. Surgery was scheduled for the next day because the doctor didn't think it would pass naturally.

The first thing Nick did when he got home was plug the phone line back in. He didn't want to miss a call from the doctor if one came. The idea that he could possibly lose Yogi was tearing him up. That night, he couldn't sleep so he drank one shot of tequila to every two cups of coffee until he finally fell into a fitful sleep filled with bad dreams and regret. For the next few days, he waited by the phone, like a soldier waiting for his marching orders. Finally, it rang and this time he answered it. The vet's office told him Yogi was ready to come home. It was 5 pm. He shot out the door to get his only friend.

❧

After a week's recovery, Yogi sat at the back door, staring out. Nick joined him and saw his yard was bare — the flowers gone, his fiancée gone. He couldn't leave it this way. Pushing through, he brought in some color — yellow roses. How could he not? He positioned the first bush at the garden's corner and ran the hose in a gentle pour. This time would be different. This time he'd follow through. The new plants would thrive, unlike the promises he had made before. New bush, new opportunity, and new life.

Except now his old life came calling. Kearney was at the front door ringing the bell, then peeking in through a window where all he saw was Yogi trying to sun himself in the smidgen that was left on the kitchen floor.

Nick turned as he heard someone opening the gate and entering his yard. His senses were numbed and slow from the beer he still relied on. Whomever it was could have killed him with ease, he thought. But seeing who it was, Nick felt more concerned about being left alive, because it meant he had to talk to him. "I was wondering when you'd show up," Nick said.

Kearney's earlier calls had gone unanswered, even at the front of the house, so he let himself in. He appeared just as improbably as when they first met. Kearney looked around the yard. "Michael really feels bad about Kate," he said.

Nick ignored him and went back to his garden chores. He turned off the hose, put down his beer and pushed a new rose bush into the hole he'd prepared. Kearney picked up the shovel and started filling in the dirt. Nick watched him blankly for a few scoopfuls then went to work adjusting the bush to make it straight.

Once the hole was filled, Nick took a trowel and pressed the dirt down hard while Kearney hammered it with the broadside of the shovel. He then stabbed the trowel down next to the shovel Kearney left against the fence. The bush was in place and looked good. He hoped it would survive. Nick retrieved his beer, still cool thanks to the early evening air, and joined Kearney who was making his way to the back porch.

Kearney sat on the loveseat, rocking back against the dolphin, and lit up a cigarette. It caused Nick to wince at the sight of him sitting in his and Kate's special place.

"Emma and I have been worried. How's Kate?"

Nick paused to take a slug then said, "She's gone."

"Sorry. I didn't know."

"Really? Thought that's why you're here." Nick could still detect pure bullshit when he heard it.

Kearney was unfazed. "Is there anything I can do? Why don't you come down and stay with us until you're doing better?"

"I just need to keep busy," Nick said.

Kearney twirled his lighter around in his fingers, a minor spectacle of surprising dexterity. Irked, Nick said, "Just spit it out."

"What?" Kearney said calmly, placing the cigarette to his lips.

"The lighter's your tell," Nick said, "when you have something problematic to say."

Kearney shot Nick a penetrating glance, his eyes narrowing with a mix of seriousness and even a bit of annoyance. "You keeping busy isn't a problem," he remarked, his tone carrying a hint of reassurance but also urgency. Eager to cut to the chase, Kearney leaned in slightly, his voice dropping to a more confidential tone as he continued, "We finally have a lead on Espinoza and where we can take him out." He paused for a moment, measuring Nick's reaction before asking, "Can you get over the Michael thing?" The question hung in the air, laden with the weight of past tensions and the pressing need to focus on the task at hand.

Nick paused for a moment before finally replying, "I'm learning to get over a lot of things." He hurled his beer into the nearby trash, the bottle clattering loudly as if to echo his determination.

Kearney locked eyes with Nick and could see a determination that wasn't in him the last time he took part in an assignment. This time it wasn't about making money or a government contract, it was more like a need to move into a different world away from the pain in his.

CHAPTER SIXTEEN

GAS CHAMBER CAR

Grief, Nick discovered, was surprisingly portable. It traveled well. It fit in the overhead compartment and asked for nothing. The job, on the other hand, asked for everything.

Nick arrived in Nicaragua unceremoniously, half asleep, and was out of the old, unmarked and unregistered cargo plane into the tropical sun in a dead sprint. The pilot took off instantly for safety's sake. Best not to show up on anyone's radar, even if his excuse was going to be that he was shuttling food and supplies to the locals.

Nick sat across from Michael, going over the assignment, though every word Michael spoke felt like salt on a wound. Clearly, Nick was still raw from the 'Michael thing,' which he couldn't shake off. Yet, he forced himself to keep a professional demeanor.

The assignment was the same pattern in a new territory, the same problem cropping up once more in foreign lands. The same thing that drove a wedge between him and Kate. He tried to distance the thoughts of home and focused on a different inevitable reality — that he might not get to go home at all if the assignment didn't go well.

That was made more than clear on the way over and on the way to the primary location. He was going up against a perpetrator of cartel activities potent enough to start a pan-American war. Nick knew he had to be on his best game. He tidied up in the freezing cold hotel shower, and waited for his opportunity. Michael guided him to the room where they met their local contact, a man named Oscar, who was to be part of the operation. He was in his forties, short and slender.

Oscar let them in and led Nick to his new "client", a man who was tied to the foot of a bed in an adjoining room. The curtains were drawn and only a dim light illuminated him. He would definitely be less willing than Nick's first overseas appointment but not impossible to break. It took some effort, but within a couple of hours Nick left the room with a tape recorder still running and stopped it as he set it on the table in front of Michael and Oscar, who first checked out Nick's handiwork. The subject was slumped over, not moving, with no evidence that he was still breathing.

"Is he dead?" Oscar asked with his slight stutter.

"Nah," Michael said passively, knowing Nick didn't leave his subjects dead, just out of sorts.

"He doesn't know anything else," Nick said.

"Back to square one," Michael added. They traded the tape recorder for a set of papers. Maps, photos, schematics, and notes were scattered across the simple little dining table. The sounds of old cars clattering and rumbling along outside provided the subtle backing for their planning session.

Oscar instructed Michael while Nick hovered around, sometimes at the window and sometimes back at the table. They started with the schematics for a car, not official factory guidelines but ones that noted several specific customizations.

Oscar said, "The car's shielded from remote detonation ... looks like the windows are bulletproof glass and the doors have steel reinforced panels."

"So," Michael said, "all we have from this guy is a way to by-pass the walls to get into the compound. Here, behind the garage," he pointed.

"Why don't we just storm the place?" Oscar asked.

Nick said, "Didn't Kearney want this to be subtle so there's no blowback?"

Michael nodded and returned to the schematics, this time to a layout of buildings that were interlaced with a topographical map. "It's a bit far from the garage to the main house." He then noticed and pointed to three red Xs on some of the areas that were outlined on the blueprints of the house and adjacent buildings. "I don't see any reference to these."

Oscar said, "They're safe rooms."

"That's why we don't storm the place," Michael said. "By the time we get past the guards and alarms, the bastard could be in one of the safe rooms."

Nick walked over and checked all the paperwork on the table. "The car's the key."

"Agreed," Michael said, "and I have something I've been wanting to try for a while." He sounded slyly excited.

"The guy said he has others start the car before he gets in," Nick mentioned.

"Won't matter," Michael said with a gruff demeanor. "Oscar, I'm going to need a few things."

"Okay, and I'll get some of my men to help."

"We only need one more," Michael said, his voice barely above a whisper as he scanned the room. "Too many will just get us found out." His eyes flicked over to Nick, a silent invitation hanging in the air. Nick shifted his weight, feeling the tension in the small space. He met Michael's gaze and gave a firm nod. There was that adrenaline pumping thrill tugging at him again.

"But I thought he's just a head guy," Oscar countered.

"He's up for this. Trust me," Michael assured him.

"Okay."

After that, things moved in a blur. Oscar collected what Michael needed and Nick tuned out the world around him and operated on his instincts to keep his senses on high alert. He followed Michael's lead and Oscar's words as they drove past various outposts along the way to their destination. The guerrilla fighter bases were all abandoned or ransacked, always being moved and renovated, never in one spot too long. It was hectic and stressful but it seemed to work. No military formality or red tape mazes. As for the team, they maintained an acute awareness to stay vigilant in the event government patrols took a look-see just in case.

Hours later, they parked in a concealed area. They double-checked their gear and waited for nightfall. Although the moonlight was bright, the passing clouds, at times, would obscure it. That would be an advantage or disadvantage for the team depending upon their need for concealment. But with everything taken into account, it was the perfect time to strike Espinoza's compound.

It was at the top of a steep hill surrounded by an uncut wilderness that led off into extremely rough terrain on one side and sheer cliffs on the other. The main road in was blocked by checkpoints and guarded by armed soldiers. That led to only one way for the team to get in, up the hill itself. Michael eyed it with grim regard. He rolled his shoulders and flexed his fingers and squatted slightly to prepare himself. Nick could tell his partner was nervous. Worse than that, he was doubtful.

He didn't have his usual cocksure all-weather smile. "This should be easy for a Marine," Nick said as a slight dig. At the same time, he was thankful that he had the forethought to take extra precaution to protect himself on this mission — a heavy-duty jockstrap and securely wrapped thigh.

Michael shored up his resolve with a "Let's do it!"

They met their bodies to the dirt and climbed for their lives. Oscar and Nick were up first and caught their breath. Michael lagged behind. He was halfway up when the other two reached the summit. Oscar kept a lookout while Nick waited for Michael and stood by to help him up. Once Michael was close enough, he reached up and Nick helped pull him the rest of the way. Michael struggled for breath and winced with pain.

"I'm okay," he said, deflecting Nick's suspicious glance. It was sad to admit, but they weren't on a job for less-than-fit men. He would hear no end of it if he offered even a passing sympathy to his trainer. Oscar then led the way, according to the blueprints, up to a high metal fence that was overgrown with foliage and ringed the perimeter around the buildings. It gave them some cover to work with as they approached. A few guards came walking down a path nearby so they all dropped into a sudden prone position and waited for the guards to pass. They were nearly invisible in their camouflage clothing.

After Michael had caught his breath, he took over the lead role as they wrapped around to the back where there was a gate that led to the deeply wooded section just outside the compound. It had been untended like most of the wall along the steep hill. There was no other way to access it so the guards and ground crew inside just ignored it. But the gate still worked. They just had to cut it free of the dense, twisting vines.

"Stop!" Michael exclaimed in an urgent whisper. The men held their positions as he pointed down to a concealed taut tripwire right in the path of their vine-cleaving knives. Michael was always prepared for any situation. He reached into his satchel and pulled out a spool of wire and cut a long section. He turned his attention to the tripwire and stripped just enough of the insulation away not to trip it and exposed the circuit beneath. He then connected each end of his wire to the tripwire. The new connection was slack enough that it sat on the ground but still carried a current. He then cut the tripwire. It curled upwards but no alarm sounded.

They cleared away the rest of the brush and accessed the gate, but as they slowly pulled it open, it began to squeak. They froze. Michael again dipped into his bag of tricks. He pulled out a zippered case, and from that, a small can of gun oil that he used to lube the gate hinges. All good. They proceeded to squeeze through. The men were soon inside the compound, close to the detached garage, and kept low and stuck to the shadows. Basic stealth tactics. The guards they could see were all standing around chatting, distracted. Nick thought it was almost too easy and hoped it to stay that way.

They got to the side door, which was locked. Nick noticed a window higher up that was cracked open. He pressed his back against the wall and cupped his hands to give Oscar a boost. Oscar went up and hinged the window open as much as possible and climbed in. A moment later, he noiselessly opened the door, allowing Michael to enter, followed by Nick. Michael and Oscar immediately turned on their miniature flashlights.

There was a choice of three identical black limos that took up the entire floor space. Michael picked one out immediately. "Only one with bulletproof glass."

"It also sits lower," Nick mentioned. He walked over to it and opened the door. "Unlocked."

Michael pocketed his flashlight and emptied the rest of his bag's contents under the illumination of Oscar's light. One pie tin, a shot glass, a jar of mysteriously reflective liquid and a small bag of crystals. He placed them separately on the floor and hovered over them with a deeply arched back. He filled the shot glass, put it dead center of the plate then winced and doubled back in pain. Michael huffed as he rolled onto his butt. Oscar quickly tended to him and helped him up.

"I'll finish it," Nick said.

"Sprinkle the crystals around the shot glass but don't get any in it," Michael warned. Nick opened the bag and cautiously sprinkled the crystals on the pie plate as his heart pounded. The sound of tiny crystals clinking on the pie tin was loud in the garage's silence. Compared to that, the sound of the front door unlatching was deafening. They held their breaths. Oscar doused his light leaving the team in darkness.

An older guard, bloated and boozy, sauntered in mumbling the words to a song. He turned on his flashlight and made his way to a workbench in the back while his shuffling feet served to mask any sound that the team might have made as they moved to better positions for concealment. With near zero visibility, Nick picked up the tin, knowing all of their lives depended on his steady hands and movement as he made it to the other side of the car and huddled up against it. Simultaneously, Oscar grabbed the bag and spare contents and helped Michael to hide behind a nearby cabinet.

The moon began to reveal itself from behind the clouds and its light streamed in through the window and filled the inside of the garage. The guard pulled open a drawer, rattled a few tools around, and took out a bottle of hidden alcohol. A few swigs later, he turned and surveyed the room which was more illuminated. He now saw that the door of the limo Nick was hiding behind was ajar and walked over. Nick stayed motionless; his hands were steady as he fixated on the shot glass. The guard checked the interior and slammed the door shut, startling Nick, as the shot glass vibrated on the plate. Nick braced but not a drop spilled. The guard then muttered incoherently and turned off his flashlight as the garage was now fully illuminated by moonlight. He walked back to the workbench where he quenched the last of his thirst, capped the bottle, and stowed it back. He took one last look around the garage, picked up his song where he left off and departed.

The trio waited for silence to return in order to complete their assignment. Oscar held the target car's passenger door open while Nick kneeled and slid the pie tin delicately underneath the seat. Oscar then carefully shut the door. The mission was over. All that was left was to exfiltrate and hope that Michael's ingenious design worked. Nick and Oscar helped Michael out of the garage and through the gate. They went back down the hill the precise way they came.

It didn't take long before Michael's experiment got tested when, later that night, the house's occupant decided to go for a drive. The chauffeur navigated the curved mountain road with his passenger in the back seat. The pie plate wobbled. Tires squealed as the car traveled around sharp curves. The shot glass tipped over, spilling the liquid onto the crystals and, instantly, a large cloud of toxic fumes overtook the limo's interior. The vehicle cascaded gloriously over a steep cliff.

By daybreak, Michael lay in bed with every movement causing more pain. Nick paced with a cup of coffee in his hand. "You should have told someone before we went mountain climbing," he said.

Michael winced in response, obviously upset at himself for not speaking up sooner. There was no position where he felt comfortable or unbroken. "I didn't think it'd get this bad."

Nick shifted in place, testing the pain level of his own chronic condition. He was satisfied that his process, along with his strapped body, had allowed him to complete the assignment in far better shape than how Michael fared. He was so used to living with whatever pain it caused him that there were times he couldn't even acknowledge it existed at all. Nick had perfected the concept of mind over matter with concentration, meditation, relaxation, and desensitization techniques gleaned from years of research and practice. But with Michael, right now, he felt nothing but irritation.

"You could have gone to the VA," he said.

"I hate hospitals," Michael said with extra emphasis on the word hate. He waved off Nick's idea.

"You could have asked me for help," Nick said.

"Wasn't an option."

Nick glared at him.

"I need to spell it out?" Michael winced again. Even raising his voice hurt. The door opened and Oscar entered without even a knock. Nick was ready to throw his coffee before he realized who it was. Oscar was in a mad rush and scrambled to find something near the TV across from Michael's bed. "I'm sorry about what happened," Michael finally said to Nick. "You trusted me and I let you down."

"That wasn't so hard," Nick said.

Oscar interrupted them both with the TV at nearly full volume. The news showed a picture of a man with a thin mustache and a wide forehead. The ticker at the bottom streamed with a few words Nick recognized as the whole broadcast rattled on in Spanish.

"A partner to Victor Espinoza, a business attorney and alleged financial advisor to the Frente Sandinista de Liberación Nacional or FSLN, was found dead in what appears to have been an accident."

The three exchanged dismayed looks. Their plan worked but on the wrong person.

Nick and Michael returned to the States later that day via the same incognito methods and were back in LA in time to get Michael admitted to the West LA Veterans Hospital. It was the better alternative to him going home to his wife and having her worry him into a different, arguably worse, hospital as an emergency. It was well-earned, too. He tore a ligament on the climb, which aggravated a hernia from the bend over. Michael's resistance to hospitalization and surgery was dissipated by Nick's helpful process.

While Michael was hospitalized, he got a group of visitors. Kearney came with Emma, who brought along Mary.

After some pleasantries, Emma and Mary stepped out. Kearney and Michael talked over a few things before Nick arrived. He hung out near the hallway, only partially paying attention to where their conversation went but his ears perked up when he heard the name Espinoza. Then Kearney spotted Nick and invited him to join them.

"What's going on with Espinoza? We have another chance?" asked Nick.

"I don't know yet," Kearney admitted.

Emma and Mary arrived with coffees for the room. Mary sat on the edge of Michael's bed and fawned over him, so much so that it actually made everybody uncomfortable.

"When Michael gets out of here," Emma said pleasantly, "you two will come straight to our place to rest up."

"Oh Michael," Mary said, "that sounds great. I'll pack tonight."

"Whoa, honey," he said with a wave of his hand, "remember, I don't get to go home for a few days."

Mary caught his hand as he lowered it and stroked it with her thumb. "I know," she said sadly. Emma stood by and smiled at them sympathetically.

Kearney turned. "Nick, a word."

They exited and walked out into the hospital's courtyard. A few veterans were outside, enjoying the air. Some had worse injuries than others. A few men hobbled on crutches and one in a wheelchair made jabs at one another as they joked. Other men sat in total silence, disconnected from their surroundings and their bodies. Nick and Kearney walked close together so their words wouldn't reach the wounded hearts that surrounded them.

"Emma told me you're no longer working with the King. We surmised the desert incident spooked him."

"All I got was a letter from the New York consulate saying my services were no longer needed." Nick tried not to sound too bitter about it.

They walked further along before Kearney said, "You know, in the desert before the shooting started, you could have run. Most men would have."

"Maybe most men are smarter."

Kearney stopped. Nick paced a few steps ahead while Kearney lit up a cigarette. He waited for the click of the lighter, then a second later, he turned to see if Kearney was playing with it. He caught Kearney mid-spin and smirked. Kearney put the lighter away.

"Espinoza's dropped off the map," Kearney reported. "We think we can get him to surface by doing what you guys did inadvertently, taking out one of his closest associates."

"Why would that make him surface?" Nick asked.

Kearney puffed some smoke straight up in the air. "We keep knocking off his associates, there won't be anyone left to help him run the organization that's been keeping Ortega in power." He reached into his jacket and pulled out a folded-up newspaper clipping with photos attached and handed it over. Nick took it and opened it carefully. The pictures were of an older, stern-looking man taken at various angles or from different sources. "This guy is the connection between the German bank and Espinoza's arms shipments to the Sandinistas. He's branched out by holding American diplomats and their families hostage for ransom." Kearney handed over a family picture of happy-looking folks. The youngest girl was wearing pigtails with little pink bows. She looked a little like a very young Kate. "His last victims." He pointed to the girl. "They found her remains scattered. Michael was going to handle it."

"So, what needs to be done?" Nick asked.

"He needs to be removed."

Nick just looked at him. "Permanently," Kearney added.

Nick's insides felt as if they were being chewed up. He could barely breathe. For the first time, he'd be on his own. Nick turned away from Kearney and took a few steps. He looked back down at the photo, scanning it for every detail as if searching for a way out. But the way out never came. Each detail of the image added impetus to the black deed he had to do. He turned back and said, "When do I leave?"

Kearney steeled his eyes against Nick's. "You start prepping tonight. I'll tell Emma I'll be late for dinner. She'll take care of your mortgage." He ashed his cigarette. The specks fell on the ground and blended in with the cobbled stone.

Nick was back in Nicaragua a few days later. Same setup, different hotel, but he was alone this time. He was using his process to bolster his mental skills in advance of performing something he had never imagined having to face. The phone rang. He picked it up. "Yes?"

A stranger's voice, filtered and slightly muffled. "Sorry, we could only arrange forty-five minutes." That was all Nick had to hear. He hung up and equipped himself. He strapped to his ankle a holstered chopped .45 and clipped a .44 revolver onto his belt in the small of his back, and covered it with his long shirt. The last piece, a small throwaway .22, was placed in his jacket pocket.

Nick left his room and went to the parking lot full of cracked asphalt and a variety of middle and working-class cars. He found the one that was described, reached under the fender and retrieved the key then drove into the night, traveling from the low-rent area to the ritzy hills. It was a long road of widely dispersed homes with enormous yards, some of which were repurposed with more tropical trees than were native to the region. A regular Beverly Hills south of the border.

Nick found his way to the home of Carlos Herrera and parked at the curb. He stepped out and took one look at the gold mosaic walkway bordered by two crouching lion statues. "You've got to be fucking kidding." Classical music grew louder as he neared the mansion as if he were walking into a busy orchestra hall. He threw his shoulders back, puffed out his chest, displaying all the confidence that his character — that of a successful investment broker and world traveler — required, then rang the doorbell.

His target answered, a man in his 60s obsessed with recapturing his suave youth. Albeit, he was a walking contradiction in that he wore a dopey red velvet smoking jacket and wielded a pipe that looked cold to the touch in his white-gloved hands.

"Hello," Nick greeted. "I'm—"

"Come in," Herrera said, stepping away to swing the door open wider. Nick accepted the invitation and was ushered into the living room. Multiple ceiling fans churned the stagnant air. The room looked like a Liberace fan tribute, all white trimmed and decorated with gold leaf. Nick waited for his host to sit before he chose the nearest seat across from him. He favored his right side and made sure his pants leg didn't ride up too far. They got right to discussing business — or at least as far as Herrera knew.

"The lessons would be for my daughter," Nick explained. "She's twelve."

Herrera laughed in a deep, throaty voice. "I love children," he said. It made Nick cringe just hearing those words. "That's why," Herrera continued, "I help them make beautiful music. I'm a humble man just trying to give back to the people."

Nick painted a smile on his face. "That's very generous of you, considering how busy you must be."

Herrera looked Nick over with a cocked eyebrow for a moment. "Busy… si. There's much to do to make things run like a well-oiled machine. Isn't that the expression?"

"Sometimes," Nick said. He looked around and tried his best to sound humble. "You have a beautiful home, Señor Herrera." Herrera smiled and leaned back with satisfaction. Nick looked over at the piano, the centerpiece of the room. "I wonder, would it be too much to ask for you to play something? Something spirited. That's the kind of music my daughter likes."

"Spirited?" Herrera repeated.

"Lively, you know, upbeat. I'd love to tell her how good you are."

Herrera, always loving an opportunity to show off, accepted the invite. He rose and strode over to the piano bench, where he adjusted his jacket with a well-practiced flourish and meticulously peeled off his white gloves, each finger unfurling a symphony of anticipation.

Nick, nonchalant, approached him from behind, giving him a wide berth as if he were just inspecting the ivory of the piano. A number of carefully arranged framed photos adorned it. Herrera struck up a lively tune, as per Nick's request, and was enthralled by his own playing. Nick closed in, as if he were observing the technique, and slowly pulled out his .22. He aimed it straight at Herrera's head, at lethal range.

Then he hesitated. His arm dropped to his side. The music kept going — bright, lively, exactly as requested — filling the room with something obscenely cheerful. Herrera's shoulders moved with the playing, self-satisfied, unhurried.

Nick's process kicked in unbidden, the way it always did under pressure, slowing everything down. He could hear his own pulse. He could feel the gun in his hand the way he hadn't since the very first time — conscious of every part of it, the grip, the trigger, the barrel aimed at the back of a man's head. A man who didn't know he was there.

Nick wasn't a hitman. He was a man who helped people, not killed them. Every instinct he'd spent a career building was telling him to put the gun away, to find another way, to talk the man into a corner. That's what he did. That's what he was. He was so close to pure evil but his brain was stalemated — caught between the therapist and the thing he'd been slowly becoming for the past two years.

Herrera reached a lull and looked up at his photos. He saw Nick in the glass' reflection, but not what he was holding.

"I have so many wonderful students," he said. Nick looked at the first picture where his and Herrera's eyes suddenly met, mirror to mirror, layered in front of a young girl's face. The same little girl with pigtails that Kearney showed him, and the reason he was there. He wasn't a hitman. But he was for this day.

He shot twice. The second one came out in a jitter. Herrera's skull was precisely pierced. His body slumped forward and slid down to the floor as blood dripped onto the sleek marble. His red velvet jacket soaked up the blood. Nick's breath stalled, eyes locked onto Herrera's lifeless form. A nauseating mix of horror and disbelief washed over him.

Then he took a stiff blow from behind. The force caused him to fall into the piano and then onto the floor. His gun flew out of his hand and he nearly lost consciousness as an enormous body of a man — Herrera's bodyguard — flipped him over like a rag doll and came down on top of him. Nick was being choked in the grip of someone far stronger than he was. The man pressed hard into him and Nick's back was severely gouged by the revolver he had stuck there. He certainly couldn't reach it and his ankle was too far away for that weapon to be of any use.

Nick resorted to desperation tactics. He reached up and stabbed at the guard's eyes with his fingers until he forced his assailant to lean back, just enough so that Nick could grab his belt buckle knife. It was small but sharp and the distance was close enough.

The bodyguard slammed Nick back down and intensified his grip. The whole time Nick fought, his air was dwindling. He felt himself start to fade but focused on staying alive and awake. Adrenaline pumped to keep him active. He stabbed rapidly into the guard's neck until fiery blood poured out across Nick's face. It flooded his eyes and ran into his mouth. The guard collapsed after a pained gasp, no longer choking Nick, but his weight rendered Nick unable to breathe or escape. Blood poured out, already a lethal amount after just the first few stabs. Nick's aim had been spot on; he cut the carotid artery. Once he and the floor were wet enough from the behemoth's blood, Nick slid out from under him.

He grabbed his .44 and waited to see who would come next. There was no one else, just Herrera and the one guard. He knew he had limited time even though the smaller gun wasn't that loud. It was barely louder than some of the piano notes and the closest house was a good distance away. He was in the clear at least for the moment.

He stood and accounted for all of his body parts. His throat and chest were sore. He spat out as much of the foreign blood as he could and staggered down the hallway with bleary eyes, looking for a bathroom. Once he found it, he cranked the shower to max and stepped inside, fully clothed. He stripped as the water soaked through and washed the blood away, then rinsed the metallic taste out of his mouth and spat down the drain. He waited to see if he would vomit too but the adrenaline kept his insides in check. When there was nothing left to scrub off, he intruded into Herrera's bedroom closet and stole whatever clothes might fit him. Herrera's shoes were too big for Nick's feet but had to do.

Nick threw his wet clothes in a small suitcase and cleaned up most of the water trail he left from the bath to the bedroom. The actual crime scene would take a professional crew to clean up. A solid puddle of blood was merged between the two bodies like two lakes meeting across a sunken land bridge. He made his way to the foyer when he spotted an open door, likely where the bodyguard came through. *Great fucking intel*, Nick thought. Herrera was supposed to have been alone. He peeked into the room, then threw the door open. It was an office full of files and folders. Nick, as a therapist, knew the importance of information, but in this line of work, information was something worth killing and dying for. He grabbed what he thought was important and slid the files into an extra compartment away from the wet clothes.

Nick diverted back to the living room to retrieve his .22. It was disposable but also evidence that didn't need to be left behind. He made sure to step into the pools of blood and made deliberate tracks right out the front door. He went to his car looking like a house guest run amok and ended his deception. Nick switched Herrera's big shoes with his own and left the tracks at the end of the walkway. His shoes squelched with moisture as he stepped into them. He threw everything into the trunk and loaded himself into the driver's seat. Then, finally, he breathed. It felt like the first breath he took in a while and it hurt. His neck was sore and bruised. He took a moment to relax before he turned on the ignition. Nick just needed a moment to put his mind in place and focus on something other than what had just happened.

CHAPTER SEVENTEEN

NICK GETS CAPTURED

Back home, Nick sat in his recliner with his eyes closed. He stayed steady and patient with Yogi on his lap, who was also in a relaxing mood and appreciative of Nick's return. Being boarded or having a neighbor feed him was never optimal but it was a necessity as Nick could no longer burden his elderly and ailing grandparents. He was grateful for the cat's presence but always wondered how Yogi internalized Dancer's absence.

Just when he decided that today was the day he'd start fixing his life anew, his pager beeped. It alerted Yogi who glared down at Nick's side. Nick checked the message. "3p Thursday skate". Then he closed his eyes again and returned to a simple, ordinary nap.

Come Thursday, Nick met with Kearney and Michael at an ice skating rink just north of San Diego, the designated lower office, that was usually used when Kearney had other business in his neck of the woods. Michael seemed in better spirits, fully recovered. He sat with a more naturally alert posture, no longer compensating for illness, while Kearney relaxed and looked out over the ice rink from their vantage point. Nick arrived to a drink already waiting for him. The first thing he noticed, other than his associates, was the empty chair with a woman's coat draped on it.

"I had to bring Mary," Michael said after he saw Nick looking. "I couldn't get anyone."

Nick nodded. There wasn't much to say to that.

Nick took in the sights and sounds of the arena, the frosty atmosphere, the clamoring kids and the patient parents. He remembered taking Kate skating once, and why it only happened once. She couldn't stand having her feet turned into blocks of ice from the cold. Two tables over, a group of teenage rowdies jeered and mocked the efforts of the skilled and unskilled alike.

Kearney leaned over to speak to Nick discreetly, using the teenage outcry as cover. "Because of what you brought back, we now know the location of Espinoza's new warehouse and that he has a second residence close by. Oscar and his associates have been surveilling both locations."

"We're going to split up…" Michael said, "… join the surveillance while setting up to move in." Kearney reached down to open his briefcase for a folder. "How's that new gun?"

Michael asked, aware that Nick had been in recent contact with gunsmith Jim Bowen.

"Jim finished it but we still have to see which loads will work best. I do some final testing tomorrow."

While Kearney assembled the information, the rowdy teens seemed to pick out a favorite among the skaters. One of them clucked like a chicken, another mimicked the skater's balancing posture, and a third jeered at her. "That one's a real loser. Ugly too." They all laughed derisively, reveling in their own disparaging comments. Michael shot to his feet when he realized their target was Mary, who was on the ice, smiling as she fumbled and bent forward to keep her balance. She was still wearing her regular shoes. He ran down to get her.

As the teens escalated their jeering, Kearney rose to confront them but Nick beat him to it. "I'll get it," he said.

It only took a few words Kearney couldn't hear over the radio blasting pop ballads into the rink, but the teens all crumpled from their energetic behavior into looks of shock and fear. Then they fled. Kearney couldn't help but chuckle to himself as Nick calmly made his way back to the table. Michael waved up to Kearney and Nick to signal that Mary was okay. Mary followed suit, waving cheerfully and obliviously, as her husband escorted her off the ice.

Kearney had details of the new assignment prepared in folders that he distributed to his associates. "We leave on Saturday." They all finished their drinks as they spitballed the assignment, apart from Mary, who was seated at the next table enjoying the twists and turns of the skaters below.

With the meet-up completed, Nick returned to his hermitage life and prepared himself for what would be his most important assignment yet based on what Kearney laid out. After critical surveillance of Espinoza's warehouse that their local liaison, Oscar, had already begun, they would go in and shut down the operation for good. A lot was riding on this because they were hoping to get Espinoza alive. A mean feat considering he'd most likely be surrounded by his private army. Nick reviewed each detail until it was burned into his memory. When it was time to leave, he left Yogi in the care of one of the associates at the vet who also ran a pet-sitting business.

This time, Kearney arranged for different transportation for them to get to their Nicaragua assignment. It was best to mix things up. He leased a small plane he would pilot himself, categorized and registered as a medical supply run funded by a Christian charity. It was fully loaded and properly documented by the time the team got to the small private runway about a half-hour's drive from San Diego.

They arrived in Nicaragua that Saturday and split off. Kearney and Michael rushed off with their contacts to complete plans for breaching Espinoza's warehouse based upon any new intel, while Nick's task was surveillance with Oscar. The plan was to all meet up at Oscar's after they completed their initial assessments.

At the airfield, Nick and Oscar offloaded the medical supplies to another vehicle with the help of two priests, at least they were dressed like priests. Nick didn't question the arrangement. After which, the priests took off in one direction while Oscar drove Nick in another. There were no hotels or in-betweens. Their base of operation was Oscar's farmhouse. They pulled up to a happy family greeting their father on his return from "work" with his new friend. Oscar's wife waved at him through the window, and his son and daughter, who were playing outside, stopped and ran to their father for a hug. They then smiled up at Nick, who smiled back at them.

"Do you have children?" Oscar asked. Nick shook his head. "Then you have less to worry about." As his kids giggled, Oscar laughed and said, "Oh, you two are such a worry." He laughed again as the kids ran back off to play. The joking exchange between an obviously loving father and his children made Nick smile. At the same time, he knew it wasn't something he'd ever experience for himself.

The men went into the barn where Oscar unveiled an old beater car from under a tarp. "Less conspicuous," he said. He got in and turned on the ignition before he invited Nick to join him. It stuttered to a start and sounded like it might not last the trip until he shifted gears once, then it purred steadily.

"Armando will be our relief," Oscar explained. "Always wears a blue bandana around his neck for some stupid reason. I haven't known him that long but he's been reliable." He backed out and shifted into second gear with a heinous metallic growl. The beater traveled down the road a long way from the homestead into the deep heart of the outer townships and villages far remote from the standard city. "Another casualty in our fight for freedom," Oscar said with a disappointed shake of his head. Nick followed his gaze and caught sight of a funeral procession being held in a small graveyard on the outskirts of town. "I know them."

They found their exit point and proceeded up a dirt road until they reached their hidden vantage. It offered a full view of the warehouse below. They parked and stayed put then watched a large truck roll into the docking area. Oscar jotted details of the truck and notes into a notepad then pulled out a thermos and a sack of food. Bread, cheese, meat slices, and homemade cookies that his wife had prepared. He divided up the contents with Nick and they engaged in banter while they sat, waited and kept a careful eye on the warehouse and their surroundings.

Hours went by. Nick checked the side mirror and saw a van approaching. "I think our relief's here."

The van pulled up right behind them. Oscar checked his mirror and saw the driver. "Blue bandana and all," he remarked.

Two men exited the van, the formerly described Armando and his partner, both around Oscar's age. Nick got out to greet them. Armando smiled and then pulled a gun on Nick before he could react. The partner did the same to Oscar and ordered him out of the car. Nick and Oscar were shoved up against the car and forced to put their hands on the roof then were patted down. There was a dent above the door with a jagged edge. Nick purposely dragged a finger across it, just enough to cause it to bleed. He smeared some of the blood on the roof above the door then covered it with his palm so the intruders wouldn't notice. But hoped that possible rescuers would.

Oscar was livid. He shot Nick a look.

"Hey, you guys are smart enough to get us, you should be smart enough to know that I'm the one you want. Not him," Nick covered.

"Open your mouth again," Armando said, "and I shoot him." All of their weapons were taken and held by the partner. Armando, or so he was called, tied Nick and Oscar's hands behind their backs and pushed them into the back of the van where they were forced onto their sides. His partner jumped in after them.

A short ride later, they stopped in front of the warehouse's side entrance. They pulled Oscar out first, then grabbed Nick by the feet and jerked him out, causing his head to slam to the ground when he cleared the door. Armando forced Nick to his feet then marched him and Oscar through the door of the warehouse. Nick quickly surveilled the place while nursing a pounding headache. The warehouse was buzzing with dozens of workers unloading shipping containers, loading trucks, crating armaments and other wartime supplies. Nick also saw 55-gallon drums, standard industrial materials, and some very expensive-looking cars that were half-hidden in the rows of metal crates. Armed guards, scattered throughout the complex, kept a keen eye on the workers. Anyone caught stealing would be immediately and permanently dispatched.

Armando pulled his hostages over to a door and unlocked it then called over four of his men who were in laborer attire. Two quickly took Oscar away.

"He doesn't know—" Nick attempted to explain, but Armando silenced him with a hit to the back of his head from the butt of his gun. Nick nearly passed out as the other men dragged him inside, but was harshly awakened by the sharp stench of chemicals. Cabinets lined the walls filled with bottles, syringes and implements more fit for an operating room. A couple of car batteries with attached cables were also in view. They passed by a metal platform, a slotted table with leather straps and stains across the surface. In the corner was a steel pole with a chain and shackle welded to it. That was Nick's destination. They latched his arm into the shackle.

One of the guards came by with a needle and shoved it into Nick's neck. He felt the sudden pain of the jab and the awful feeling of some foreign substance surging into his body. Just a moment after they retrieved the needle, Nick felt his body give out and fell to his knees. The men turned off the lights and exited, leaving him alone in the darkened room. Nick tried to touch his thumb to his little finger before he passed out. His breathing went from rapid to less than one breath a second, and then everything went dark.

CHAPTER EIGHTEEN

NICK GETS TORTURED

Nick awoke to an extremely bright light with his head pounding and a litany of new pain sources across his body. He was cold and exposed, strapped to a metal table. His ankles, waist, wrists and neck were all bound hard by leather straps, making it impossible to struggle. And when he did, the straps dug deeper into his skin. He hadn't been moved far, but his new situation was far more dire than what he last remembered. He saw three shadowy figures stand over him, one with a familiar face, and with a familiar goatee. Victor Espinoza himself, clad in a beige linen suit.

"Keep struggling," Espinoza said, "and you won't be wearing your ears or nose."

Nick took a few calming breaths and worked to un-tense his body. Espinoza disappeared into the shadows above Nick's head. He couldn't angle his head to see around him but heard the clatter of metal on metal. Espinoza reappeared with a mobile cart. On it were a scalpel, a glass straw, a rubber mallet, and large-sized pliers. They made Nick's heart race as Espinoza placed them one by one on the table. "You have caused me a considerable amount of trouble," Espinoza said, "money and valued associates."

"Hey, I don't know what's going on here. I just got paid to keep an eye on the place."

Espinoza picked up the scalpel. "You must have a special eye for them to bring you all this way." The men with Espinoza laughed.

"Come on, guys, I have no idea what you're talking about." Nick firmly denied.

Espinoza leaned down with a knowing glare. "Maybe after a nice cup of coffee."

"And a donut," another man spoke. Nick recognized the voice. It was Rojas from the black site. He stepped into the light and put his hand on Espinoza's shoulder.

Espinoza smirked. "How can you forget a face like this?" he said as he patted Rojas on the cheek, then immediately sliced his throat with the scalpel. Rojas was just as shocked as Nick was. He grabbed his throat as he slumped to the floor. Espinoza looked down at the body and said, "How could I ever trust you again, sapo?" He turned away from Rojas, who choked and gurgled his last breaths unseen, while Espinoza's men set up the next horror show.

They pulled back the curtain to a connected room and angled Nick's table up so he could see past his restraints. Nick's eyes adjusted to the lower light as he saw what Espinoza wanted him to see. Oscar, beaten and bloody, in a heavy wooden chair. His arms were shackled to the armrests and his ankles were shackled to the legs. Both looked broken. To his left was a small table with a large knife on it, and kneeling on the floor in the corner were his wife and his two kids. They were all in tears of fear and desperation. Armando and his partner from the van stood behind them with guns aimed at their heads.

Nick was forced to watch through the window as the unthinkable happened. He couldn't hear, only see the results of the actions unfolding. The men instructed Oscar and released one of his arms. His hand twitched toward the knife. His blood, sweat, and tears streaked down his face onto his chest. Oscar's wife pleaded with him as he tried not to meet her eyes and focused on the knife. He said something to her, sorrowful. An apology for what happened, for bringing them into the mess of his life.

The rest was impossible to watch but Nick had no choice. He was the sole outside witness to Espinoza's evil.

Oscar put the knife to his own throat and sliced. A deep wound, lethal, but not immediately. He missed the jugular and went across the throat instead. Instead of dying from blood loss, he guaranteed a slow choking death by drowning.

He turned to look at his family on their knees. He was in shock and panicking but hopeful they would be saved.

A muzzle flash filled the room. It came from behind Oscar's wife. Through her head and out the other side. A spray of brain matter flew out and hit Oscar in his face. His eyes went from sorrowful to maddened. Then two more shots, one for each of his children, aimed so the residue would hit him. Oscar couldn't breathe, let alone scream, but his eyes let out a painful wail no voice could match. Nick screamed on his behalf at the glass. Oscar's head dipped down, eyes wide and chest covered with his own blood.

The curtain between rooms closed and left Nick in the dark again. He wrenched his body against his restraints and masked the pain because none of what bound him hurt worse than the illness he felt in his soul.

"You motherfucker," Nick growled. Espinoza went to work despite Nick's protest and undid the last piece of his shame by taking the bloody scalpel to Nick's underwear to cut it off. "Wait," said Nick, "we—"

"No waiting," Espinoza interrupted. "No we. The damage has been done." He motioned toward the sealed window. "He has paid for his mistake, and now," he turned to Nick, "you must pay for yours." Espinoza replaced the scalpel with two other items from the tray. The mallet and the glass straw. He held the thin tube up to Nick's eyes, so close he could see the light coming through it. "When I am done inserting this and smashing it to pieces, you will remember me every time you piss."

This is surreal. This isn't happening. Nick's mind raced as he repeated the sentiment over and over in his head. He pushed his own head back against the slab and focused on his breath. Espinoza picked up the pliers and clamped them around Nick's penis to begin the grotesque procedure. Nick felt the pressure escalating and worked on focusing and redirecting his thoughts to anything else. But his mind was filled with the horror he had just witnessed and it all brought him back to his terrible reality. It felt as if a fiery ice pick was being shoved into him. Then —

Multiple gunshots and flash grenades echoed through the warehouse. Men screaming in Spanish, "¡Vamos!" Espinoza dropped what he was doing and ran out with his men as more gunshots rang out.

Some moments later, two armed rebels wearing camouflaged fatigues rushed into the area. They were the same two priests unloading medical supplies at the airstrip. As they passed the open door to where Nick was, they gasped when they saw him — once at the state he was in, and again when they realized he was still alive. They undid the straps and helped Nick sit up. All three men were unsure how to handle the rest of the situation. Nick grit his teeth and gently pulled the glass tube out. It came with a sudden sting of pain, and then a moment of burning soreness which followed a sudden flush of adrenaline-fueled relief. Like he'd just taken the worst piss of his life. Nick got up and looked around. He hobbled to the medicine cabinet and got a bottle of rubbing alcohol, the only thing that looked like it wouldn't make matters worse. More gunshots and explosions pounded the warehouse. Nick splashed his hand and spread the alcohol around his body like aftershave, wincing at the sharp, cold pains — but accepting them. They were far better than the alternative.

"What's happening?" Nick asked. The rescuers cringed as they watched Nick soldier through. Nick wrapped himself in gauze strips and paid careful attention to his penis, which he bound and taped up. Once he was properly mummified, he got his clothes from the heap nearby and threw them on.

"When you didn't come back, your friends—"

"Where are they?" Nick interrupted.

"They're coming in from the north side with some of our men."

Nick pointed in a direction he thought was north. They nodded and one of them handed Nick a gun.

Nick moved to the door to pursue Espinoza and the rebels followed. Before they could extricate themselves, gunshots came from above, on a catwalk that spanned the warehouse. Armando shot, just missing Nick but killing one of his rescuers outright while the second man was shot in the gut. Nick fired a couple of quick rounds and nailed his captor in the chest. Armando catapulted from the catwalk, some 15 feet, and splattered onto the warehouse floor. A satisfying end for him, although Nick would have preferred something slower and more wrenchingly painful.

Nick slammed the wall switch to douse the lights then dragged the injured guy back into the room. He retrieved the dead man's gun and extra ammo then went back to the injured man to see what he could do to help but the man appeared dead. Nick crouched to check for a pulse. There was none. The pain of Nick's own injury shot through him as he stood to leave. He wasn't sure if he could outlast it, but he couldn't take the time to suppress it.

Nick ran into the warehouse, keeping a low profile and using anything he could for cover. He was deep in the enemy's stronghold and it felt like every gun was shooting his way. The concrete floor got chewed up by scattered suppressing fire from above.

Nick glimpsed men up ahead; one of them was Espinoza. He tried to keep him in sight as he positioned himself behind a storage container. Espinoza was easy to track because of his suit. He was dodging his way behind and between containers as he tried to make his way to the exit, all the way across the warehouse floor. Nick fired back between the volleys, eliminating some of the threat.

He edged his way along a large container to follow Espinoza but lost sight of him when he was forced to dive between two crates to avoid getting hit by the continuing gunfire. Nick crawled past the crates and sidled up next to a custom Lamborghini. The window was tinted dark and offered a reflection instead of a clear view in. Nick saw the reflection of two figures moving above and behind him. He turned and aimed up at the catwalk just as the men spotted him and raised their rifles. Nick fired and hit them both. One of them, Armando's partner, fell and met the same fate as his wretched ally.

Nick busted out the car's window with his gun, opened the door from the inside, and used it more as concealment rather than a shield. It wasn't strong enough to protect him; he knew that. Even at long distance, rifle rounds would penetrate it.

He reached for the horn and hit it nine times, three short, three long, three short again. S-O-S. The sounds blared through the warehouse, somewhat stifled by the sound of gunfire. He waited and tried again as bullets slammed the hood. The sound of gunshots died down as Espinoza's forces were reassessing and scrambling to make up for their lost numbers.

The tentative silence was broken as a gillie-covered jeep rumbled in and screeched to a halt in front of the shot-up Lambo. Two men exited in Kevlar vests. Kearney tossed Nick a vest then immediately took a kneeling position with his M16 rifle and checked every sightline. The second was Michael with his M1 Garand. He positioned himself next to Nick.

The enemy forces were scattered and trying to regroup but without their boss, Espinoza, who had disappeared.

"You okay?" Kearney asked. He looked down and noticed the deep red stain that was growing at the crotch of Nick's pants.

"I'll live."

Michael asked, "Where's Oscar?"

Nick shook his head in response to Michael's question and then broke the sad news. "He didn't make it, or his family."

"Where's that motherfucker Espinoza," Kearney spewed.

Nick put his hand up — *wait a minute* — which caused Kearney to pause as Nick was forced to apply his process to numb the pain that now struck with a vengeance. Nick then wordlessly pointed to the direction Espinoza had taken.

"Espinoza?" asked Kearney. Nick nodded and they proceeded as a unit.

Michael and Kearney entered a large space simultaneously but split to the left and right with weapons at the ready. Nick followed in after them, taking more of a center approach, and spotted Espinoza huddled next to a large truck closer to the back. The dry storage space had different cargo than in the main warehouse. It was sealed off by multiple loading dock steel doors. The contents were all labeled explicitly. Weapons, ammo, and explosives in crates and barrels were piled up around the room, and some were still left in the truck. The big-ticket items.

Nick signaled Michael and Kearney to alert them to Espinoza's position and to flank him. Two fingers up — two targets. He waved his hand down to his chest and pointed his fingers out. He'd take point. They executed the maneuver quietly and stalked across the floor. Nick wound up behind Espinoza and his last remaining ally. He fired a headshot and caught Espinoza's comrade in the temple. It was a through-and-through so it struck the truck's metal bumper. Espinoza spun around to see the smoking barrel of Nick's gun and his bloody crotch. He quickly slid over his gun and threw his hands up from his position on his knees. "I want a deal," Espinoza said, almost choking on his words. He looked uncharacteristically terrified. It reminded Nick of the look on Oscar's face when he was forced to watch his family murdered. It was a face pleading for mercy that Espinoza didn't deserve to wear.

Just then, Kearney and Michael appeared behind Nick. Espinoza knew there was no dealing with Nick, not after what he had done to him, but he figured the other two might be easier to manage.

"Meet Dr. Mengele," Nick said to his associates.

"Victor Espinoza!" the man insisted with renewed fury.

Kearney looked at Nick, at the bloodied area of his pants. "He did that to you?" Kearney asked, catching Nick's reference to Hitler's infamous "Angel of Death."

Nick's silent, smoldering expression gave the answer.

"You can't kill me for following orders," Espinoza said. "I'm a patriot."

Kearney sniffed in disgust then went to the back of the truck and grabbed a few cargo straps that bound some gas canisters. He threw the straps over to Nick who began tying up Espinoza then Kearney and Michael inspected the rest of the contents. There was plenty to see, namely in the crate marked 'Explosives' — bricks of C-4, a type of malleable plastic explosive, a spool of detcord, and easy-rig timers with detonators.

Michael looked over at Nick and said, "Let's kill them all and let God sort it out." He turned to Kearney for approval and got it.

But Espinoza scrambled. "Wait," he said as Nick was finishing up with him. "I'm too valuable to your President Reagan. We can work this out."

Nick stared at Espinoza for a long moment as his mind drifted back to the metal table that imprisoned him. "No waiting. No we." He tightened the straps to the same level he had experienced which pulled at Espinoza's shoulders and chest. He screamed in pain and struggled. Nick wadded up Espinoza's tie and stuffed it into his mouth. The man was effectively immobilized, the same way Nick was, which made the fear in his eyes so much more profound. Michael and Kearney began assembling the explosives.

"What the fuck are you doing?" asked Nick. "The rebels could use all of it."

Kearney gave Michael a look and a nod that said — *you tell him.*

"We would do anything to bring back Oscar and his family but we can't and there will be thousands of more Oscars."

Nick was dumbstruck. Michael insisted, "You were right, what you said at the party… it's all bullshit!"

On one hand, it felt good to Nick to know that he was right about something in this insane business. But what a shitty thing to be right about.

Kearney stepped to the side and pulled out his walkie-talkie, his connection to the rebels, and in Spanish, told them. "Fall back. Immediately."

Michael pocketed a couple of grenades then picked up the pace of his work on the C-4 as the gunfire slowed to nearly a stop.

Nick turned his attention to Espinoza and wrapped some of the detcord around Espinoza's waist and attached a timer nearby, in sight, so he could watch the countdown to not just his doom but the obliteration of everything he worked for.

Michael looked over and noticed that Nick hadn't tied up Espinoza's legs. "I'll get his legs."

Nick said, "That won't be necessary." He turned back to Espinoza. "This one's for Oscar," and shot him in the left kneecap. He then blasted Espinoza's right kneecap. "And that one's for his wife and kids."

Nick's gunshots triggered a new scramble in the main warehouse and shouts. He realized that he just gave away their position and offered Kearney and Michael a look of apology. The men moved faster. Nick helped Michael spread and connect the rest of the C-4. "They'll hear this in California!" Michael cheered.

Once everything was completed, Kearney stepped away from his handiwork and motioned at the large steel roll-up door on the exterior wall. And further, to ready themselves. The whole compound was on alert. Rebel forces stationed outside would be ready to pick off Espinoza's men should they try to flee. They hopped into the cargo truck and got ready to drive it out.

Espinoza's remaining men streamed in. Kearney worked the gears and drove toward the roll-up door. Meanwhile, Nick fired from the cab and Michael held his ground behind a wooden crate in the back. A shot clipped the crate and ricocheted into Michael's shoulder. He braced through the pain, courtesy of what he remembered from Nick's mind-over-matter process. It gave him steady enough aim to spray suppressing fire while Nick's precision dropped the strafing Sandinistas as they entered and ran for cover.

Kearney shifted into first gear and pushed aside a huge wooden crate then slammed it into reverse to get some distance so he could build up speed. The tires squealed as he shifted from reverse back to first gear as the engine's RPM hit the roof. Once the tires found grip, the truck leaped forward and Kearney slammed it into second. The truck sped forward into the roll-up door. All three were thrown forward and back as the truck sprang off the solid warehouse door. Kearney's head hit the wheel and left him dazed. Michael jumped out and opened the driver's door and he and Nick helped Kearney out. They maneuvered to one side of the door that had been dislodged just enough for them to escape.

The trio stumbled out onto the loading docks, lit only by the amber of a harvest moon. Michael then rolled in the two grenades. BOOM! BOOM! The gunfire stopped as Espinoza's forces were held back. It gave Kearney's group a brief break as they heard sirens closing in from a distance. "They can't find us here," Kearney said, fully out of breath.

Nick passed Kearney off to Michael then hobbled fast to a row of cars off to the side where he found an old station wagon with the keys in the ignition. His groin injury was pulling at him while his newly inflicted injury throbbed wildly. Nick was holding it together by sheer will and years of practice. He then helped Kearney into the passenger seat while Michael climbed into the back. By now, the arm of Michael's shirt was fully soaked with blood.

Nick floored it as soon as the keys tumbled the engine. He rammed through the weak perimeter fence and drove up a bumpy cutaway of grass that extended out to the road. It didn't matter where he went. He turned and drove at full tilt. The old wagon shuddered and a metallic rattle came from the engine as it mis-shifted up the hill.

Inside the warehouse, Espinoza continued to struggle against his restraints as he watched the timer counting down from ten. He saw a few of his men bearing down on his position.

Then everything flashed white. Kearney's team heard and felt a massive explosion from behind. Then the sound wave hit them, causing the car to bounce up like it'd hit a massive pothole and it crashed back down on its creaky suspension. Nick slammed on the brakes as soon as he could and looked back to check the situation. His lap throbbed and bled from the concussive force.

Kearney was unconscious now, one bump on the head too many, while Michael pressed a rag he found against his wound to keep the bleeding under control. Nick's eyes wandered out the back window and he saw an immense cloud of dirt and debris rise. It was deep red, like a bloodstain, and slowly faded to a dirty brown-gray. The entire warehouse compound was obliterated, along with any kind of evidence that could have been there. The assignment was over. Success or not.

CHAPTER NINETEEN
THE END OF THE LINE

Nick heard a metallic clatter, a banging of tin and alloys being bashed together. He sprang out of bed, as if under attack, and rolled onto the floor. The pressed-down carpet smelled a bit like dog urine. From a time long, long ago when Dancer wet himself, waiting for Nick to get out of bed for a walk. Despite years of scrubbing and vacuuming, the scent was still there and it reminded him he was home. He wasn't in Herrera's house with a gun, in the warehouse where Oscar died, or on the metal slab with a mallet smashing his manhood. Those were now just bad dreams. Made from worse memories.

He stayed on the floor for a moment and let his breathing slow. This was the ritual now. Wake up somewhere wrong, figure out where he actually was, talk himself back into the present. Some mornings it took longer than others.

The banging was the product of his trash cans being emptied. He checked the street through the blinds and saw only a flash of white from the brightness of the sun. It stung his eyes. Nick leaned on his nightstand and disturbed a small pile of unpaid bills and unopened envelopes. While the team had been battling it out on behalf of the rebels, government funding, despite all the agency's manipulations to keep Congress in the dark as to where the money was actually going, had completely dried up. No notice. No fanfare. The CIA was forced to quickly tie up loose ends. No one on Kearney's team got paid. Even the last mortgage payment on Nick's behalf had bounced. Emma did her best to keep everyone solvent, even juggling whatever personal funds she and Kearney had socked away and doled some out toward Nick's and Michael's expenses. It just wasn't enough. He had been burned — again.

After a glass of water to wash out the taste of sleep and throwing on some clothes, he went about his business of staying in and being unseen. He was back to sporting a weeks-old beard. Why bother? A 3-day Notice was taped to the refrigerator door. The house was full of packed boxes as this was to be his last days in the place. He was done with it as much as he was with the government, the CIA, all of it. He sorted a few boxes in the morning, then alternated between sleeping and drinking for the rest of the day until he was too awake to sleep at night.

Early the next day, Nick sat uncomfortably, naked from the waist down, on an examination table at Dr. T's. The doctor unwrapped the silver cloth from Nick's penis and gently removed the stitches. Nick winced momentarily, not from pain but from the particularly odd tugging sensation. "Looks good… strictly from a medical perspective," Dr. T said. Nick almost laughed. "You won't need to wrap it anymore. Just let me know if anything develops… out of the ordinary."

"Humor suits you, doc." That was the most pleasantness Nick could muster. And that was just about the most pleasant the doctor had been with any client. He could tell Nick was in a bad way, not just physically. He smiled slyly, as if he had taken lessons from Michael, and gestured for Nick to get dressed. Nick was out of there like a shot.

Later that evening, Nick retired to the garage and continued packing the last of his remaining possessions. He was interrupted by Yogi, who jumped up onto his workbench and stretched out in front of him. Nick lazily hoisted the cat up and placed him on his bed at the end of the bench. Before he could return to work, he was interrupted again by a knocking at the side door.

His heart started pounding as he approached the peephole. Then it went quiet — almost stopped — when he saw it was Kate. He let her in. She was not surprised, or happy, by what she saw. There was someone, though, who was surprised; it was Yogi. The moment he heard Kate's voice, he opened his eyes and lifted his head to watch her every move.

"Thanks for letting me come by," she said. "Sorry, it's so late."

"Sure," Nick said. "But I couldn't find it."

She looked around and saw most of the boxes stacked up. "Oh, you're moving?" She made the tiniest sound as she spotted the Scrabble Board tucked away and dusted over.

Nick returned to the workbench. His face was hollow, too tired to show emotion. "It's not here," he said. Kate looked down and saw, lodged between two boxes, Yogi's little foam rubber ball. She picked it up and dusted it off. Yogi moved to a sitting position now seeing that Kate had his favorite toy.

"Are you sure?" she asked. "Did you check…" Nick cut her off by opening a drawer to sort through and started pulling out loose drill bits and screwdrivers to pack in a shoebox. Kate looked away and scanned the garage, one square foot at a time. She spotted a bunch of dead yellow roses in a vase, a stark contrast to what she had seen earlier. "I stopped by that little Italian restaurant today. The waiter sat me across from a young couple sitting at our table." Kate hoped for a reaction from Nick. When she didn't get it, no matter how much she tried, she couldn't mask the bitterness in her voice. "Anyone could see how much they were in love. Except for one man sitting alone, right next to them."

Just then, she spotted her dolphin keychain hanging above his workbench, partly obscured by a large wrench. Kate calmly walked over and reached out, her hand gliding right past Nick's face to the wall. She took her keychain from the peg and finished with, "He had the same vacant look."

Kate then wandered over to Yogi and petted him. She gave him a kiss on the head and placed the ball next to him. She then turned, walked to the door and paused without looking back. She then left.

For a long time afterward, Nick sat there with Kate's words echoing in his head. When he came to, Yogi was sitting by Nick's arm with his ball. Nick was in no mood to play, but in the eyes of the only friend he had left was a look of unconditional love, something Nick thought he may never experience again. He threw the ball across the garage, causing Yogi to jump off the bench to the floor with such energy that he did a somersault on his way to fetching the ball. Yogi trotted back to Nick with the ball in his mouth and as Nick watched him, he felt in that moment, a special type of serenity that is only experienced by a few at the end of a very long battle.

Nick's last task in the old neighborhood was a trip to the bank, a mere block away, to apply for a desperately needed loan. Having sold just about everything, his guns and much of his furniture, Nick's last resort was the bank, although he didn't know how helpful they would be since he was being evicted and had no verifiable employment. He entered the bank's back parking lot and stopped for a moment to look over his paperwork a final time. Nick then heard some yelling coming from the bank, then saw the back door burst open as a man ran out carrying a paper bag and revolver. He crossed Nick's path toward an old sedan.

A few yards from the car, the bag blew up, covering him with blue dye. The surprise caused him to drop his gun as blue money flew everywhere but he kept on running. Nick took off after him, dropping his papers in the first few strides.

The robber jumped into the passenger seat of the sedan and the driver sped off. Seconds later, a yuppie driving a BMW pulled up next to Nick and the driver asked him what was going on. Nick was agitated and bizarrely excited. "Guy just robbed the bank. They're probably headed to the freeway. We can still catch them."

"What?!"

"With the traffic, we can catch 'em."

"What the hell for?"

"They just robbed a fucking bank!"

"Are you nuts?!"

Nick exploded. He yanked the yuppie partially out through the window. The only thing keeping the guy inside was his seatbelt. The man flailed, trying to slap Nick's arms away, but Nick pulled back, ready to punch him in the face.

The terrified man was shaken to his core. "Please stop. I'm sorry."

Nick stopped, shaken by his own fury. He pushed the yuppie back and the man immediately hit the gas to distance himself from what he determined was a crazed lunatic.

Police cars sped in and officers jumped out and ran into the bank. They were completely unaware of the interaction that had just occurred between Nick and the BMW driver. Nick dropped to a sitting position on the curb, his papers scattered about him. He couldn't move. He couldn't think. But somehow, deep inside, he knew it was the last straw. He questioned his own sanity.

Weeks later, Kearney and Michael drove by the house to check on Nick but were surprised to see kids playing in the front yard. African-American. And a father in the doorway calling them inside. Nick had slipped away from his old life, his old contacts, and his old self.

That was how he ended up in the small, equally dark apartment, now enlightened only by a police helicopter's searchlight. He had sat there tracing his steep fall back as far as he could. There were two of him at some point, two Nick Bryants who fought for control over the sole body between them. He stared at the photo of himself with Kate. It reminded him he was someone who used the powers he'd harnessed over self-control and discipline for the good of others, to calm them and teach them to control their own pain. But the hidden gun, the knife, and the tequila betrayed the other side of him, someone who knew the same techniques, the secrets of pain and the causes of suffering, of someone who had spread them wide at the request of others. One self-motivated to enlighten the world, the other propelled to darken it. Two wolves that ate at each other for the scraps of Nick's attention.

But no matter how miserable or lost he seemed, Nick was still a fighter, still ready for anything. That gunshot — it wasn't Nick's gun that fired. It came from the street below. He stepped out onto the balcony to inspect. A body lay on the ground and a team of cops surrounded it with weapons drawn. Whatever the problem was, it was over, and this time it had nothing to do with him. No longer did Nick have a country to fight for or an institute to create. All the people he could have helped and fought for were gone.

Yogi brushed up against his legs. He bent and looked at the cat until it sat back and stared up at him. Nick walked to his kitchenette, put the gun on the counter, and took out a can of cat food from a cabinet. He keyed open the lid for his friend who fortunately only knew the one side of him.

Nick watched Yogi for a long moment as he ate. The police helicopter came back around at a different angle and its spotlight shined through a stained glass ornament sitting on the windowsill. Nick became mesmerized by the rainbow of colors that danced around the room. He couldn't help but remember the good times from what felt like so long ago. Grandma Ruthie would come in with a pie the second their forks hit empty plates from their dinner. Billy would be ready with a knife to stab in and claim a piece while it was piping hot. And all the while, they would sit at a table underneath the same stained glass ornament that splashed the room with a beautiful kaleidoscope of colors.

Nick drove into the night and ended up in front of what was once a happy memory but saw a house that was vacated and weathered down. He sat in his car, an old beat-up sedan, and just stared at it as a flash of lightning lit the sky. A few thunderclaps accompanied the creaking of an old "Estate Sale" sign swaying in the middle of Ruthie's beloved flower garden that was nothing but piles of dark, rotten soil.

He left the warmth of his car and pulled his jacket tighter against the icy wind as he walked up and pulled open the door to Billy's workspace. He entered, feet crunching on broken glass. The garage had nothing but the outlines of where tools used to hang and the scrapped remains of wood and metal.

He stood still for a moment and let the lightning do the work. Flash by flash, the outlines on the wall came back to life — the shape of the handsaw, the drill press, the sander that had hummed under Billy's hands the day Nick first saw the loveseat taking form. He could still hear him. *Didn't I teach you that everything is connected?* He could still smell the sawdust and the particular oil Billy used on his tools, a smell that had meant safety to Nick since he was a boy. None of it was here anymore. Just the shapes of what had been, like shadows left behind by things long gone.

In a corner, the wolves no longer fought. They lay in pieces in a swept-up pile of trash. The thunder clapped; lightning flashed. The garage was lit for a moment, revealing the light-colored wolf staring up at him. Nick took off his jacket and wrapped the pieces in it.

He got back into his car and now felt the pain of ages overtake him. Pain he'd worked hard to suppress. Just like every controlled wound he had reopened under his moment of torture, every heartache and sorrow revisited him and drenched him like rain from the sky that was now pounding his windshield. He had to let it go.

EPILOGUE

The farmer's market was modestly busy. A decent crowd of people toured the vendor stalls to take their picks of freshly grown produce. One stand that stood out as being especially popular was the fresh-brewed French press. They had their own roast of beans that was ground by hand and pressed for customers on request.

Nick Bryant stopped by to get a cup to go. He was a regular in recent months after having clawed his way back among the living. He paid for his cup, inhaled the luscious aroma, and thanked the vendor.

Nick headed off for his next stop, a toymaker's stall run by a Polish family. Not a popular destination but a unique one in the farmer's market that attracted visitors just to look at what the family-owned business brought to sell that week. They specialized in wooden dolls and other woodwork gifts. Nick held back a bit and watched as a lady, presumably the toymaker's wife, entertained a small child with a simple stick-controlled marionette. The little girl giggled in her mother's arms.

The old toymaker himself smiled as he spotted Nick and ushered him forward. From behind the counter, he hoisted a large paper bag then unveiled the repaired battling wolves' sculpture, blended together at the chest, fighting for dominance, with the full inscription intact. A few seam lines showed where the repairs were made and the filler that bound the wood together where chunks and splinters went missing were filled in by wood of the same shade. Even the grain was the same. The toymaker handed it to Nick, who stood admiring each of its many details before handing over the cash that was due.

"Thanks," Nick said simply and left.

He followed the crowd out of the market to the car park. Everyone, including Nick, walked past a homeless man wearing a worn-out army fatigue jacket, who was laying off to the side. Nick stopped; his mind went elsewhere. The people around him kept moving.

Nick turned and walked back against the flow toward the homeless man. What he saw was a man struggling, split between two choices: self-destruction or the hard climb of restoration, a choice Nick made and made again. He saw someone in need of illumination to help them decide which wolf to feed — or simply to feed themselves. Nick sat, planted the sculpture beside him on one side and placed the coffee next to the man on the other. And did what he was put on this Earth to do.

THE END

BASED ON A TRUE STORY

Author J Bartell Offers Up Some Background to the
Events Portrayed in "The Wolves Within"

J Bartell (Nick Bryant) demonstrates controlling pain,
blood flow and the slowing of his heart rate

Chauncey Marvin Holt (William Kearney)

J Bartell & Michael Harries at the gun range

Michael Harries (Michael Davies) and
his famous Flashlight Technique

Michael's "War Wagon"

Ruthie & Billy, the Grandparents
(the only picture remaining)

J Bartell in Morocco at the Palace Gate

J Bartell - Some awards and trophies

J Bartell's car driven during the desert shoot out.
Sheriff counted 26 hits from gun fire.

Additional information and photos can be found at
BijouEntertainment.com

AUTHORS

J Bartell, M.A., is an author, screenwriter, and behavior specialist, renowned for developing and teaching his process known as 'Left-Right Brain Suggestibility.' He was previously a licensed Marriage, Family, and Child Counselor in California. In his mid-thirties, J became Chief of Staff at one of the world's largest therapeutic/educational institutes. At that time, he gave lectures and live demonstrations of Pain, Bleeding, and Muscle Control at UCLA and other venues. His clients included people from all walks of life, but it was his worldwide travels on behalf of affluent, private individuals, including heads-of-state, that put him on the radar of the CIA. For more information about J, visit his website at http://jbartell.com.

Ginger Marin is an actor, author, screenwriter, environmentalist and animal rights advocate. As a former network TV Journalist at NBC News NY, Ginger served as producer and writer for the network's top news shows and various special reports. Ginger is also the author of "Monster on Mars" and "Adventures in Avalon: An Offbeat & Quirky Adult Bedtime Story". To learn more about Ginger's acting and film projects, visit her IMDB page at http://www.imdb.me/gingermarin or her personal website https://gingermarin.com. If you want to read how she bemoans the world, check out her blog at http://bioniclady.com.

www.ingramcontent.com/pod-product-compliance
Lightning Source LLC
Chambersburg PA
CBHW011139310726
48972CB00009B/2777